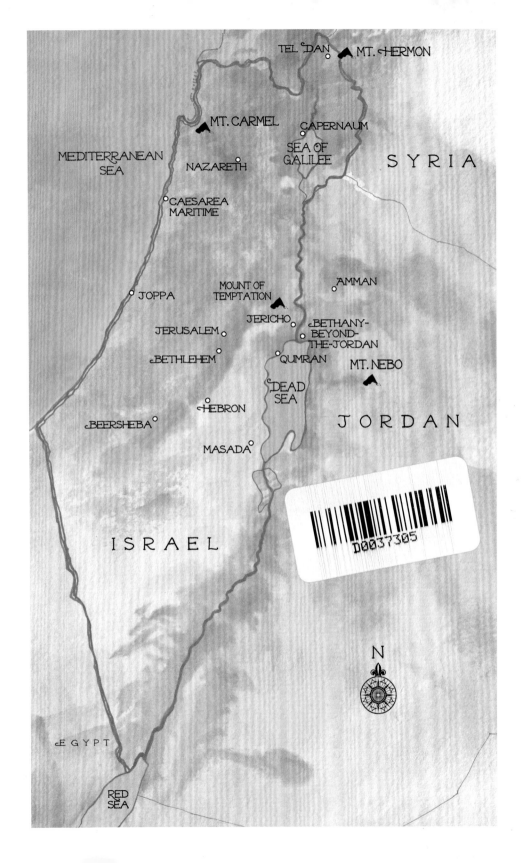

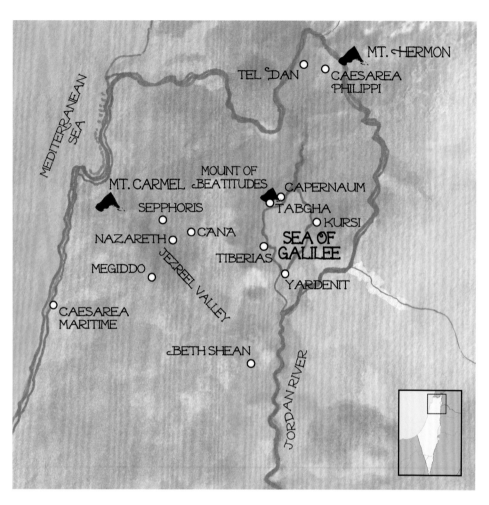

Northern Israel, around the Sea of Galilee

Caves at Qumran, where the Dead Sea Scrolls were found

Capernaum, where Peter lived and Jesus established a home base

The Sea of Galilee, the lake where Jesus spent much of his ministry

Caesarea Maritime, where Pontius Pilate was headquartered

Herodium (near Bethlehem), Herod's man-made mountain palace

Caesarea Philippi, an ancient center of Pan worship

"In this wonderfully creative book, René Schlaepfer has once again done what he does best. He has built a bridge from the ancient world in which the biblical drama unfolded to the issues of contemporary life. As you make your way through the book it soon becomes evident that your author-tour guide is a masterful storyteller, which will remind you of the gifts of a first century rabbi named Jesus."

REV. DR. M. CRAIG BARNES, pastor of Shadyside Presbyterian and author of *When God Interrupts, Sacred Thirst, Searching For Home,* and *The Pastor as Minor Poet.*

"As cliché as this may sound, when you journey into the Holy Land, reading your Bible truly does move from 2-D to 3-D. What a privilege we have getting to experience some 3-D of the land where Jesus walked as René brings us right into the world where Jesus lived. Without understanding the world that Jesus lived in, you won't fully understand all of Jesus' words and teachings.

"I had the joy of living in Israel for several months and revisiting it since, and René does an amazing job of bringing the land where Jesus walked into our living room—and not just into our homes, but into our hearts and lives. I am very grateful René wrote this and so thankful as I think of the incredible impact it will have on readers as they journey into the land and teachings of Jesus."

DAN KIMBALL, René Schlaepfer fan, teaching and mission leader at Vintage Faith Church, and author of *They Like Jesus But Not The Church*

"If you've always wanted to visit Israel to walk where Christ walked and to see where he ministered, here is your opportunity — and you don't have to leave home to do it. René Schlaepfer takes readers on just such a trip in *Jesus Journey*. He blends insightful commentary, biblical accuracy, and touches of humor from his own journeys to Israel that make this book a spiritual adventure you will enjoy taking again and again. Don't miss it!"

KAREN O'CONNOR, speaker and author of *Squeeze The Moment*, *Basket of Blessings*, and many more

"In *Jesus Journey*, René Schlaepfer weaves exotic travelogue, historical mysteries, and the story of Christ into a daily devotional that will motivate and inspire. René knows how to put the reader on the ground in the Holy Land in a way that is compelling and illuminating. His writing will fascinate enthusiasts of Holy Land trips as well as those looking for an excellent personal or small group study."

BILL BUTTERWORTH, speaker and author of *The Short List*

JESUS JOURNEY

40 DAYS IN THE FOOTSTEPS OF CHRIST

BY RENÉ SCHLAEPFER

"JESUS JOURNEY: 40 days in the footsteps of Christ"
© 2012 René Schlaepfer
ISBN 978-1-4675-4473-3

1st printing: 2012

Cover photography: John Eric Paulson (www.johnericpaulson.com)

Printed locally on recycled paper with soy-based inks at Community Printers, Santa Cruz, CA.

If you would like to reproduce or distribute any part of this publication, please contact:
Twin Lakes Church, 2701 Cabrillo College Drive, Aptos, CA 95003–3103, USA
or email info@tlc.org

CONTENTS

CULMINATION

SMALL GROUP STUDY GUIDES

EXTRAS

JESUS JOURNEY

40 DAYS IN THE FOOTSTEPS OF CHRIST

Now Jesus did many other signs in the presence of the disciples, which are not written in this book; but these are written so that you may believe that Jesus is the Christ, the Son of God, and that by believing you may have life in his name. JOHN 20:30–31 ESV

INTRODUCTION

People who return from a visit to the Holy Land often find it hard to put their experience into words. But they usually try. Here are a few comments I've heard more than once:

"The Bible is so much more interesting to me now!"

"I felt closer to God there than ever before!"

"It changed my spiritual life!"

"I loved the hummus!"

Why the enthusiasm?

My theory: For the first time, many visitors to the Holy Land are seeing the Bible the way it was *meant* to be seen, as a book grounded in a real culture with real geography and real history. And the hummus really is delicious.

MEETING JESUS

I've been to the land of the Bible as a member of a study group, on a personal visit to friends, and as a tour leader. Each time, I too was surprised by the depth of my emotion toward God, and by the many "Aha!" moments of sudden insight into familiar Scriptures

It's not just that I understood Jesus better. I felt like I was *meeting* Jesus.

Maybe it's because, when you visit the Holy Land, you're seeing and touching and feeling and smelling and hearing (and tasting!) some of the same things Jesus did.

Suddenly you know what it means to walk on a Roman road, to sail on the Sea of Galilee, or to stride up the Temple Mount, because you're doing it. *Just as Jesus did.*

But it's more than that.

JESUS JOURNEY

It's realizing that Jesus came as a real human to real people in answer to real deep problems in a real place. *This* place. It's here he steps out of the stained glass windows and into our stained lives.

That's why the Holy Land has been called "the fifth gospel." Here the old Bible stories — stories that can take on an almost mythological blur back home — leap off the page and right into sharp-focused reality. And they take your breath away. Because now you see the setting, the culture of the place, so that the stories make so much more sense. They're not happening in a far-off flannelgraph world anymore. They're happening in a real world!

That's the sensation I'm trying to capture in this book.

WHAT IS THIS?

In each daily devotion, I've given you a Bible passage to read, and then I describe how I encountered that very same place, or someplace similar, on one of my trips (Please read those Bible passages; they're the most important part of this book!). Many of these devotions stem from my own journal, written during and after my most recent trip as the leader of a group from our church.

While there, we also filmed small group videos on location that tie into each week's theme — they're available on DVD or online at WWW.JESUSJOURNEYBOOK.COM. A sermon series tie-in is also online at the same place.

The small group videos are designed to be incorporated into the start of each week. For example, you or your group can watch the first video and then begin day 1.

WHY 40 DAYS?

This book is divided into 40 short chapters, each set at a different location in the Holy Land. I designed it this way so you can read straight through *Jesus Journey* if you like, or you can choose to use each chapter as a daily meditation in a 40-day journey of discovery.

INTRODUCTION

Forty days is the exact duration of several crucial periods of teaching in the Bible:

- At the beginning of his ministry, Jesus spent 40 days praying and fasting in the Judean wilderness (MATTHEW 4:2).

- After his resurrection, Jesus spent 40 days teaching the disciples (ACTS 1:3).

- Moses spent 40 days on Mount Sinai receiving God's commandments (EXODUS 24:18).

- Elijah traveled 40 days to reach "the mountain of God" and receive instruction there (1 KINGS 19:8).

Almost every 40-day period in the Bible leads people to a time of discovery and learning. I pray that this does the same for you!

LETTING THE MUSIC PLAY

Jesus Journey is not intended as a definitive chronology of Christ's life, or to answer every question about Jesus that might be asked. In fact, I had to leave out some of my favorite stories because of the limited scope of this book! But I tried to include the major *themes* of the gospels.

That's because the four gospels don't exactly tell a simple story, like a movie. They're more like a symphony.

A *movie* is usually a narrative with one grand plot. But a *symphony* introduces different themes, different melody lines, and then weaves them together and repeats them in new variations until an overall impression is created.

That's what the gospels do. Themes appear, fade away, and then reappear, until they give you a sense of this amazing living person: Jesus.

JESUS JOURNEY

Don't imagine you know all about him already. Set aside the critics' opinions for a season. Just let the symphony play.

ENJOY THE JOURNEY

In John 1, Jesus calls his first disciples to join him on the journey. Here's the way one translation, The Voice, describes it:

> *The next day Jesus set out to go into Galilee; and when he came upon Phillip, he invited them to join them.*
>
> *Jesus: Follow me.*
>
> *Phillip, like Andrew and Peter, came from a town called Bethsaida;* **and he decided to make The Journey with Him.** *Phillip found Nathanael, a friend, and burst with excitement.* JOHN 1:43–45 (THE VOICE VERSION)

My prayer is that you decide to make The Journey too, and find yourself bursting with excitement as well. Because Jesus — the same unpredictable, living, unique Jesus that Philip knew — is journeying right alongside *you* the whole way, right now!

So let's go to the Holy Land! Grab some hummus, and enjoy the trip!

0 SEEING STARS

READ JOHN 1:1-5, 9-14

I see the moon's rocky craters in razor-sharp detail. Its silvery surface dust seems close enough to sift through my fingers.

Slight shift. The glowing planets Venus, Jupiter and Mars hang together in alarmingly close alignment.

I turn east, and face the famous rings of Saturn.

After two weeks of journeying through the past, I'm travelling into space.

It's the last night of our trip to the Holy Land. An amateur astronomer has set up his telescope on the Jordanian shore of the Dead Sea and I'm enjoying his tour of the solar system.

Then, a surprise.

"You know, telescopes aren't just for stars," he says. "Check this out." He spins the telescope so it points horizontally, straight west. Across the Dead Sea. Into Israel.

I bend down and take a peek. And suddenly I'm standing on the hills of Jerusalem. I see its buildings as if I'm right there on a city sidewalk. He moves the telescope slightly to the left. And I land in Bethlehem. The lights of that town fill my vision.

I glance over my shoulder at the moon and planets I'd just been watching. I bend back down to peek at Bethlehem. And I see something in a way I've never seen it before. I see the greatest distance anyone has ever travelled. I see the road map to a rescue mission. I see the journey a love-struck God took to bring his lost children home.

From far beyond the light of the Moon and Mars and Sun and stars, the true Light came into a dark world.

INTO THE BREACH

He had the means and the motive. If there is an all-powerful Being who made everything, surely visiting us — as one of us — is child's play for him.

And if this Being is not just infinitely powerful, but, as the Bible teaches, infinitely loving, then such a Being would have the motivation to visit and save the fallen objects of his love.

So in love he came into the breach, to be with us, to communicate his love to us, to woo us, and to rescue us.

He didn't just shout a message. He gave himself.

The God who breathed out the galaxies came to breathe our air. The One who strolled the stars came to walk our streets. The angel-maker came to touch lepers.

I stand there on the shore of the Dead Sea during our last night in the Holy Land and think of all we've seen on our *Jesus Journey* so far.

We'd arrived two weeks before and hit the road hard, visiting site after site. Places Jesus lived and walked and taught.

We thought we'd traced his steps. But illuminated by the glow of the stars above me, and an ancient town in front of me, I see more steps. The steps he took to reach us began much longer than two thousand years ago, and much further away than Bethlehem.

PONDER: What does it mean to you that God came to earth out of love for the world – including you? How does this impact your attitude and confidence?

PART 1
BEGINNINGS

1 PREPARING A LANDING SITE

READ ISAIAH 9:1–7; ISAIAH 53

TIME: Several days before my telescope peek.

PLACE: The other side of the Dead Sea.

Our group stands amid the dry and dusty two-thousand-year-old ruins of Qumran on a desert mesa in Israel. We stare across canyons that encompass us, and notice caves dotting the faces of the cliffs — possibly the most significant caves in biblical archaeology.

In 1947, a Bedouin shepherd boy searching for his lost goat threw a rock into the entrance of one of these caves and heard the crash of breaking pottery. Investigating, he found several huge clay jars containing ancient documents. Among these parchments were copies of the Old Testament from before the birth of Christ: The Dead Sea Scrolls.

To understand the gospels — to get a grip on the ministry of Jesus — you have to start here. You have to go way back, before the New Testament was written. Back to the Hebrew Scriptures, known as the Old Testament to Christians.

They end with a longing for the appearance of God's anointed one, the Messiah, who will judge wickedness and free the oppressed, restoring God's people to glory.

SINGING THE BLUES

The last books of the Old Testament written, the books of the Prophets, sound almost like an old American blues song.

Something like (humor me and imagine a blues guitar riff after each line):

Oh we've brought ourselves so much sorrow,
And we wonder if God is real,

8

1 PREPARING A LANDING SITE

Will we be as stupid tomorrow
Or will we accept God's deal?

Before false idols we've kneeled
And our worship of God is a joke
His will is plainly revealed
Help the poor, hungry, sad folk
Need to help the oppressed folk

God won't you please come back,
And finish your promised story
Protect us from all attack
Restore the kingdom to glory

One day you'll send a Son
Anointed to set things right
He'll be the promised One
And shine with your heavenly light
Need to see that radiant light
Want to see the Son of Man's light

OK, so I'm not a blues writer, but that pretty much sums up the themes of the last books of the Old Testament.

These were the ideas echoing in the minds of the Jewish people when Jesus was born. If a classic blues song longs for a love relationship, the prophets longed for God and his chosen agent, the Messiah, to soothe all sorrows and bring the Kingdom to true magnificence.

THE KING IS COMING

The oldest of the Dead Sea Scrolls, a 2,250-year-old copy of the Book of Isaiah, predicts the coming of a Messiah in riveting detail:

> *Look! The virgin will conceive a child! She will give birth*
> *to a son and will call him Immanuel (which means 'God is*
> *with us').* ISAIAH 7:14 NLT

9

For a child is born to us, a son is given to us. The government will rest on his shoulders. And he will be called: Wonderful Counselor, Mighty God, Everlasting Father, Prince of Peace. ISAIAH 9:6 NLT

Other Messianic prophecies found in the scrolls add more detail:

Rejoice greatly, O Daughter of Zion! Shout, Daughter of Jerusalem! See, your king comes to you, righteous and having salvation, gentle and riding on a donkey, on a colt, the foal of a donkey. ZECHARIAH 9:9

There before me was one like a Son of Man, coming with the clouds of heaven... He was given authority, glory and sovereign power; all nations and peoples of every language worshiped him. His dominion is an everlasting dominion that will not pass away, and his kingdom is one that will never be destroyed. DANIEL 7:13–14

There are hundreds more. But—why were scrolls with all these prophecies preserved in caves at Qumran?

Apparently, members of an ancient Jewish sect, the Essenes, lived here in strict separation from what they considered to be the corrupt Temple leadership in Jerusalem. They were forbidden to marry, own any property, or eat hummus (just kidding about that last one). Their entire existence centered on the preservation and study of the Hebrew Bible.

When the Romans marched toward them in 70 AD as part of Caesar's campaign to brutally suppress a Jewish rebellion, the Essenes hid their treasured scrolls. And they hid them well. The scrolls stayed hidden for nearly 1,900 years.

The caves also contained something else: Hundreds of Essene writings about the Messiah based on their studies of these prophecies.

So thanks to the Dead Sea Scroll discoveries, we know that

prophecies about the Messiah in the Hebrew Scriptures were not added back in by later Christian editors. They were there for hundreds of years before Christ's birth. In fact, the teachings of the Essenes refer specifically to the "Servant Songs" of Isaiah, the "Seventy Weeks Prophecy" of Daniel 9, and various psalms as clues to the Messiah's identity.

THE KING IS CLOSE

Then, around the time of Jesus, the preaching of the Essenes shifted. They began teaching that *the time was now at hand*, that the prophets' predictions were coming true, that in their lifetimes, the Messiah would be revealed.

And what you could call "Messiah-Mania" swept through this part of the world in the first century. People knew the prophecies. They'd been singing those blues for hundreds of years. Now they were actively looking for the Messiah.

As I stand near the Dead Sea caves, I marvel at how God readied a landing site for the earthly ministry of Jesus. The idea of a Messiah didn't just drop out of heaven on Christmas morning to an unprepared population. It was an inspired concept that God cultivated for centuries, furrowing and fertilizing the world for the seed to come.

The oppressed were hoping. The oppressors were fearing. Expectations were sky-high.

And then the hopes and fears of all the years were met just over the hill from Qumran, in Bethlehem, one night.

Yet no one, not even the Essenes after centuries of study, exactly predicted the kind of radical Messiah who showed up that day.

PONDER: How does it help your faith to know that Christ fulfilled ancient prophecies about the Messiah?

2 THE MOUNTAIN AND MARY

READ LUKE 1:26-55

I can see it all the way from our hotel on the other side of the Dead Sea. From here, it looks like the silhouette of a massive volcano. Its slopes rise 2,500 feet above the surrounding valleys.

But this wasn't always a cone-shaped mountain. And it wasn't always this tall. This strange place is largely man-made. And it's over two thousand years old.

It's called the Herodium.

One of our best sources outside the New Testament for descriptions of the Holy Land in the time of Christ is the ancient Jewish writer Josephus, who lived at the end of the first century.

He described this place as "a hill raised to the height of a mountain by the hand of man." He says that thousands of slaves reshaped the slopes and added hundreds of feet of elevation by using dirt shaved off a neighboring summit.

At the top today: The ruins of a pleasure palace and military fortress. Among other wonders, in the time of Christ it had a huge swimming bath twice the size of a modern Olympic pool. An aqueduct brought water from springs four miles away. Using mirrors to reflect the sun and send coded messages, the castle staff kept its inhabitants up-to-date with the latest news from Jerusalem.[1]

VOLCANIC RULER

The man who built it was the powerful and paranoid Herod the Great, who ruled Judea as Rome's representative from 37 to 4 BC.

Excavations in 2007 unearthed Herod's long-lost tomb on the side of the mountain, and in 2010 a 450-seat theater that had apparently been built exclusively for use during Herod's funeral was discovered.

2 THE MOUNTAIN AND MARY

But what's particularly interesting is the tiny village that this mountainous fortress overshadowed — literally.

The little town of Bethlehem.

For centuries it had been just a wide spot in the road, known primarily as King David's birthplace, after which it receded again into obscurity. It was called *"the least of the cities of Judah"* (MICAH 5:2). In Joshua 15 there's a list of Judean cities, and Bethlehem isn't even mentioned.

After the Herodium rose to dominate the horizon, this little cluster of poorly constructed homes and shepherds' caves shrank even further by comparison. The Herodium was a statement of power and importance, a destination for the elite who had earned the king's favor, a glittering crown jewel in King Herod's collection of palaces. Bethlehem was like the famous description of Oakland, California: "There's no there, there."

What's worse, the volcano-like silhouette of Herod's massive fortress would have been a grinding daily reminder for beleaguered Bethlehem residents of the threat of violent eruptions from their temperamental king.

MAD KING AND MEEK MAID

Herod clung to power against any and all challengers. Ancient sources say he had two of his own sons strangled, later executed his favorite wife, and on his deathbed ordered another son beheaded, all for suspicion of treason.

The contrast between the fortress mountain and the tiny village was much like the difference between the power-mad Herod and the meek mother of Christ, Mary.

A young teenager when visited by the angel, Mary had no aspirations of glory, no hunger for power.

She was not a pampered princess, she had no expectations of giving birth to a King.

She hadn't even been praying for a message from God.

But she got one. *"You have found favor with God,"* says the angel. *"You will bear… the Son of God."* (LUKE 1:30–31, 35 ESV)

Mary's response? Simply awe and thanksgiving at what God was doing by his grace.

"My soul glorifies the Lord and my spirit rejoices in God my Savior" (LUKE 1:46–47) she sings, inspired by the Spirit as she reacts to God's awesome favor. The Father sent the Son through the Spirit in the life of Mary.

THE MARY MIRACLE IN ME

And the Mary miracle continues: Although of course Mary holds a unique and honored place as the mother of Jesus, this is exactly the way God works in you and in me today.

"You have found favor with God." Those are words you and I also hear. The word for "favor" there is the word for grace, which God pours on us before we've done anything to deserve it.

Just as he did for Mary, God is always the One who initiates, acting unilaterally, without any advance contribution from us to earn his favor.

OUR MAGNIFICAT

And we can react the same way Mary reacted, with praise and thanksgiving for the wonders he has done, is doing, and will do, in us.

Later when she visits her cousin Elisabeth, Mary bursts into a song we know as *The Magnificat*, the Latin word for "magnify."

"My soul magnifies the Lord," she sings. Her lyrics are rich with

imagery from the Old Testament and focus on God's grace to the unsuspecting and weak.

You can sing the same song, and for the same reason. Paul's words in Ephesians about God's grace to all of us sound a lot like Mary's response:

> *All praise to God, the Father of our Lord Jesus Christ, who has blessed us with every spiritual blessing in the heavenly realms... Even before he made the world, God loved us and chose us in Christ to be holy and without fault in his eyes... This is what he wanted to do, and it gave him great pleasure. So we praise God for the glorious grace he has poured out on us... He has showered his kindness on us...*
> EPHESIANS 1:3–8 NLT

THE MEEK OUTLAST THE MIGHTY

It's interesting for me to trace the influence of first-century lives by the popularity of names two millennia later.

No one names their kid Herod. Or Pilate. Or Archelaus or Antipas, two of Herod's surviving sons who had hoped to further the family dynasty ("Archelaus Schlaepfer" — now that would be a mouthful).

But names in the extended family of Jesus? Mary, Joseph, James, Elizabeth, David... Their popularity demonstrates their influence.

In the end, it would not be the power-mad king in the impregnable fortress who furthered the dynasty, but the pregnant teenager in the tiny village. The meek would outlast the mighty.

It was a pattern Mary's son would continue. In the disciples he chose, the missionaries he deputized, the miracles he performed, he kept choosing the poor in spirit to confound the proud and powerful.

He chooses the least likely suspects. Like you and me. That's the good news of grace. What's your response?

JESUS JOURNEY

Why art thou troubled, Herod? what vain fear
    Thy blood-revolving breast to rage doth move?
Heaven's King, who doffs himself weak flesh to wear,
    Comes not to rule in wrath, but serve in love;
Nor would he this thy feared crown from thee tear,
    But give thee a better with himself above.
Poor jealousy! why should he wish to prey
    Upon thy crown, who gives his own away?
— Richard Cranshaw [2]

PONDER: Why do you think God chose to enter the world through a person of no apparent significance? What does this teach you about God? How does it impact you to know that "you have found favor with God"?

THE CAVE OF CHRIST

After the Jewish rebellion known as the Bar Kochba revolt of 135 AD, the Roman government attempted to wipe out all the Jewish and Christian holy sites near Jerusalem. But their strategy of building pagan temples over these spots eventually backfired, because generations of Christians remembered that their holy sites were under the Roman shrines. For example, in Bethlehem, about six miles south of Jerusalem, the Romans noticed a cave that Christians believed was the birthplace of Jesus. So they built a temple to the Roman god Adonis there.

Then in about 326 AD, Helena, mother of the first Christian emperor Constantine, was told by local Christians that the Adonis shrine was over Christ's birthplace. She had workers tear down the pagan temple and build a church over the grotto she found underneath.

Is this the very cave where Christ was born? There's no way to know for sure. But that Jesus might have been born in a cavern, instead of the wooden stable of Christmas card iconography, is not surprising. Several ancient writers point out that shepherds regularly used the many caves in the area as barns.

It's moving to think that when God came to earth, he didn't choose to enter through a silk bed in some palace. Instead he was born in a hole in the ground, descending all the way into the anxiety of a temporarily homeless young couple forced to welcome their first child in animal dung and darkness.

To me, that's a foreshadowing of the ministry of Christ. He did this very thing for the rest of his life, and does it to this day. He descends all the way into your darkest dead-ends. Things seem hopeless, you're in a cave, and suddenly Christ is born, right there in your heart.

3 LIKE FATHER LIKE SON

READ MATTHEW 1:18-25

The men and women are separate here. That's part of keeping it holy, I'm told.

So my wife is on the other side of the fence as I wander alone through crowds of men at the Western Wall in Jerusalem, the giant retaining wall that stands as the only visible remnant of Herod's first-century Temple.

Jesus saw this very wall. And as he approached the Temple which then stood above it, he saw people much like the devout men I'm witnessing.

Just as they did in Christ's day, these men wear phylacteries — small boxes containing Scripture — strapped to their foreheads to show their devotion. Many dress in centuries-old style: robes and prayer shawls with long tassels.

Foremost in their minds: Ritual purity. Strict observance of the law.

Their forerunners two thousand years ago expected the coming Messiah to be the purest of all, to restore perfection to Temple worship, to be the one man untouched by the impurity of the world.

And that's what they got. But not at all the way they thought they'd get it. The strictly religious people were always surprised by Jesus, by the way he acted, the people he hung out with, the message he brought.

And the very first strict religious person to be surprised by the Messiah's methods? *Joseph.*

Matthew calls him a "righteous man." That phrase is a technical expression. In Hebrew it was a single word: *Tsadiq.*

This word meant Joseph was righteous according to the strictest interpretation of the Torah (the first five books of the Bible, also known as the Law of Moses).

Whatever Torah said, Joseph did. He was one of the men with the phylacteries and shawls and tassels, devoutly attending synagogue, attending to his prayers, reciting scripture.

He was pure. He was separate. He was *tsadiq*.

But, as John Ortberg puts it, Joseph was *tsadiq* with a problem. [3]

Because, guess what the Torah says to do in his situation?

If a woman pledged to be married was found with child, and the child's father is not her husband-to-be...

> *She should be brought to the door of her father's house and there the men of the town shall stone her to death.*
> DEUTERONOMY 22:21

The Gospel of Matthew's phrase "public disgrace" is a soft euphemism for what awaited the pregnant Mary. But even though Joseph was one of the *righteous*, he finds he cannot lead the parade to his father-in-law's house. And so he decides on plan B: a private divorce. Send Mary away. Get her out of town. End the engagement. But quietly.

This must have torn him apart, because already he would have been compromising his purity.

Then an angel appears. And tells him to do something else, something he would never have dreamt of doing before this.

"Take Mary home as your wife...." MATTHEW 1:20

This meant scandal. This meant rejection. This meant an end to his status as *tsadiq*.

Even though *we* know the child within Mary was conceived by the Holy Spirit, the people around them only knew what their eyes told them was true: Mary was pregnant before she and Joseph ever lived together as a married couple.

And yet Joseph acted in bold mercy toward Mary.

THE MESSY SCANDAL OF GRACE

I like to think that maybe, just maybe, when Jesus was leaping over the walls put up by his society to separate the religiously pure from the "sinners" — when he was forgiving the woman caught in adultery, talking to the Samaritan woman, teaching the "sinful" women — he wanted to be like his dad.

Like his heavenly Father, to be sure. But also like the man Joseph.

Joseph, who though ritually pure and devoutly observant, chose to obey God and live in scandalous grace –- rather than please the religious performers.

And maybe when Jesus taught that *"your righteousness"* — your *tsadiq-ness* — *"must surpass that of the Pharisees,"* he was thinking of his earthly dad: obedience that went beyond the rules and into reality. Mercy that got messy. Grace that got gritty.

PLOT TWIST

And then this righteous man hears an angel tell him the life mission of the child he will raise as his own:

> *"...give him the name Jesus, because he will save his people from their sins."* MATTHEW 1:21

His name *was* his mission. The very word *Jesus* means "Jehovah saves." But the angel adds an unexpected twist to the Messiah's mission: *"...from their sins."*

And suddenly the Messiah's purpose is crystal clear. It's not primarily to judge the people *for* sins, or teach the people what *is* sin, or turn the righteous *against* sin. It's to save people *from* sin.

The people were expecting a Messiah to help them fix problems with their religion and their government. But from the very start, the angel reveals a plot twist: The Messiah's mission is not to streamline a bureaucracy or overthrow a king. Those would have been mere patches on the problem, Band-Aids on a much deeper wound. His was a mission of transformation at the *soul* level.

Matthew adds this was all meant to fulfill a prophecy: *"They will call him Immanuel, which means, 'God with us'."*

Here he focuses on another theme of the prophecies about the Messiah that had been overlooked: The Messiah was not just to be the *representative* of God with us. He *was* God with us.

This is the motion, the direction, the movement of the gospel: God stooping down to meet us, not *us* trying to get up to *God*.

These few verses contain the genetic code for everything that follows. Every action of Christ, everything he taught about himself, all that's about to unfold, it's all in seed form right here.

And after Mary and Joseph, the next people to hear of the Messiah's mission are the most outcast of all.

PROJECT: Think of one person you're struggling to show grace to right now and write down one way to show them grace today.

4 BRIGHT LIGHTS & BIRTH ANNOUNCEMENTS

READ LUKE 2:8-20

We had told ourselves before the trip to try to be cool, to try not to be obvious, wide-eyed American tourists.

Well, that lasted about an hour.

It's our church tour group's first morning in Israel. We're driving from the coast to Galilee when our cool detachment is shattered for good. And by such a simple thing.

Our guide Kenny proclaims that our bus is fast approaching a real-life, Holy Land shepherd boy.

"On your right! On your right, everybody!! Sheep with a shepherd!"

All dignity is abandoned as cameras are whipped out of backpacks and we rush to that side of the bus, anticipating the stained-glass scene from our imaginations: Powder-white, freshly washed and shampooed sheep in a Thomas Kinkade landscape.

Instead we see a dozen dingy dreadlocked lambs that seem to be grazing on rocks, watched over by a boy of about ten years old wearing jeans and a dirty Manchester United soccer shirt. He waves and grins through a mud-streaked face as our bus rolls by.

"He's Bedouin." Kenny announces. "Not the Omar Sharif of your imagination, is he?" He explains that Bedouin tribes are rapidly leaving their nomadic lifestyles, partly because, as Israeli society grows, their roving bands of shepherds are seen as unwanted trespassers.

The same kind of stigma was attached to shepherds of the first century. Only worse.

They were *despised* by the "respectable" people — seen as thieves and tramps, because they didn't own land for grazing their sheep, but wandered from field to field. Their livestock stripped vegetation and angered farmers. In fact, in the caste-like society of first century Israel, the only people considered lower than shepherds were lepers.

One rabbi of the time said this about shepherds: "Most of the time they are dishonest and thieving; they lead their herds onto other people's land and pilfer their produce." [4] Consequently, he warned people not to buy anything from shepherds because it was probably stolen property. Shepherds weren't even allowed to testify in court because they were considered so dishonest. [5]

They were *religious outcasts*, too, ceremonially unclean because of the dirty nature of their job, and therefore prevented from participating in the religious festivals at the Jerusalem Temple.

And don't forget: The Bible says they were *"living out in the fields… [with] their flocks…."* If you do a word study on this sentence you'll find it means they were *living out in the fields. With their flocks.* And I'm sure they smelled like it and looked like it.

And to *them* the angels came.

THEY'RE SINGING TO YOU

Listen to how the angel makes it so personal: I bring *you* news. Unto *you*. A sign to *you*. *You* will find…

Ron Mehl was a friend who pastored a church in Oregon for many years. He loved to tell about one memorable Christmas concert at his church. Ron watched a little boy he knew—a child with a severe hearing impairment—who sat in the audience and stared, somewhat bored, as the choir and soloists sang. Even when the children's choir went on stage, this child was not interested.

Until, for one song, the children's choir used sign language. He sat up and excitedly began flashing signs to his mom.

After the concert, Ron asked her what he had been signing with such enthusiasm.

It was: "Mom!! They're singing to *me!* They're singing to *me!*" [6]

I'm sure the shepherds could hardly believe their ears. God sent the angel choir to sing to *them*. And God is singing to *you*. To *you*, who may feel as despised and isolated and religiously undeserving as a first-century shepherd. To *you* he comes with an amazing message!

NEWS, NOT ADVICE

Did you notice how the angel characterizes his announcement? It is *good news*.

As Tim Keller points out, this is different from how we perceive religion. Religion is fundamentally *advice*. The gospel begins and ends with *news*.[7] These are completely different things. Most religions are based on the principle that you connect to God by being good, and so they give advice on how to be good. There are a thousand variations, but "they all have the same logic: If I perform, if I obey, then I'm accepted."[8]

The gospel is *news* rather than *advice* because it announces something that has happened that changes everything: God has come to earth, making a way for me; therefore, I am motivated to follow him out of love.

Do you see how good this news would have seemed to the shepherds, of all people? They were unable to follow the *advice* of their religion because of their occupation. It made them ceremonially unclean even as they were raising sheep for potential use at the Temple, an aggravating catch-22. The angels' message of a Savior for *them* was truly great news.

FAVORED ONES

The phrase "favor" in the angelic announcement is the same word the angel Gabriel earlier applies to Mary the mother of Jesus: "*Greetings, you who are **highly favored!**"* (LUKE 1:28) It's also the word translated elsewhere in the New Testament as *grace*.

The message is not that God is rewarding the shepherds for their

Temple sacrifices or their synagogue tithes or their religious purity. They could claim none of that. It was that they were simply the *objects of God's favor.*

Just like you and me.

Before writing this devotional today, I received an email from a man who reminded me of the shepherds:

> I thought that while everyone else may have been loved and saved, I was a lost case. I was positive God judged me because I was unable to stick to what I thought God's rules for being a good Christian were.

> I stopped going to church after a while and eventually stopped praying all together. I was convinced that I was this terrible person and if my deep dark secrets got out, everyone, not just God, would hate me.

> I am blessed with friends who care and convinced me to visit church with them. I didn't make it easy. I fought them the whole time.

> Well, my friends never gave up on me and I eventually made it to church. I had never understood how people could cry when talking about God's love, until I found grace. I felt the ice break off my heart. I felt my demons leave me. I felt free. I am God's beloved and he loves me no matter what. I believe in Jesus Christ who died on the cross and through him I am forgiven. I come to church smiling now. I'm not a perfect being. But I know… God loves me and knows my heart.

Maybe you, too, feel unclean; you're disqualifying yourself from the presence of God because of your shame.

But that's why Jesus came.

INTO THE TROUGHS

One last detail: The angels then tell the shepherds the sign of the Messiah. I'm sure the shepherds were waiting for something dramatic. In those days, *signs* were expected to be amazing, heavenly, astrological miracles. For example, at Caesar Augustus' birth, a blazing comet was said to be the sign of his "divinity."

So what would be the sign of the Messiah for the shepherds? Not a star in the sky. The Son in a stable. *A baby lying in a manger.* Don't miss it. A manger… that was a feeding trough for livestock. Now, how many feeding troughs do you think the shepherds had seen? Lots! They had probably used every manger within the vicinity to water or feed their flocks.

Only this time, *one of their own feeding troughs* would be holding their *Savior*.

The point? When God comes down, he comes *all the way* down. All the way to *your world*. All the way to *you*.

From the very start, his message was all about grace. From the start, he did not judge by outward appearance. From the start, it was about the heart.

PRAYER: Thank God today that he gives his favor to the least deserving.

5 LITTLE SPROUT

READ MATTHEW 2:19-23, LUKE 4:16-32

We just drove past the shepherd boy, and already our sleepy group is struggling to stay awake during this first jet-lagged afternoon in Israel. I look around and watch everyone sway, half-lidded, as our diesel bus grinds up a steep grade to the top of Mount Precipice.

As I drowsily glance to the east I see stunning views down into the agricultural Jezreel Valley — and then suddenly the scene becomes very urban. Brick walls and telephone wire flash in front of the bus window. We have turned a corner, and are right in the middle of a modern city.

I realize we have just driven up the famous cliff of Nazareth. This is the spot where many believe Jesus was nearly thrown to his death by villagers from his own hometown. They felt insulted by him — just minutes after he started his ministry! He sure didn't waste any time before he ticked people off.

NOWHERESVILLE

Most tour groups roll right through Nazareth on their way to more colorful locations. Although it's developing some interesting new sites, the town has a somewhat lackluster reputation as a destination today — and in Jesus' time, it had a similar identity.

During much of the first century, Nazareth was a tiny village with a big P.R. problem. One of Christ's own disciples expressed shock that Jesus called it his hometown: *"Nazareth! Can anything good come from there?"* (JOHN 1:46)

On the day before Christmas 2009, archaeologists announced the discovery of some small dwelling places here, the first that have been conclusively dated back to the time of Christ. The clues they discovered "suggest that Nazareth was an out-of-the-way hamlet of around fifty houses on a patch of about four acres." [9]

The Bible says Jesus' family settled here when he was a small boy. They'd been living in Egypt, where they'd fled to escape the wrath of Herod. Why move to Nazareth?

THE KING IS DEAD

The Gospel of Matthew says *"When Herod died..."*

Now stop there for a second.

That's Herod the Great, the father of all the other Herods in the Bible. He was the mad genius who built the Herodium we saw earlier outside Bethlehem, along with other spectacular monumental structures that were known as wonders of the ancient world.

He also killed most of his own family because he suspected them of treason. And in a failed attempt to kill the Messiah, Herod murdered all the babies in Bethlehem when Jesus was born.

Back to the verse:

> *When Herod died, an angel of the Lord appeared in a dream to Joseph in Egypt. "Get up!" the angel said. "Take the child and his mother back to the land of Israel, because those who were trying to kill the child are dead...." But when Joseph learned that the new ruler of Judea was Herod's son Archelaus, he was afraid to go there.* MATTHEW 2:19–20, 22 NLT

Joseph's fears were well-founded. Archelaus was the most bloodthirsty of Herod's surviving sons. He once killed three thousand men just for suspicion of treason, without a trial. When fifty of Jerusalem's leading citizens complained to Caesar about this, Archelaus had them all killed too.

So Joseph wisely decides to go right past the powerful city of Jerusalem and its small suburb of Bethlehem, and he takes Mary and the child Jesus all the way up north to the sleepy, seedy little town of Nazareth. He has relatives there, and because it's so tiny

5 LITTLE SPROUT

and so unimpressive, it's very much off the radar of anyone in Jerusalem. It's a great place to hide out and raise a family quietly.

And by so doing, Joseph is fulfilling prophecy.

GROWING UP IN BRANCHTOWN

Scholars believe the ancient town name *Nazareth* came from the old Hebrew word *netzer*, which means a sprout or little branch. So Nazareth literally means "Branchtown" or "Sproutville."

In Isaiah 11:1 there's a prophecy of the Messiah:

> *Out of the stump of David's family will grow a shoot — yes, a new Branch bearing fruit from the old root.* NLT

The word there for branch is the Hebrew word *netzer*.

In this section of Isaiah, written hundreds of years before Christ, the prophet is promising that after the destruction of Israel by foreign armies (which happened in 586 BC) there will still be hope — because out of a remnant of King David's family will come a *netzer*, just a little sprout that no one really notices — and out of that little shoot, a whole new olive tree will grow.

To understand what Isaiah is saying you need to know that olive trees have amazing longevity, much like the redwood trees we enjoy in California. The whole tree can seem to die, but if just a little sprout remains from the stump, an entirely new tree can form.

That's why olive trees can grow to be as old as redwoods. There are olive trees in the Holy Land over two thousand years old. They might get cut down or burned in a fire, but as long as they produce a little *netzer*, they're okay.

Jesus was that sprout! Descended from King David, he grew up unnoticed, in a land ravaged by war.

And the branch grew up... in *Branchtown*.

JESUS JOURNEY

One of the many things I love about the Bible is that God is so poetic. You don't have to see the poetry to understand the message, but it's there at so many levels if you look for it.

SCANDALIZING SERMON

Fast forward through time. It's about thirty years after the birth of Christ. People gather for the weekly synagogue meeting. Hometown boy Jesus gets up to read, and turns to Isaiah 61, one of the messianic passages the Essenes popularized in his day.

> *He unrolled the scroll and found the place where this was written: "The Spirit of the Lord is upon me, for he has anointed me to bring Good News to the poor."*

The word "anointed" is important. That's the way kings were crowned in Israel: Not with a circlet of gold, but with the anointing of oil. That's what "Messiah" means, the *anointed* one. In Greek, the word for Messiah is *kristos*, from the Greek verb *krio*, which means to anoint. That's where we get our word "Christ." It's not Jesus' last name! It's his title: *Christ, Messiah, Anointed one.* They're all just different words for the same thing.

But let's listen as Jesus reads on…

> *He has sent me to proclaim that captives will be released, that the blind will see, that the oppressed will be set free, and that the time of the Lord's favor has come.*
> LUKE 4:18B–19 NLT

Then he sits down.

And says, *"Today this Scripture is fulfilled in your hearing."*

That Messiah character? Yeah. It's me.

I imagine a brief pause as the worshippers take in his audacious claim. And then all pandemonium breaks loose. People get upset, fast. The favor Luke says Jesus had enjoyed with his fellow villagers evaporates in an instant.

5 LITTLE SPROUT

WHAT JESUS LEAVES OUT

Why would they be so upset with him? Well, it's interesting to look back at Isaiah 61 to see what Jesus leaves out. He stops right in the middle of the sentence. The rest of Isaiah 61:2 reads, "*...and the day of vengeance of our God...*" But Jesus chops off the verse just before this line. Because the judgment of God was to come *later*.

I suspect that, for the people listening, this omission was a big problem. *They* knew the whole verse. Probably had it memorized. Remember, we know from the Dead Sea Scrolls that the expectations of the time were that the Messiah would *start* with the *vengeance* part—some good old-fashioned *smiting!* That's what they wanted. Not *grace* to the Gentiles. *Smite* the Gentiles.

But grace to *all* is what, Jesus goes on to clarify, he *is* offering. In fact he boldly says he will do miracles for Gentiles, just as the other Jewish prophets did!

> *When they heard this, the people in the synagogue were furious.* LUKE 4:28 NLT

There was massive tension going on at the time between Jews and Gentiles—especially in little villages like Nazareth.

It was a poor place, yet all around it during the life of Christ, the Gentiles, and Jews in league with them, were erecting amazing monuments full of the latest technology—cities like Caesarea and Sepphoris were gorgeous towns even by our standards today.

How do people in impoverished neighborhoods today feel when rich foreigners come in, buy up the land, and build their lavish homes and shopping centers?

These Jews felt they were being humiliated by foreigners who were bulldozing their country and disrespecting their heritage. Saying nice things about Gentiles is not going to provoke a positive reaction.

THROWING JESUS OFF A CLIFF

They erupt into a riot, and the enraged mob tries to push Jesus off a cliff just outside town. In those days, you could stone someone in two ways. Throw stones at the person. Or throw the person at the stones. That's what they try — but Jesus slips away.

He starts a pattern here. For the rest of his ministry, he consistently confounds everyone's expectations of what a Messiah should do.

And of course it's still true today in *all* of our lives. When Jesus' agenda surprises us, we're sometimes ready to throw him off a cliff. We find ourselves saying things like, "I don't know if I believe in a Jesus who would act like that."

> On some level, Jesus disappoints everyone. Jesus is an equal opportunity disappointer. He disappoints not only the people of Nazareth who tried to throw him off a cliff because he wasn't the Messiah they wanted, he disappoints his own disciples at times too. — John Koessler [10]

Jesus came *for* us, but that does not mean he came to *please* us. He will not subject himself to our agenda, no matter how good we may think that agenda is. The little sprout grows undeterred right through our thickest walls.

Where does Jesus go, now that he is kicked out of his hometown? A spot so strategic that he becomes an international name overnight.

Meanwhile, down in the Judean desert about ninety miles south of Nazareth, Jesus' cousin John is attracting a crowd.

PONDER: Where in your life have you been outraged that Jesus hasn't been following your script? It's always a lot more interesting to follow Jesus as he works off *his* script.

6 THE MAN

READ LUKE 3:1-9, 21-22; JOHN 1:19-30

She tells me she ran from God for years.

She's still running.

But now she's running into his arms.

Mary Lou is just one of the thirty people in our group being baptized today. Others tell me of years lost to drugs or alcohol. Some have simply never been baptized after confessing faith decades ago. But for all of them, this is clearly a big deal.

A crowd gathers to watch. I look each person in the eyes, one at a time, and ask, "Have you placed your trust in Jesus Christ as your Lord and Savior?" I can see tears in their eyes and a glow on their faces.

They all know: Jesus is not just Savior of the World. He is Savior of *them*.

We're baptizing in the Jordan River at a place called Yardenit, close to where the river exits the Sea of Galilee to flow toward the Dead Sea. This is the same *river* Jesus was baptized in by his cousin John. But not the same *spot*.

Leafy trees cast comfortable shade on cool waters for our baptisms. John's baptisms took place ninety miles to the south, in a climate more suited to his scorching sermons: The hot Judean desert, at a place called "Bethany-beyond-the-Jordan."

HOT EXPECTATIONS

Remember how the Essenes, who also lived in that desert, helped spread the expectation that a Messiah was coming? Well, John's message is that the long-awaited Messiah is *almost here!*

Like the Essenes, John criticizes the religious power structure in Jerusalem. And it was a bureaucracy worthy of criticism.

In fact, you can find scathing, sarcastic comments about the high priests and the religious power structure in the sayings of other Jewish voices of the time as well. That first century Jewish historian Josephus characterized the family of high priests led by Annas as "heartless judges." [11]

Why were John, and many others, so critical of the Temple leadership?

PRIESTS AS POWER BROKERS

In 167 BC, about two hundred years before Jesus begins his earthly ministry, there was a revolution in Israel. The foreign oppressors are kicked out. The Maccabees, a Jewish rebel army, free Jerusalem. The Hasmonean dynasty begins.

And one very important change is introduced that has implications for years to come: They make the office of high priest not just religious, but political as well. The high priest becomes the leader of the nation, the top diplomat, the authority over every living Jew in the world, more powerful in many ways than even the king.

And when the mighty Roman army rolls into town, the ruling Jewish dynasty agrees to a peaceful transfer of power, as long as they retain just one small privilege: the right to appoint the high priest. After all, they insist, what interest would Romans have in Jewish religion? The Romans, perhaps not entirely aware of just how powerful the priesthood had become, agree.

For years afterward, the high priest is selected not on the basis of religious credentials, but on his ancestral connection to the Hasmonean family. The leading priestly families become the "godfathers" of life in Israel. Little is accomplished in the country without their cooperation and approval. And the capo di capo, the head of the families? The high priest.

6 THE MAN

Of course, an elaborate Temple system evolves to line the pockets of these priests. One way or another, the high priest's office charges for nearly every religious service — enough to pay for at least ten thousand priests in the city of Jerusalem alone.

CRUEL KINGS

On top of all this religious bureaucracy, there's the corrupt secular government.

In John's time, although Herod the Great had died, his family members were still political power brokers. Two of Herod's sons, Antipas and Philip, were the short-tempered, corrupt rulers of the Galilean provinces, while the Roman prefect Pontius Pilate ruled Judea. All of these rulers had one response to criticism: violence (John will experience this later when, after he criticizes Antipas, he is imprisoned and beheaded).

This religious and political background explains why the Essenes withdrew to the Judean wilderness near the caves at Qumran. With the government controlled ultimately by the pagan Romans, and in practical terms by a corrupt line of high priests who are all part of the same family dynasty, they see no hope for reform — until the Messiah arrives to kick all the bums out.

So now here comes John, preaching that the Messiah will soon set all things right. This is why Luke sets up the historical context for John's ministry so deliberately, with the names of Pilate and Herod Antipas and Philip and the high priests Annas and Caiaphas and others. These names are like a rogue's gallery of scoundrels and tyrants.

YOU'RE THE MAN

But John's preaching isn't just aimed at the bureaucracy — "The Man" — and how corrupt he is.

John makes his message very personal for each one listening. John says, essentially, "You're the Man." He does not allow the people to get self-righteous and point fingers just at the power structure. He warns them to see the evil in themselves too, and repent of their own sinfulness.

John says each individual must get ready for the Messiah's pending arrival, because, he implies, who knows what the Messiah will do? He may just decide to wipe out all the corruption by smiting anyone who is corrupt!

So the people who turn out to hear John are eager to know: *What does God want me to do as I prepare for the Messiah's arrival?*

I imagine a tense silence as people wait for John's answer.

Importantly, John does *not* tell people to go to the Temple to atone for their sins.

He doesn't talk about keeping the religious law, either.

He doesn't ask them to withdraw from society. Or give up hummus.

He even discounts the importance of their ethnic Jewishness: He says God can create children of Abraham for himself out of whatever and whoever he wants!

Instead, John preaches that what really matters is individual repentance of the *heart*. And real *inward* repentance will result in changed *outward* behavior.

John's message is a recovery of the prophet Isaiah's emphasis on sincere faith — resulting in a changed life — not religious law, an emphasis that Jesus will continue.

THE CURTAIN FINALLY OPENS
Then Jesus shows up. And John points to him and says…

Not: *Behold the King who replaces the Romans.*

Not: *Behold the Priest who purifies a corrupt religion.*

But: *"Behold the Lamb of God who takes away the sins of the world."* (JOHN 1:29)

John knows. Corruption runs more than skin deep. Or even system-deep. It's soul-deep. And so we need a soul-Savior.

There is so much in what happens in the next instant.

From heaven the voice of the Father booms: *"This is My Beloved Son."*

Then the Gospel of Mark says: The heavens were *"torn open and the Holy Spirit descended on him like a dove."* (MARK 1:10)

Don't miss the wording — the heavens did not just *open*. Something merely opened can be closed again. They were *torn* open. What's torn open *stays* open.

When the curtain opens to reveal the Messiah, it is ripped apart. And that tear is never mended. In fact, it gets bigger.

Mark's only other use of the word "torn"? Stay tuned for that part of the story. It'll rock your world.

But what happened right after Jesus was baptized was like a scene from a horror movie.

PONDER: Think back over the first few days of focusing on Jesus. How has it impacted you so far?

HOW MANY HERODS?

Bible readers are often confused by the various references to Herod in the New Testament. In the Gospel of Matthew, the evil King Herod orders all the babies in Jerusalem killed, then dies himself. In Mark and Luke, King Herod is still alive years later and orders John the Baptist beheaded. Much later, in the book of Acts, a young King Herod persecutes the early Christians.

The solution to this mystery? The name "Herod" appears in the New Testament 44 times—but it refers to three different men. [13]

THE FATHER: HEROD THE GREAT

The first Herod was the most infamous. Known as "Herod the Great," he was the ambitious builder of the Jerusalem Temple and ruthless murderer of anyone he suspected of scheming to steal his throne, including one of his own wives and several of his children. He was the ruler of all Judea, under the authority of Caesar himself. This first Herod died about two years after the birth of Christ, in 4 BC.

THE SON: HEROD ANTIPAS

After Herod the Great's death, his kingdom was divided into three parts, ruled over by three of his sons. They all used the title "Herod" at times, but the New Testament only refers to one of those sons as "Herod," the powerful Herod Antipas, who ruled over Galilee until his death in 39 AD. This is the Herod who had John the Baptist beheaded and presided over one of the trials of Jesus.

Herod Antipas' even more brutal brother, Herod Archelaus, ruled briefly over Jerusalem and Samaria but was removed from power in 6 AD by the Romans. He's referred to in Matthew 2:22 simply as "Archelaus." Another brother, Philip, controlled the eastern side of the Sea of Galilee. He and Antipas were deeply at odds, partly because Antipas stole Philip's wife. Philip later married his own niece Salome, the notorious dancer who had demanded John the Baptist's head.

THE GRANDSON: HEROD AGRIPPA

A close friend of two Caesars, Caligula and Claudius, Herod the Great's politically astute grandson Agrippa was able to convince Rome to unite the three regions ruled by his uncles when he came to power in 39 AD. He is the Herod who persecuted the church in the Book of Acts, then died after accepting worship from spectators in the theater at Caesarea.

7 / THE FIRST TEMPTATION OF CHRIST

READ MATTHEW 4:1-12

We're on a high.

After our baptism in the Jordan, we drive southward toward Jerusalem. Everyone on our bus is still giddy with the joy of the baptism, when our guide directs our attention to a craggy mountain looming over the city of Jericho.

It looks barren, dangerous, and, well… evil. We can barely make out a gravity-defying ancient monastery clinging to its sheer cliff face.

I understand how the monks who once lived there could be convinced this was the very spot where Jesus faced down the devil.

What's known as the Mount of Temptation sits on the edge of the Judean Desert. In contrast to the lusher areas of Galilee to the north, this spot gets an average of one inch of rain per year. It can get up to 125°F in the summer. The treacherous cliff falls four hundred feet to the town below (although these days you can reach the old monastery by taking a modern aerial tram). If the temptation of Christ didn't happen right here, this is an easy place to imagine it!

The Bible describes how Jesus headed to this region right after his baptism — just like our group today (I can only hope we don't meet the same character!).

Think of this. Jesus was alone here for forty days. The only human witness to these three temptations was Jesus. That means the disciples' source for this story must have been Christ himself.

Now ask yourself: Why would he relate this event to his disciples? What was he teaching? Was it just a really good scary story for one of their late night campfires? I believe Jesus used this story to explain the rules by which he operated. Though he was divine, he would not use his power in certain ways.

7 THE FIRST TEMPTATION OF CHRIST

FIRST TEMPTATION

1 The devil suggests that Jesus use his amazing power to *provide* for himself in a way outside God's timing…

The Bible says that after fasting forty days and forty nights, he was hungry (I guess so!). And the devil says, *"If you are the Son of God, tell these stones to become bread"* (LUKE 4:3). But Jesus will not use his power for his selfish benefit. He'll multiply bread and fish for the hungry masses, but not for a personal snack. He chose to be subject to the same physical weaknesses as you and me. He got hungry, tired, lonely.

SECOND TEMPTATION

2 Then the devil suggests that Jesus *prosper* himself in a way outside of God's will…

He shows Jesus the kingdoms of the world and offers them all to him, if Jesus will bow to him. Just one time.

Imagine being Jesus, and knowing that you could bring instant justice to the corrupt kingdoms of the world for this small moment of compromise.

So many people have taken this bargain. They think of all the good they could do with power, splendor, authority — and they are willing to compromise to get there.

But for Jesus, worshipping God *alone* trumps anything else. Any good he could have done outside of God's plan is not worth it.

THIRD TEMPTATION

3 Finally, Satan suggests that Jesus use his position to *prove* himself beyond a shadow of a doubt to all those who would mock him.

Again, imagine being Christ. Thousands of angels have worshipped you for eons in heaven. And yet here on earth, on a mission of love, you are reviled and hunted by sinful humans who call you crazy and demon-possessed. Wouldn't you want to prove to them all, conclusively, who you really were — and what ignorant jerks they were being?

Satan says, "Do it. Jump off the pinnacle of the temple and float to the ground!" Amaze the crowds! Compel belief!

Jesus is not interested in that kind of belief. He's interested in *love*.

We often want God to give some undeniable proof to the whole world at once of his existence — but as C. S. Lewis wrote, "Are we sure that he is even interested in the kind of Theism which would be a compelled logical assent to a conclusive argument?" [12]

NO COMPELLED CONVERSIONS

Christ's responses to these three temptations answer so many questions I have about him, and that others in his lifetime had too. For example, "If Jesus is God, why doesn't he help himself out a little — like, come down from the cross? Why doesn't he just put all the bad guys away and take control, right now? Jesus, why don't you give an undeniable proof, do a personal miracle on request for everybody, so no one could possibly doubt?"

Jesus is saying, "That's not the way I work."

He is the King of Kings. He is God. He does do miracles.

But not on demand. Not to grab authority. And not to help himself.

The bottom line to all these temptations? Jesus will not use his divine power for his own benefit. Not even to force belief. He is here to reach out in love.

JESUS IS A GENTLEMAN

In the ridiculous movie *Bruce Almighty,* Jim Carrey actually does a decent job of showing what happens when someone yields to all three temptations. Bruce gets to use divine power for a few days to provide for all his needs and wishes, to prosper himself wildly, and to prove himself to his girlfriend and compel her to be with him.

And he loses any hope that her love will be given to him freely. And this is his greatest desire.

If Jesus had yielded, he would have lost the very object of his quest: Our love.

Or think of it this way: Ask people what they don't like about Christianity, and what are they going to say? The Crusades. The Inquisition. Judgmental Christians.

They know intuitively that at those times the church did not operate the way Jesus did. At those times, the church yielded to the temptation to power — to belief compelled by a show of force.

But Jesus is a gentleman. He stands at the door and knocks. And waits for you to answer.

Why? He is building the foundation for what's to come. The kingdom of God begins one human heart at a time. This is how the new heaven and new earth will be populated — not by slaves or robots, but by those who have willingly turned their hearts toward him. And he longs for as many to join him as possible.

But this wasn't easy for Jesus. After he's nearly killed in his hometown for announcing that he is the Christ and then facing down the devil, Jesus finds a new headquarters, a place so strategic that it enables him to reach the whole world without traveling more than a few miles.

PONDER: Write down one temptation you're currently struggling with. How can Jesus' example help you face that temptation?

PART 2

MISSION

8 MESSIAH HEADQUARTERS

READ MATTHEW 4:12-16; 23-25

The Philippines. Sri Lanka. India. Brazil. Iraq. Eritrea. Italy. Switzerland. Martinique. Mexico. Ethiopia.

All responses to my question, "So, where are you from?" And all heard just this morning.

Our group is walking the pilgrim path into Capernaum. We're far from alone. Just like in the days of Jesus' earthly ministry, he still has crowds of followers eager to meet him. And they are from all over.

It's expanding my vision of the Body of Christ. I'm getting a worldwide, God's-eye view.

But it's a view Jesus had from the start.

You can tell by looking at a map.

ON THE WAY OF THE SEA

After he's kicked out of Nazareth, Jesus very strategically chooses the town of Capernaum to be his headquarters for much of his ministry.

Why? Capernaum was not big or important or well known. But as you'll see, his choice was deliberate — and brilliant.

Capernaum is on the northern shore of the Sea of Galilee. That's the largest freshwater lake in Israel. It resembles the shape of a harp when seen from the surrounding hills, which is where it gets its Hebrew name, "Sea of Kinnereth" or, in Greek, "Sea of Gennesaret." These words are related to the Hebrew *kinnor,* meaning "harp."

In ancient times, an international trade highway called the *Via Maris* skirted a few miles of Galilee's shoreline. One of the most important roads in the entire ancient world, *Via Maris* literally means "The Way of the Sea." Remember that phrase.

The *Via Maris* connected three continents. It came down from Europe and Asia in the north via Damascus to the top of the lake. Then it ran down the northwest shore for a few miles until it shot further westward toward the coast, and from there it led south to Egypt and Africa.

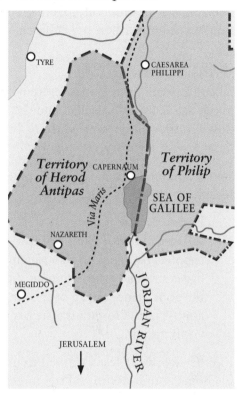

Capernaum, in a narrow valley between the lake and the mountains, was the official toll station on the Via Maris as travelers entered or left Galilee.

That meant virtually any traveller between Rome, Greece, Syria, and Persia in the north, and Judea, Egypt, Ethiopia, or the rest of Africa in the south, had to travel *right past this village.* Little Capernaum would have seen much more international traffic than even Jerusalem, which was far larger and more famous, but in an inland valley away from the trade routes.

BORDER TOWN

What's more, Capernaum was almost right on the border between the two regions ruled by warring sons of Herod the Great: Herod Antipas governed the more Jewish western side of Galilee, and his hated brother Philip ruled the eastern side.

So when things got hot in one lakeside territory, Jesus could just hop on a boat and sail over to the other side of the lake, which was controlled by a different government. This kept him safe until the time was right for him to lay down his own life.

FAR FROM THE MEDDLING CROWD

Since Capernaum is on the extreme northern side of the lake, it's about as far from Jerusalem and the meddling religious authorities down in the southern province of Judea as you can get — and still be in Jewish territory.

And Capernaum is a very nice place. The ancient Jewish writer Josephus praised its climate. He wrote,

> Its nature is wonderful as well as its beauty... Its soil is so fruitful that all kinds of trees can grow upon it... it supplies people with the principal fruits, with grapes and figs continually during ten months of the year; besides the good temperature of the air, it is also watered from a most fertile fountain. The people of that country call it Capharnaum.... [14]

In other words, if Jesus wanted to influence the whole world from his home country with as little interference from religious authorities as possible, and live in a nice place to boot, Capernaum was the best choice.

It worked. Matthew talks about the instant, international extent of Jesus' popularity:

> *News about him spread as far as Syria... Large crowds followed him wherever he went — people from Galilee, the Decapolis, Jerusalem, from all over Judea, and from east of the Jordan River.* MATTHEW 4:24–25

This was not only intended by Jesus; it was specifically prophesied. Matthew describes how Jesus...

8 MESSIAH HEADQUARTERS

...went and lived in Capernaum, which was by the lake in the area of Zebulun and Naphtali — to fulfill what was said through the prophet Isaiah: "Land of Zebulun and land of Naphtali, the Way of the Sea (Notice this phrase? The Way of the Sea was the *Via Maris*), *beyond the Jordan, Galilee of the Gentiles — the people living in darkness have seen a great light; on those living in the land of the shadow of death a light has dawned."* MATTHEW 4:13–16

PARTY AT PETER'S HOUSE

In the ruins of Capernaum, archaeologists have discovered several buildings that actually date to the time of Christ!

The most impressive ruin in Capernaum today is the limestone synagogue from around the fourth century AD, dated by thousands of coins found beneath the pavement. But it's easy to see how the white limestone was laid on top of another building made of black basalt rock. Dated by pottery found on the floor, this older synagogue is from the time of Christ — probably the very building in which he taught!

And the story behind another ruin is even more astounding. Experts discovered, under an ancient church, the ruins of a house from the time of Christ. It was about a block from the synagogue, right on the lakeshore — apparently a fisherman's house.

Ancient Christian graffiti in Aramaic, Greek, Syriac, and Latin naming both "Lord Jesus Christ" and "Simon Peter" has been found on the walls. Excavators believe that, shortly after the ministry of Christ, this was venerated as the house of Simon Peter!

The house was apparently used as a church as early as the mid-first-century AD, remodeled over the years to accommodate bigger crowds. It remains the most ancient Christian place of worship yet found. Its location fits the evidence in the Bible; the house of Peter was a short walk from the synagogue in Capernaum (SEE MATTHEW 8:5, MARK 1:29).

Since its discovery, a unique glass-bottom church was built over the site. You can now sit in modern pews and look down beneath your feet at a two-thousand-year-old house Jesus probably ministered in.

On this afternoon, I watch as many of those very pilgrims I met earlier in the day enter the church. Some pray. Some sing. Others weep. I find the atmosphere charged with joy and excitement.

From across the world, speaking languages unknown to one another, we have all been drawn here, bound by something stronger than the name of the country on our passport: We were sought out and found by the one we worship today. We were lost sheep of other folds, who heard the call of the one shepherd.

Even in his choice of Capernaum as a headquarters, Jesus is continuing to reveal the DNA of the gospel. It's always been about cross-cultural, international outreach. From the start, Jesus was showing that God is a God for all humanity. He is concerned about redeeming *all* people, everywhere.

From the very beginning, the Messiah came not just for Israel, but for the entire planet — and that includes you!

Now that he's got an amazingly strategic headquarters, what kind of talented, A-list, high-capacity people will Jesus recruit when he puts together his staff? You will be surprised.

PONDER: What implications are there for your own attitudes and priorities when you see how intentionally Jesus reached out to the whole world?

9   FIRST FOLLOWERS

READ MATTHEW 4:18-22, LUKE 5:1-11, LUKE 6:12-22

I stand in a museum along the shore of the Sea of Galilee looking at one of the biggest finds in the history of marine archaeology. And I'm getting goose bumps.

The story of this discovery is amazing.

A misty rain broke a long drought here on January 24, 1986. Because of the drought, the water level in the lake had receded dramatically.

On an early morning sail that day, two fisherman brothers saw something curious poking up from the mud in shallow water. They couldn't believe their eyes: It looked like an ancient boat. In a curious coincidence, at the very same moment, they both looked up and saw a double rainbow.

They suspected they were on to something big, and immediately contacted famous marine archaeologist Dr. Kurt Raveh and Texas A&M biblical archaeology professor Dr. Shelley Wachsman.

Three independent precision carbon-14 tests confirmed the amazing truth: The brothers had found an intact wooden fishing vessel from the time of Christ — the very kind Jesus and his disciples travelled and fished in! It's now housed in a building near the lakeside community of Kibbutz Ginosaur where we stand and stare.

One curious detail about this boat: It can comfortably seat about... *twelve people.*

A cooking pot and a lamp and some first-century coins were found in the shipwreck and are also on display at the museum — just normal artifacts of daily life in the first century.

ORDINARY BOAT, ORDINARY MEN

What's striking about this boat is that it's so ordinary. Just like the boats Peter and Andrew and James and John used. Or I should say, just like Peter and Andrew and James and John themselves!

In today's readings, Matthew gives the quick sketch and Luke fills in the details.

These men are busy with the day-to-day responsibilities of fishermen: Fixing nets. Prepping for the next trip. How many times had they done this, over and over again? Following Christ isn't even on their agenda. Their minds are elsewhere. But Jesus calls them.

This is a huge departure from the way other first-century rabbis gathered disciples. In those days, potential *disciples* travelled to the *teacher* they hoped to follow, and asked his permission to become a disciple. In a sense, they applied for an internship.

So in the normal social and cultural protocol of the day, this story never would have happened.

Put yourself in their sandals. Here's Jesus, standing on the beach, interrupting your day, calling you to follow him.

And Jesus does not even go into long explanations. He simply says, *"Follow me."*

Living the Christian life does not mean understanding everything God is doing, or everything Jesus meant. It means following along as Jesus does his thing, around you and in you and with you. Then telling others about this amazing person.

CHOSEN TO FOLLOW

As Jesus will later remind his disciples,

> *"You did not choose me, but I chose you and appointed you that you should go and bear fruit and that your fruit should abide." John 15:16*

9 FIRST FOLLOWERS

I don't think Matthew is writing this so that we can admire these guys and think, *Wow, how awesome of them to leave everything and follow Jesus; they were spiritual giants!* I don't think Matthew is pointing to the disciples at all; he's telling us something about how Jesus operates.

He comes to you and me in the middle of our busy lives and says, simply, *"Follow me."* It's not about your worthiness or your performance or your potential. It's about his grace.

And notice: *"Follow me."* Not "Work for me."

Most Christians who burn out in their faith have, at some point, gone from *walking with* Jesus to *working for* Jesus. When you think of yourself as working for Jesus you will get resentful and burned out (think of the oldest son in the Prodigal Son parable: "All these years I've been slaving for you!" he spouts off to his father, who responds, "My son, all I have is yours...").

GOD USES NOBODIES

I love that the very first followers Jesus picks seem to be very average. Just normal people doing ordinary things. They weren't showing promise. They didn't earn an internship. He is not picking proven A-players. He is showing what he can do with *anyone*. God can do more with a nobody than anybody else can do with a somebody!

And look who he calls next. Jesus didn't just call fishermen. The other people represented in his inner circle were an even bigger surprise.

There were three main religious groups in first-century Israel, and they despised each other. They were all focused on getting that longed-for kingdom reboot prophesied in the Scriptures, but they had radically different ideas about how this would be achieved.

ZEALOTS

Here's the way John Ortberg describes the first group: "Zealots believed that the Kingdom of God would come to Israel when there were enough people who were angry enough to revolt. They chose the way of *attack*. This was an extreme nationalist party. They were dedicated to bringing in the Kingdom of God by overthrowing the Romans; they would use any means necessary, including violence." [15]

PHARISEES

Pharisees believed that rigid adherence to the Law of Moses and all of its 613 commandments was the way for the Kingdom of God to come to earth. They essentially withdrew into a holy huddle to avoid pollution by the pagan world. They wouldn't even enter a Gentile house. Their strategy was basically *withdrawal and rule-following*.

SADDUCEES

The most powerful group, the Sadducees did not believe in the Resurrection, the afterlife, angels or spirits. They were interested only in the here and now. The Sadducees looked at the Romans, and thought, *Well, if you can't beat 'em, join 'em.* Their strategy was *collaboration*. They worked with the tax collectors to get money for the Temple system. They had an uneasy alliance with the Roman political powers.

These three groups all despised one another.

Then who does Jesus choose to be his followers, after he starts with the fishermen?

How about… Simon, the *Zealot*. One of the attackers.

Then there's Nicodemus, the *Pharisee*, one of the rule-followers.

And Matthew, the *tax collector* — one of the Jews who happily collaborated with the very Romans the Zealots wanted to attack.

9 FIRST FOLLOWERS

And how about the Samaritan woman? As Ortberg puts it, in the eyes of all the rest she's the wrong gender, wrong nationality, wrong religion, and has the wrong sexual history. She stands outside *all* the walls. [16]

But Jesus, as always, is not about walls. He's about grace.

COLORFUL KINGDOM

Even in his choice of followers, Jesus is showing what kind of a community he came to create. He picks a group of people about as diverse as possible in the first century. A group where what matters is not your ethnicity or history or bank account, but your heart. And he still does.

I look at the group on our Israel tour bus right now. People range from 13 to 73 years of age. Men and women, Republicans and Democrats. English and Spanish and Russian and German speakers. People sporting close-cropped Marine haircuts and Grateful Dead-style ponytails.

But we find our unity in following him.

Maybe you feel like you've never really belonged. Like you've always been cut from the team, or never invited to join in the first place. Jesus says, *Come join my community.*

PONDER: Jesus chose widely diverse followers. What implications does this have for your own actions and attitudes? Thank God today that he chooses you!

10 SLOW AND SNEAKY KINGDOM

READ MARK 1:14-15, LUKE 17:20-21, MARK 4:30-32, JOHN 18:36-37

I'm standing above one of the most stunning archaeological sites in Israel: Beth Shean.

This spot is mentioned in 1 Samuel 31 as the place where the Philistines hung the bodies of Saul and Jonathan after they were killed in battle. A thousand years later, it was the capital of the cities of the Decapolis, a region the Bible says Jesus visited.

The ruins here are spectacular: Beautiful, colonnaded sidewalks border shops, temples, and gymnasiums decorated with mosaics and marble. This city stood strong and proud until

it was destroyed by an earthquake on January 18, 749 AD. In a moment, dozens of massive columns toppled over in the same direction, and were simply left there as sandstorms slowly buried the city. It was all but forgotten when it was uncovered in the 1920s by archaeologists.

Today Beth Shean, or Scythopolis as it was known in the time of Christ, is a great place to be reminded that first-century residents of Israel were rather sophisticated. In cities like this there were beautiful fountains, smoothly paved streets, and art and culture everywhere.

LAYERS OF KINGDOMS

This is also a great spot to note the variety of governments the Holy Land has had.

Monuments with hieroglyphics detailing the reigns of the Pharaohs Seti I and Ramses II were discovered here, as well as a life-sized statue of Ramses III. As I stand on top of the hill in the ruins of the Egyptian governor's house, I can look down past Canaanite and Israelite fortifications all the way to the Roman and Byzantine ruins in the valley, one powerful civilization after the next.

That's typical in this part of the world. The Holy Land has probably seen more of the world's kingdoms reigning over it than any other piece of real estate on earth. And there's a simple explanation.

THE LAND BRIDGE

This is a land bridge between Africa and the Arabian peninsula to the south, and Europe and Asia to the north. Picture a thin strip of hospitable country with the ocean on one side and the desert on the other. That's Israel.

From prehistoric times, humans and animals have travelled back and forth across this space, funneled by geography into a narrow channel about seventy miles wide (at its widest).

All of the world empires that ever existed anywhere close to this strip of land longed to control it because of its strategic importance. The flags of Egypt, Babylon, Assyria, Greece, Rome, Turkey, England, and many more empires, have flown over this small area. For a brief period that became the stuff of legend, there was even a united kingdom of Israel led by David and Solomon.

To understand the mindset of the long-suffering Jewish inhabitants of this land in the first century, understand: *This was a place of constant kingdom replacement.*

Consequently the people here saw the solution to all their problems in terms of regime change. After this parade of foreign kingdoms, the idea of a great and good ruler leading a kingdom that once again actually originated right here was seen as a kind of paradise.

Since *kingdoms* had brought so much pain and so much progress, that was clearly, people figured, both the problem and the solution: Get rid of the old kingdom. Get a new kingdom. A kingdom of God.

THE KING IS COMING!

Jesus, as the people would have expected from a Messiah figure, does indeed use a lot of "kingdom" language. But he slowly and surely changes their idea of what God's kingdom is all about.

He says his kingdom is *in* the world, but not *of* the world. It is really *in* the world. It's not merely a spiritual kingdom. It's just as real as Rome. But it is not *of* the world. In crucial ways, it's not *like* any earthly kingdom.

LIKE AND UNLIKE THE KINGDOMS YOU KNOW

Parable after parable is introduced with the words, *"The kingdom of heaven is like..."* and then Jesus gives a surprising metaphor designed to explain the kind of kingdom the Messiah was here to establish. It's like a buried treasure. It's like a pearl in an oyster. It's like a tiny seed that grows into the biggest tree.

What can you learn from the details of those parables and sayings? Jesus makes clear that the kingdom of God has a ruler and citizens and power and authority, like earthly kingdoms. But in at least five ways the kingdom of God differs from the paradigm the people had when they thought of the kingdom:

First, *it starts in the heart.* It starts at the soul level before it gets to the system level. Then saved souls are like a good virus inside the system, changing it from the inside-out, even as they've been changed.

Second, *it's already here.* God's kingdom isn't something we have to sit and wait for anymore. It's here *now.* That's good for us to remember, too. It's already in prisons. In oppressed countries. In hospitals. In nursing homes. In businesses. In schools.

Third, *it starts small and grows until it fills the whole world.* God's kingdom starts inside individual hearts and souls. Then one day the very planet will be transformed by the Messiah himself when he returns to perfect what has begun.

Fourth, *followers of the Messiah are like advance ambassadors for the fully realized kingdom.* Through the way we live, the way we treat others, we show people what living in the kingdom of heaven is like. We proclaim that the Messiah will return one day to make the whole world a place of such peace — permanently. Being part of the kingdom in this way is worth any sacrifice we can possibly make.

Fifth, *it grows through love, not violence or political manipulation.* God's reign on earth is typified by the poor and hungry being fed, by sinners being forgiven, by the sick being cared for. This is what the Messiah came to do, and what his followers do. These good deeds are not the good news; the gospel is the simple message of God's rescue mission in Christ. But these acts flow from lives changed by the gospel.

IN OUR WEAKNESS HE IS STRONG

It's easy to feel that the kingdom of God is weak because its soldiers go about feeding the poor and healing the sick instead of waving weapons and crowning kings. And it is often weak in the eyes of the world's power brokers.

True, the kingdom of heaven is powered not by political alliances or gunpowder. But it has power.

It's powered by the same loving God who makes every wave that seems weak but shapes the shoreline, every tree that grows quietly until it splits pavement, every creeping glacier that almost imperceptibly carves valleys, and it's just as slow and just as deliberate and ultimately just as relentless.

Make no mistake: *earthly kingdoms will oppose God's kingdom.* No one gives up a kingdom easily. Even though God brings a kingdom of love, this is still seen as a threat by earthly powers. Somehow they understand the revolutionary nature of this concept. Followers of the Messiah should expect opposition. But we can also expect ultimate victory.

Jesus still corrects our concept of God's kingdom today.

When his first-century audience heard that phrase, they thought only of earth, of thrones and soldiers and crowns and kings — a purely physical government. Even today some want to see God's kingdom advance with weapons of this world. They promote violence, fear, and anger, all in the name of religion. But his kingdom is not *of* the world.

We can err in the other direction, too, often imagining Jesus is speaking only of heaven. One day, we think, we will see the kingdom of God, in the sweet bye-and-bye. But Jesus says his kingdom is *in* the world. Now.

> ...the point of God's split-level good creation, heaven
> and earth, is not that earth is a kind of training ground
> for heaven, but that heaven and earth are designed to
> overlap and interlock... and that one day — as the book
> of Revelation makes very clear — one day they will do so
> fully and forever, as the New Jerusalem comes down from
> heaven to earth. —N. T. Wright [17]

PONDER: How can you bring God's kingdom closer to your world today? What does it mean to you when Jesus says to "seek first the kingdom of God and his righteousness"?

THE URBANITY OF CHRIST

Somehow an image of Jesus developed over the years — perhaps a result of low-budget Bible movies — of an illiterate peasant who wandered nearly empty country roads, without exposure to the wealth of art and literature blossoming in the Roman world at the same time.

Now we know this is inaccurate.

Visitors to the Holy Land are often astounded at the advanced technology in the Greco-Roman-style cities built here during Christ's life. Archaeological digs in Tiberias, Caesarea Maritime, Sepphoris, Jerusalem, and other first-century cities have unearthed beautiful theaters, paved streets with sidewalks, colonnaded marketplaces very much like modern shopping malls, aqueducts, the advanced use of building materials like hydraulic cement, and more. Jesus would have walked right past these first-century marvels many times.

And Galilee, where Jesus spent most of his time, wasn't a place of rural emptiness. Josephus describes the cities of Galilee as much larger than we tend to imagine:

> The cities lie here very thick, and the very many
> villages here are everywhere so full of people,
> because of the richness of the soil, that the very
> least of them contain above fifteen thousand inhab-
> itants... (Josephus, *War*, 3:3)

It all paints a picture at odds with the hayseed savant Jesus and primitive followers we often imagine. As I tell my group, "These were not the Flintstones!"

11 WON'T YOU BE A NEIGHBOR?

READ LUKE 10:25-37

We sit in a medical clinic near a church. Palm trees sway outside in the warm twilight breeze as traffic noise filters in through the open patio.

I listen as the wealthy young businessman describes life in this Muslim-majority country. When someone in our group asks him what it's like to be a Christian here, he lowers his voice. Perhaps without even realizing it, he glances quickly toward the window.

After ten days in Israel, we have crossed the border into Jordan, where we meet several local Christians. While they're all careful to endorse the many good works of the present government, they also admit to the pressure of being a tiny minority in their own country.

I can understand why. The secret police are always lurking here. From their perspective, they're just trying to keep order. There's so much potential for explosive violence in this society, with its volatile mix of religions and political loyalties, that the police monitor every organization to root out any troublemakers.

But for many Christians, the constant presence of the secret police, or *mukhabarat* in Arabic, can be chilling. Simple evangelism, part of the basic DNA of any believer, feels dangerous. The conversion of Muslims to Christianity is against the law in this country, so any religious conversation with anyone outside the small circle of known Christians is tinged with risk.

Even the U. S. State Department, which considers Jordan an ally, says the lack of accountability within the *mukhabarat* underscores "significant restrictions on freedom of speech, press, assembly and association." It reports that agents "sometimes abuse detainees physically and verbally" and "allegedly also use torture." [18]

So what's it like to be a Christian in a place like this?

11 WON'T YOU BE A NEIGHBOR?

THE HOLY HUDDLE TEMPTATION

One Jordanian friend tells me that the temptation is to retreat to the "holy huddle," to just hang out with other people who are like you. It's safer. It keeps you out of trouble. It keeps you clean.

It reminds me of what was happening in the Judaism of Jesus' time. Because of the sometimes brutal oppression of the Greek and then Roman rulers, rabbis debated the meaning of the word "neighbor" in this command from the book of Leviticus:

> Do not seek revenge or bear a grudge against anyone
> among your people, but love your neighbor as yourself.
> I am the LORD. LEVITICUS 19:18

Does "neighbor" include the sneering soldier, the foreigner, the enemy?

By the time of Christ, popular teaching excluded all non-Israelites from this Levitical command to love and not hate. Pharisees even excluded non-Pharisees. Other rabbis in Christ's time said this didn't include any *personal* enemies (which seems to miss the whole point, doesn't it?). [19]

So the lawyer in Luke 10 wants to know Jesus' opinion. *Who is my neighbor?*

And as he almost always does, Jesus says, *Let me tell you a story.*

THE SURPRISING NEIGHBOR

Once upon a time, a man walked from Jerusalem to Jericho.

This 17-mile drive was notorious in ancient times. It wound through steep desert canyons, descending 3,600 miles from the high plateau of Jerusalem to the desert oasis of Jericho along the Wadi Qilt gorge. Ever hike into the Grand Canyon? Think of something like those narrow paths and you'll have an idea of what this road was like.

Robbers wait around a sharp turn in the road. The man is robbed, stripped, beaten, and left for dead.

Then three people happen along.

First, a priest. In those days, thousands of priests worked on rotation in Jerusalem but lived in Jericho, known as the city of priests. Because this man is headed "down" the road, it's clear he's headed home. But he crosses to the other side of the path, stepping carefully around the body, perhaps because he can't touch a corpse without becoming "unclean," which would interfere with his job.

He's focused on ceremony, on cleanliness, on career. Not compassion.

Second: A Levite, one of the thousands of clerical assistants in the temple, who also had rules against touching corpses. He too passes right by.

Third: Well, most scholars agree that Christ's original listeners would have expected him to introduce a Jewish layperson at this point. But Jesus, the master of the plot twist, introduces a *Samaritan.* The most despised ethnic group in the region.

One night when Jesus was about ten, Samaritan terrorists infiltrated the Jewish Temple in Jerusalem and defiled it by scattering human bones all over the sanctuary, halting worship for quite a while until it could be ritually cleansed again.

Those Samaritans had been exacting revenge for the time a few years earlier when Jewish soldiers had destroyed the Samaritan temple.

And this cycle of attack and counter-attack had been going on for centuries.

FAMILY FEUD

Hundreds of years before this story, the Jews were conquered by the Assyrians. Most of the Israelites were taken captive and moved out of the country. But a few, especially the poorer ones, were left in Israel. They intermarried with the Assyrian soldiers to survive in the ruins. When, years later, the other Jews moved back, these people were despised, seen as collaborators. They weren't even allowed to worship in the Temple.

So the Samaritans, as these people came to be called, said, "Fine. We'll build our own temple." They went to a place called Mount Gerizim, and built a house of worship there.

The tension thickened to the point where most Jews would never even eat or talk with Samaritans. They were considered heretics, deviants, blasphemers.

A Samaritan would *never* be the hero of a Jewish story.

But not only does this Samaritan rescue the man, he gives him shelter at an inn nearby and leaves two denarii — enough to pay for about twenty-four days at the inn — and promises to bring back more money if needed.

SURPRISE ENDING

Then, the second twist at the end of the story. I think almost everyone misses it, the way Jesus spins the lawyer's question around on its head. The lawyer was asking, "Who is my neighbor?" But Jesus asks him, *"Which of these three do you think was a neighbor to the man who fell into the hands of robbers?"* (LUKE 10:36)

In other words, "neighbor" is not about the label I choose to apply to other people. "Neighbor" is a term that may or may not describe *me*.

The question is not who is the lawyer's neighbor; *the question is whether the lawyer is a neighbor.* [20]

Jesus is telling a story about the tendency of religion to degenerate into an *us vs. them* system; a way to distinguish the good people from the bad people; a way to socialize with the *insiders* and avoid unclean contact with *outsiders*.

CHOOSE TO BE A NEIGHBOR

In December 2000, Wheaton college professor of New Testament Gary Burge was given the remarkable opportunity to preach the sermon at Friday prayers at the influential Abu Nour Mosque in Damascus, Syria. Because the relationship between the minority Christians and the majority Muslims in Syria is often strained, he chose to speak on the parable of the Good Samaritan. He concluded:

> Being a neighbor is meaningless if it refers only to those inside my religious or cultural or national circle. Being a *neighbor* is about courage, about taking risks; it is about walking across the road and helping — and not using religion as an excuse to stay away. [21]

It is certainly a risk for Christians to do this in the Arab countries of the Mideast. The businessman we're listening to in Jordan explains that this is why he, and many other Jordanian Christians, have opened health clinics, such as the one we're sitting in now.

Clinics like this are designed to be places where low-income people — many of them Palestinian refugees from the West Bank — can receive free care, without any strings attached. The ones who've been left on the side of the road can find help here, in these places that remind me of the Inn of the Good Samaritan.

"Muslims will not read our Bibles or listen to our sermons," one Jordanian says. "But they will see us. So the one question is, what do they see when they see us?"

Christians in every culture must consider this. Jesus continually emphasized the role of good deeds — not to earn salvation, but to show the new kind of kingdom that Christians are spreading: A kingdom of love.

Ours is not a kingdom of this world. There are no borders, no ID checks. No secret religious police. But there are ambassadors. Emissaries of the kingdom to come.

11 WON'T YOU BE A NEIGHBOR?

The next place I visited in Jordan gave me a stunning, border-free, God's-eye view of the Holy Land.

PROJECT: Think of a person or group of people you're struggling to treat as your neighbor. "Cross the street" today and do something that demonstrates God's love to that person or group of people.

12 JUST ONE LOOK

I stand on Mount Nebo facing east, thousands of feet above the Jordan Valley. The land of Jesus unfolds before me like a 3-D Google map:

On my left and to the south, there's the Dead Sea, where those prophecies about Jesus were preserved for two thousand years.

A little to the right of that, I can trace the contours of the Mount of Olives overlooking Jerusalem.

Directly below me, snaking to my right and north, the Jordan River, where Jesus was baptized.

Just beyond it lies the city of Jericho, where the vertically-challenged Zacchaeus climbed a tree to get a better view of Jesus above the crowd.

Looming above Jericho are the mountains of the Judean wilderness, where Christ was tempted by Satan himself.

Because the Jordan River valley sits below sea level, a 3,300-foot mountain on its edge has quite a spectacular, unobstructed vista. In fact, this mountain is in the Bible *because* of its view. It's the place where Moses—1,400 years before Christ—saw the Promised Land.

SNAKE ON A POLE

There's a church behind me on the mountain commemorating that story, the Church of St. George. And immediately to my right, behind the church: A metal statue of a snake twisting up a pole.

This weird sculpture comes from a fascinating story in Numbers 21:6-9. Because they had rebelled against God, the Israelites were punished with an infestation of poisonous snakes.

They were dying from the poison in their blood. The situation seemed hopeless.

And then God instructs Moses to do something strange: Make a bronze serpent on a pole. It's an image similar to the icon of the medical profession, the caduceus. God says to lift it high in the air. Anyone who simply looks at it will be miraculously healed.

So what did it mean when Jesus said in John 3, *"Just as Moses lifted up the snake in the wilderness, so the Son of Man must be lifted up, that everyone who believes may have eternal life in him"* (JOHN 3:14–15)?

NICODEMUS THE TOP DOG

To really understand this, you have to know who Jesus is talking to here. He's saying these words to *Nicodemus*. Thanks to John's detailed description, we know a lot about this guy.

Nicodemus was a *Pharisee*. That meant he was one of the few, the proud, the spiritual Marines of his day. There were never more than six thousand Pharisees, even in their heyday. That's because, to become a Pharisee, you had to take a vow to devote every moment of your life to keeping God's law *perfectly.*

They wrote down volumes of extra rules they'd invented to ensure they wouldn't even come close to breaking one of God's laws. Eventually, their rule book developed into something called the Mishnah. Just one example of how strict they were: There are twenty-four chapters in the Mishnah on how to keep the Sabbath holy. That's two dozen thick volumes on *one commandment alone.*

Nicodemus was also a member of the *Sanhedrin*. This was a select group of men who ran all the religious affairs of Israel. They had authority over every Jewish man in the world.

Not only that: In verse 10, Jesus calls him *the* Teacher of Israel. Nicodemus apparently had a position of prominence and celebrity.

So you filter the general population down to six thousand elite Pharisees, then to seventy more elite members of the Sanhedrin, and finally to one Teacher. That guy was Nicodemus.

If you had asked Nicodemus about God's plan of salvation, he would probably have handed you a few heavy volumes of rules and said, "Start reading!"

Jesus tells *this* guy, let's talk about God's plan: You know that story about the Israelites and the poisonous snake bites? Well, the Son of Man will be lifted up just like that bronze snake. And everyone who looks to him will be healed spiritually. Period.

THE LIGHT GOES ON FOR NICK

What did Nicodemus think of all this? Well, he is mentioned later in John as one of the men who took charge of the body of Jesus and placed it in the tomb, so he was probably at the crucifixion. Apparently he was a follower of Jesus by this point.

I wonder when the light bulb went on above Nicodemus' head? Maybe it happened when he witnessed Christ lifted up on the cross and remembered this reference. *Jesus Christ was actually lifted up on a pole at his crucifixion. And all who look to him are saved.*

And maybe he also remembered how Jesus gave him a God's eye view of the situation:

> *For God so loved the world that he gave his one and only Son, that whoever believes in him shall not perish but have eternal life.* JOHN 3:16

Not "whoever is strict";
not "whoever understands";
not "whoever jumps through every hoop."

But *"whoever believes."*

Simply look to God's Son and be healed. Not of snake venom, but of a much more serious blood disease: Sin.

70

12 JUST ONE LOOK

JUMPING TO GOD?

If you think about it, this is the only way of salvation possible. God is so far above us in purity that our absolute best attempts at living holy lives must seem quaint to him.

Imagine I spied through my telescope a group of people below me on the plain of the Jordan River trying to jump up to my perch on Mount Nebo. Some could be Olympic athletes and others couch potatoes, but no amount of effort would make a perceptible difference from my perspective. All their efforts would be similarly in vain.

God is much further above us, in moral perfection, than I am above the Jordan Valley. None of our efforts could ever reach him. None of our thoughts could ever comprehend him. None of our writings could ever accurately describe him. Unless God himself became both Revealer and Rescuer.

And Jesus explains to Nicodemus that this is exactly what has happened.

God made the jump. All the way down.

Why? Why would an all-powerful deity care about little ants down in the valley? Jesus says God has a strong motivation for not leaving us distant and dying. In fact, it's the strongest motivation in the universe.

Love.

God so *loved*...

This is a mind-blowing revelation. God's Son speaking to Israel's Teacher says that, for all his knowledge, Nicodemus has missed one thing. God's love. For...

...the *world*. Not for Israel alone, or any other group or country. The Messiah's kingdom is universal precisely because people can simply look to him for healing. They don't need to convert first to any culture or system.

THINGS ARE LOOKING UP

You might feel you're stuck in the wilderness with a poison in your blood and without the means to heal yourself. You'd be right. But God so loved *you* that he sent his Son.

Look to *him* instead of *yourself.*

Like those ancient Israelites, our problem also began as a rebellion. Since the poison in our blood was introduced because of our decision to *reject* God, the poison begins to be removed with our decision to *receive* God. One heart at a time.

My time on Mount Nebo recalling Christ's conversation was enriching. But I was about to discover what it's like to lose a loved one in the ancient maze of streets in Old Jerusalem.

PRAYER: Thank God today for his love for you. Pray that you will shift your focus from yourself to him.

13 THE LOST LAMB

READ LUKE 15

Oops. We lost one.

Our guide Kenny says it's the first time it's ever happened to him.

We walked into the Church of the Holy Sepulcher about an hour ago with forty-three people in our group. Now there's only forty-two. And we cannot find the lost lamb.

The church had been so crowded that people could barely move. As we were leaving, a shoving match started, jostling the mob. Then we heard something like breaking glass and somebody screamed and a fight broke out. I sure hadn't expected to experience this in the somber setting of an ancient church.

People began to push in panic. Kenny said it was time to leave. Right away. So we got out.

Now we're in the alleyway and after a quick count we realize Marlene is missing. We send a delegation back into the church but the crowds make any search all but impossible.

Kenny says we have no other choice but to move on, that either Marlene will find us or he'll go back and find Marlene later, so we go to the next spot on our itinerary minus a member.

But before we start the tour of another church, we're all distracted and worried. We can't just go on like nothing happened. So I ask our group to stop and pray for Marlene to be found. I tell God that Marlene is such a gentle, soft-spoken senior citizen that I simply can't imagine her all by herself in the rather rough-and-tumble crowds choking the old city that hot afternoon.

"But God," I pray, "You said you came to seek and save the lost, so please find our little lost lamb Marlene today."

Something tells me to be specific. I say: "God, please remind

Marlene that our guide Kenny's mobile phone number is on the back of the name tag she is wearing around her neck, and help her to figure out how to place a call to him. Amen."

Within seconds after the "amen," Kenny's phone beeps. He answers it. We watch as his face goes pale. He blinks twice. And after a brief conversation, he hangs up and says, "That was Marlene. She said she suddenly remembered she had my number on her name tag."

A bone-rattling cheer goes up from our group. Right before this everyone had been so dejected. Now there's euphoria!

I can tell Kenny's a little shaken by the immediacy of the answer to prayer, and to tell the truth, so am I. But after all, we were praying to the one who came to find the lost.

LOVER OF LOST THINGS

Luke 15 is the only time Jesus tells three parables in a row. And they're all on the same theme: *Lost things.*

The Pharisees and other religious people had been wondering why Jesus spent so much time with notorious "sinners" (unlike us! I'm sure they were thinking). So he tells them.

These parables all have three elements in common: In each one, something's lost. Then an all-out effort is made to search for it. And then — don't miss this part — there is a huge party.

As Bill Hybels says, the point Jesus is making to the religious people is clear: *Lost people matter to God.* And they should matter to *you* too. [22]

The shepherd doesn't just hope the lost sheep will wander back, and he doesn't just drop a trail of sheep snacks. He leaves the others and goes looking for the lost one.

The woman doesn't say, "I'll look for one-tenth of my wealth tomorrow." She lights a lamp immediately and does a full house search.

13 THE LOST LAMB

The father, when he sees his son returning, hikes up his robe and runs to meet him! In the culture of his day, this kind of display would have been humiliating — but the father couldn't care less.

Jesus' own life mission statement is this: *"For the Son of Man came to seek and to save the lost."* (LUKE 19:10) It's why he's here.

Have you ever considered what this says about how valuable you are to God? He came to earth as Jesus because he treasures you. You're worth more to God than you can imagine, worth so much that he put together a search and rescue effort to find you, his lost sheep, lost coin, lost child.

And doesn't this motivate you to be a part of God's great search and rescue team, too?

SEARCH PARTY

Jesus says a party in heaven is thrown whenever one lost person is found. That means when you prayed that prayer to receive Christ, angels threw a party.

I don't know what an angel party looks like, but I'm guessing there's singing, celebrating, praising (maybe even some pita bread and hummus). And they repeat that over and over, millions and millions of times, each time a lost person comes home — they never tire of searching, and they never tire of partying!

I think that in a lot of churches today, there's not enough searching *or* partying.

Somehow we've gotten it into our heads that Jesus came to bring organization or information, and we gauge our Christian lives on how big our organizations are, or how much information we know. But he came to bring transformation; to seek and save the lost!

ONCE LOST, NOW FOUND, FOREVER CHERISHED

Marlene was the recipient of several gifts from people in our group just overjoyed to see her again — and I treated her to lunch the next day. She became an object of special affection precisely because she'd once been lost, and now was found.

We later discovered that Marlene had been separated from our group right when the fight broke out in the church. The security guards had been putting up some barricades to keep the crowd in order, and she was trapped on the other side.

Then, at the exact moment we prayed for her, Marlene stopped panicking (yes, she'd been a little freaked when she realized we were gone). She suddenly remembered she had Kenny's number. But she had no phone. She asked God to send her someone who could help. And a kind English-speaking priest stopped and let her use his mobile phone.

And I think the angels rejoiced.

Of course, the parable of the Prodigal Son is told to the Pharisees not just to explain that this is how the Messiah lives; it's told so they can see how *they* should live. Because they are the final character in the story — the stodgy, duty-bound and bitter older brother.

Seek the lost, Jesus is saying. It's what matters — and in the end, it's a lot more fun!

Now, if "fun" is not the first word you think of when someone mentions religion, Jesus is about to agree with you.

PONDER: How did today's devotional help you understand Jesus' love for others? How does it help you understand his love for you? What implications does this have for your priorities and actions?

GENUINE JESUS JOURNEY

It's easy to think that "walking where Jesus walked" means visiting the Holy Land.

And that's true, in a strictly geographical sense.

But what if I told you that you could go somewhere and actually meet Jesus, live and in person?

To really journey with Jesus today, go where Jesus went — to the outcasts, the sick, the poor, the disenfranchised.

You'll find him there today.

> *"I was hungry and you gave me something to eat, I was thirsty and you gave me something to drink, I was a stranger and you invited me in, I needed clothes and you clothed me, I was sick and you looked after me, I was in prison and you came to visit me... whatever you did for one of the least of these brothers of mine, you did for me."*
> MATTHEW 25:35,36,40

Dearest Lord, may I see you today and every day in the person of your sick, and whilst nursing them, minister to you. Though you hide yourself in the unattractive disguise of the irritable, the exacting, the unreasonable, may I still recognize you, and say, "Jesus, my patient, how sweet it is to serve you." —Mother Teresa of Calcutta [23]

14 STAIRS TO A BLANK WALL

READ LUKE 18:10-14

Left. Right. Left.

I'm actually taking video of my feet.

Can you blame me? I'm walking up steps once ascended by Jesus. This is the place I've been looking forward to visiting since our plane touched down in Israel.

I'm on the Southern Steps, a massive first-century stone staircase.

If you had visited Jerusalem before the early 1980s, you wouldn't have seen these steps; they were buried under tons of dirt and debris. No one knew they were even here. Archaeologists since then have discovered not only this staircase, but whole streets and shops from the time of Christ.

These stairs lead up to the southern side of the Temple Mount wall in Jerusalem. Today they end at a blank, bricked-up gate near the Muslim mosque, but in Christ's time they led under arches in the massive Herodian retaining wall and then up through the dark substructure of the vast temple platform, surfacing into bright daylight on the paved surface near the Court of the Gentiles.

Back then these would have looked very much like the wide steps going up to the U. S. Capitol, or, from the top, like stairs emerging from an underground subway.

It was a very impressive structure, far more complicated and "modern" than we usually imagine from our old Sunday School pictures of Jerusalem. But what makes this really special for Christians: Jesus stood right here, many times in his life.

The first time he was here, it was as a baby — Mary and Joseph carried him up to the Temple for his dedication (LUKE 2:22). Since these steps were the public entrance into the Temple for commoners, it's certain they walked here.

As Jesus grew up, his parents made the Jerusalem pilgrimage annually (LUKE 2:41), and Jesus was probably with them each time, watching as Herod's master architects slowly crafted the Temple complex into what many considered the most beautiful building on earth.

Then at twelve, Jesus was discovered as something of a childhood prodigy here, astounding the teachers at the Temple with his questions and answers (LUKE 2:42–50).

During the three years of his public ministry Jesus came down from Galilee to speak at the Temple a lot; during those times Luke says he'd teach at the Temple *"every day"* (LUKE 19:47; 20:1; 21:37–38; 22:53). The Southern Steps would have been one likely place for these teachings. We know that large crowds of both men and women listened to him together, a detail that favors this location, since genders were separated up on the Temple Mount.

I don't think it's any accident that most of the stories told by Jesus on these steps are meant to puncture religious pride. There was plenty of that to go around here; the magnificence of the buildings was apparently producing in many people a kind of spiritual cockiness. Jesus said a lot to comfort the weak, guilt-crippled sinners. But he said a lot to correct the strong-willed, self-righteous people too.

My favorite of these stories is told in Luke 18:

> *Two men went up to the temple to pray, one a Pharisee and the other a tax collector. The Pharisee stood up and prayed about himself, "God, I thank you that I am not like other men — robbers, evil-doers, adulterers — or even like this tax collector. I fast twice a week and give a tenth of all I get."*
>
> *But the tax collector stood at a distance. He would not*

even look up to heaven, but beat his breast and said, "God, have mercy on me, a sinner." I tell you that this man, rather than the other, went home justified before God.
LUKE 18:10–14A

I imagine a twelve-year old Jesus ascending these steps with Joseph and Mary, watching the proudly religious Pharisees wearing outward symbols of their piety, and then, looking down, he sees the sad, humbled "sinners," so desperate for God that they dare not even ascend the steps. And he finds his heart going out to those people. And he never forgets them.

His point in the parable? Be like the second guy.

STAIRWAY TO HEAVEN

The long stairway to the Temple I'm standing on is, in many ways, a metaphor for what religion had turned into for people in Jesus' time — and in ours: a stairway to heaven.

The "stairway to heaven" idea is not thinking you have to listen to Led Zeppelin to see God, although a friend of mine in high school did try that, with some additional stimulants, but that's another story (didn't work).

The "stairway to heaven" idea is thinking that you get closer to God, step by step, all the way to the top, on your own effort. Every prayer, every tithe, every time you go to church, every time you help someone, you're an incremental step closer. But every time you sin, you slip down a step or two.

It's the popular view of religion, really. It's religion that accurately sees we're sinners separated from God. He's way up there, we're way down here. Something must be done!

And then someone always says, "I know! We'll make a list of rules! And we'll keep score! And we'll teach people! And then God will look down and say, 'These good guys kept the rules — and those other ones didn't keep the rules. I'll save the good guys!'"

So naturally, it becomes a source of pride: "God, you're obligated to me — you *have* to save me. Because I'm a good person. Look at the score sheet I have handily devised. I did good things. I'm better than *that* guy, that's for sure." [24]

I find myself slipping back into this stairway mentality all the time. Don't you?

If you think that going on a mission trip, or reading a certain Bible translation, or having an ecstatic religious experience, or doing Bible study gets you extra credit from God, you're on the stairway.

Even if you're not religious, if you think you're going to heaven because you're better than most people, you're on the stairway.

"Thank you God, that I am not like other people! I am further up the steps!"

In this way of thinking, you become self-obsessed instead of God-focused.

Left. Right. Left. You focus on your feet. Look at me go, as I progress up the staircase.

Jesus talked *a lot* about this danger:

> *"You give a tenth of your spices — mint, dill and cumin. But you have neglected the more important matters of the law — justice, mercy and faithfulness."* MATTHEW 23:23

The Pharisees were so focused on the steps *to* God they forgot *God*.

Standing here on these steps, I think to myself: How dare I think that any effort of mine gets me an inch closer to a God who is infinitely beyond me in power and perfection? If there was a stairway to heaven, it would stretch not to the top of some hill, but all the way out of our galaxy, all the way to the furthest star.

And then I realize it does. And someone already has travelled it. All the way down.

The Pharisees were right: Something must be done! And Jesus is the One who did it.

HOW DO I REACH GOD?

One time, some people who only knew the stairway-to-heaven idea asked Jesus, "What must we do to do the works God requires?" They realized Jesus was criticizing their system—but then what system was he advocating, they wondered? What new stairway was he building?

> *Jesus answered, "The work of God is this: To believe in the one he has sent."* JOHN 6:29

No steps for you. Just believe.

For years I didn't get this. I tried to climb the steps myself, to do all I could to get closer to God. But nothing seemed to work. In fact, the harder I tried, the further away I seemed to get. Then I discovered *grace*. And my whole life changed.

The sad thing is, if you're trying to climb some stairway to heaven, even if you get to the top, you find it bricked off. Like the gates at the top of the Southern Steps. You just can't get inside from here.

Your efforts might help you get more disciplined. They may help you learn manners. They might help you with anxiety. *But you can't get through the wall of separation.* Only God can pierce that veil.

The way to the very top is at the very bottom.

Did I say Jesus once stood on the long staircase leading to the House of God?

Correction: *He's still there.*

He's at the very first step, extending his hand. To you.

PONDER: Why do you think the idea of a "stairway to heaven" is more appealing to many than the idea of grace? How do you fall back into the "stairway" worldview?

PART 3

MESSAGE

15 MORE THAN SKIN DEEP

READ MATTHEW 5:1-12

I'm a little intimidated as I stand with the group from our church at the Mount of Beatitudes just outside Capernaum.

For some reason I cannot now fathom, back when I put together our schedule I had thought this would be a great spot for me to deliver a sermon.

Of course, now that I'm here, I can't help but think of the first sermon preached at this spot. The most famous sermon in history. The Sermon on the Mount.

While we can't be certain Jesus preached that sermon here, it seems likely, because: (1) this place forms a natural amphitheater with amazing acoustic properties, and (2) it's on a big hill right outside Capernaum, very close to Bethsaida and Chorazin, the other two cities most often mentioned as places Jesus ministered.

In a rare bout of wisdom, I quickly realize that no words I can conjure could compare with Christ's, so after a short prayer I encourage our group to open their Bibles, wander the gardens, and just read Jesus' sermon.

I do give them this short orientation:

The lines that start the sermon are known as the *beatitudes*. That term comes from the Latin adjective *beatus*, which means happy, fortunate, blessed, or blissful. In Matthew 5 we have the Greek word for this eight times in a row, as sort of a poem.

Jesus says, here's where true happiness is found.

When you're poor in spirit — as opposed to the spiritual pride of the Pharisees.

When you're meek — and not a preening religious show-off.

When you realize you're starving for righteousness — and don't think you can feed yourself.

When you're pure in heart — as opposed to pure on the surface.

Someone said you could summarize the beatitudes with one line: *Blessed are the desperate.* To those who admit need and to those who hunger and thirst, Jesus says, a feast awaits.

WHAT'S IT ALL ABOUT?

These first few lines give a clue to what can be a perplexing mystery: What is this sermon *about?*

At times it seems so random. Jesus talks about prayer and giving and worry and judging and all kinds of varied topics. But is there *one unifying theme?*

Yes: God starts with the heart, not external religiosity.

Most of the other religious teachers of his day were emphasizing *externals:* Either Temple worship, or keeping the ritual religious rules, or both, as proofs of your devotion. Those teachers might have said, "Blessed are those who keep all their Temple duties" or "Blessed are those who do not work on the Sabbath."

But Jesus doesn't even *mention* those things in this sermon — except to say they fall far short as a measure of true spirituality.

Jesus emphasizes a person's *heart*, and the *actions of love* that flow *from* the heart.

ON BEYOND RULE-KEEPING

After he introduces his sermon with the Beatitudes, he states the theme of his message:

> *"I tell you that unless your righteousness surpasses that of the Pharisees and the teachers of the law, you will certainly not enter the kingdom of heaven."* MATTHEW 5:20

85

The people's hearts must have sunk when he said those words. The Pharisees were the most religious people on the planet. If religion was a basketball team, they'd be the Dream Team. If religion was a movie studio, they'd be Pixar. If religion was a restaurant, they'd be Emeril and Thomas Keller and Julia Child put together.

They were unbelievable religious performers. They added hundreds of rules to the Ten Commandments. Took it to a whole new level. When you washed your hands, the water had to drip off your elbow or it didn't count. You couldn't pick up a bucket on the Sabbath, or raise a certain weight of fork to your mouth, or gargle, because it was all considered work. No one could possibly keep all these rules. But the Pharisees took solemn vows to follow them as perfectly as possible.

So how could normal people hope to surpass that kind of achievement?

Jesus meant for the people to *move beyond rule-keeping.*

The Pharisees indeed performed well. But it had become all *about* the performance. They had complicated God's command to live a holy life so much that it became less about loving God or people, and more about "Do you gargle on Saturdays?"

Jesus basically says, if that's what you call righteousness, you need to move way beyond it!

RULES OR RELATIONSHIP?

For the rest of the sermon, Jesus elaborates on this theme.

And for the rest of his ministry, this becomes *the* issue between Jesus and the Pharisees. He will quote them this verse from Isaiah 29:13:

> *"These people honor me with their lips, but their hearts are far from me. They worship me in vain; their teachings are but rules taught by men."* MATTHEW 15:8–9

15 MORE THAN SKIN DEEP

He will tell the people, *"Everything they do is done for people to see...."* (MATTHEW 23:5A)

They were all about the performance. While Jesus was all about a heart change stemming from a life-changing relationship with God.

That doesn't mean you can live as a rule-breaker. It means your *motive* for holiness has totally changed, to the point where you're living a holy life almost before you realize it. Because you're focused on the Holy God, not on your attempts at holiness. You're centered in the *Who*, not the *how*. You "seek first the kingdom of God" and all the rest is added.

It reminds me of the dance lessons we were forced to take as part of our P. E. class in fifth grade. I felt awkward, clumsy, and focused entirely on the steps of the dance. Once I had them memorized, and the teacher said, "Begin!" I grabbed my poor partner Becky's hand and tried to stomp around as precisely as I could — *right, left, left, right!* — while avoiding all eye contact with her — until the end of the dance, when my sweaty hands slipped from hers and I immediately went back to sit with the other embarrassed boys.

Compare that to the time I entered a dance contest with my first girlfriend a few years later. It was the height of the disco era, and you could not stop us! We not only memorized steps, we made up new dances — and we won! The funny thing is, I was focused not on the steps, but on how much fun I was having with this wonderful girl.

Both of those events were called "dances." When I was a fifth grader, my steps may have even been more technically perfect. But unless my dancing surpassed that of the fifth graders at Athenour School in San Jose, I was never going to understand the joy of the dance. In fifth grade I knew the steps — but I completely missed the point.

Jesus is saying, essentially, just take my hand and follow my lead and you will learn the steps. This is not a dance class. It's a love relationship.

That kind of surrender only happens when you admit the dance class approach isn't doing it for you. When you admit you're weak, hungry, thirsty, needy. That's why it's those who realize the depth of their need who are truly blessed.

Next, Jesus has a very modern metaphor for those whose religion is only skin-deep.

But for now, why not join us here on the Mount of Beatitudes? Read the opening lines of the greatest sermon ever preached. And imagine Jesus saying them to *you*.

PONDER: How has the joy of your "dance" with Jesus been reduced to technical steps recently? How could what you've learned about Jesus so far help you restore joy to your "dance"?

INSIDE OUT

One major theme of Christ's message: True change happens from the inside out.

> For it is from within, out of a person's heart, that evil thoughts come — sexual immorality, theft, murder, adultery, greed, malice, deceit, lewdness, envy, slander, arrogance and folly. All these evils come from inside... MARK 7:21–23A

The story goes that, when a London newspaper asked readers to submit answers to the question, "What's Wrong with the World?" the novelist and Christian philosopher G. K. Chesterton wrote this:

> Dear Sirs:
> I am.
> Sincerely Yours,
> G. K. Chesterton. [25]

Why is this world so full of suffering? To quote Tim Keller: "Jesus is saying: We are what's wrong. It's what comes from the inside. It's the self-centeredness of the human heart." [26]

The famous Russian novelist Aleksandr Solzhenitsyn criticized his communist party's attempt to create the perfect society this way: "The line between good and evil passes not through states, nor between classes, nor between political parties — but right through every human heart." [27]

There's your trouble. This is why we speak of receiving Christ *into your heart*. It's there that the change begins.

16 ALL AN ACT

READ MATTHEW 6:1-5

I ask our driver to take a detour to the next hill on the horizon. Although it's not on the list of sites to see for most Holy Land visitors, it holds rare treasures for those willing to leave the well-trod tourist path. It's the active archaeological excavation of the ancient town of Sepphoris.

It's a fascinating site, because this village was being built when Jesus was a young man.

Was Jesus ever here? Well, an old tradition says this was his mother Mary's hometown.

But even more persuasive to me: The Bible says Joseph (and probably Jesus, as Joseph's son) was a *carpenter*. In Greek the word for carpenter is *tekton*, which is a general word for builder, or artisan, not just someone who worked specifically with wood. In fact, there was a lot more *stone* than *wood* in the land of Jesus, so *stonemasonry* probably more accurately describes the trade Jesus learned from Joseph.

There was not a lot of stonework available in Nazareth, which in Jesus' time, as we've seen, was just a tiny village. The small first-century village currently being excavated there had no paved roads, mosaics, or other stone features beyond the rock walls of the few modest homes. So it's logical to assume that Joseph, probably with Jesus as an assistant, worked his trade in neighboring Sepphoris.

This city was being developed in lavish Greco-Roman style during Jesus' early years. Josephus called it "the ornament of Galilee." It had a lot of stonework, large and small. We stroll down ruins of paved, colonnaded streets and ooh and aah at artwork—mostly mosaics—inside the ruins of ancient homes.

Sepphoris was the capital city for the area west of Galilee governed by Herod's son Antipas until about 20 AD, when he replaced it with Tiberias, the city he built on the lakeshore and named after his friend Tiberius Caesar.

THE THEATER, THE THEATER

One of the most impressive buildings in Sepphoris was its beautiful theater.

It's unlikely that, as a Jew, Jesus ever attended one of the plays here, since they were often based on pagan myth. But ancient writers explain that actors in the first century would regularly come out to the city streets and, to attract crowds to the show that day, blast trumpets and bang drums, and then perform parts of their drama as a "teaser," sort of like movie trailers today. So Jesus would definitely have seen these previews of coming attractions.

I can imagine Jesus and Joseph on their way to a job in Sepphoris, walking past a busy street corner where actors loudly strutted while wearing their grotesque theatrical masks (in Greek theater, actors typically wore masks to portray their characters instead of make-up as modern actors do — in fact, the Greek masks repre-senting comedy and tragedy are the icons of the acting profession to this day).

Jesus' impression of these street performers might even be evident in the Sermon on the Mount. He used the word "hypocrite" several times in this message. That's a word that has developed a very specific meaning in English, but in the Greek language of Jesus' day it meant one thing:

An *actor.*

In the gospels, Jesus uses this word *seventeen times* in his critique of the religious leaders of his day! Try reading Matthew 6:1–5, sub-stituting the word "actor" for "hypocrite":

> *"Be careful not to practice your righteousness in front of others to be seen by them..."*

91

The phrase "to be seen" there contains a verb in the original Greek, *theomai*, which is directly related to our English word *theater*, further establishing the possibility that Jesus is developing a theatrical metaphor.

> "*...So when you give to the needy, do not announce it with trumpets, as the **actors** do in the synagogues and on the streets, to be honored by others...*"

> "*When you pray, don't be like the **actors** who love to pray publicly on street corners and in the synagogues where everyone can see them...*"

> "*When you fast, do not look somber as the **actors** do, for they disfigure their faces to show others they are fasting...*"

Or Matthew 23:25:

> "*Woe to you, teachers of the law and Pharisees, you **actors**! You clean the outside of the cup and dish, but inside they are full of greed and self-indulgence.*"

Adds an interesting angle, doesn't it?

He didn't say they were jerks. He didn't say they were stupid. He said they were actors. And when we misunderstand the term "hypocrite" we miss the way it could apply to *us*.

THE GREAT PRETENDER

Ferdinand "Fred" Demara, Jr., must have been a great actor. The world was his stage. Literally.

Throughout his life, he masqueraded as a monk, a surgeon, a civil engineer, a deputy sheriff, a doctor of psychology, a cancer researcher, a teacher, and a prison warden. Faking credentials as a Navy doctor on a ship during the Korean war, he even performed several surgeries—successfully. While each patient was prepped, he would disappear to his room with a textbook on surgery and speed-read the relevant section!

But ultimately, he was always caught. He did well fooling people for a while, but each time the mask eventually slipped.

He finally settled down when he became a Christian and graduated from Multnomah Bible College in Portland, Oregon. He then moved to Los Angeles, where he worked as a well-loved hospital chaplain for the rest of his life. But after a lifetime of pretending, Fred Demara found the satisfaction of authenticity. He said that for years he was afraid to be real, that he was trapped in pretending.

END THIS CHARADE

Jesus looks around at the Pharisees and sees people trapped in pretending too.

In fact, one of Christ's biggest criticisms of his own religious authorities was that their system actually *encouraged* "acting." Legalistic systems *always do*.

If there is a religious system with external gauges for spirituality, a checklist of behaviors to accomplish, people will naturally want to become high achievers, to get gold stars and merit badges and standing ovations. And their spiritual lives become less about a relationship with God and more about the applause.

Grace, because it emphasizes God's unconditional, initiating love, encourages *honesty*. That's because you know you can't do anything to make God love you more, and you know you can't do anything to make God love you less. You might as well be authentic.

So in what areas of your life might Jesus say you were an actor?

Drop the mask. God sees the heart. You don't have to perform for him.

And you can stop living for the applause of others. You already have the grace of the Father. What more could you need?

Jesus does not call you out of one performance-oriented religious system into another. He calls you from acting to honesty, from performing to reality. Dropping the mask is the first step toward becoming a real Christ-follower!

But Jesus doesn't just skewer superficial religion. Next, he speaks to the superficiality of fame and fortune.

PROJECT: When you're tempted to play a role today make a conscience effort to drop the mask and let Jesus shine through.

17 SAFELY STORED TREASURE

READ MATTHEW 6:19-24

I stand wind-blown on the highest spot at Megiddo, which was one of King Solomon's fortress cities a thousand years before Jesus walked this country.

The site is a "tel," the archeological name for a rounded hill that looks natural, but is in fact a man-made mound of layers of previous civilizations all buried under centuries of dust and dirt.

Excavations at Megiddo have unearthed twenty-six layers of ruins. This site was inhabited from approximately 7000 BC to 586 BC—that means it was occupied for five thousand years before Abraham moved to the Promised Land.

Since 586 BC, it has remained uninhabited, the sand of centuries slowly burying its remains. The same fortification stones that once stood as intimidating, imposing reminders of the king's wealth and power now lie broken, eroded, sun-bleached and worn. Walls that kept out armies at war are hopped over by children at play. Yet these walls keep secrets still.

Archaeologists began unearthing the city in 1903, and they are still at it today. Shortly after our visit, researchers revealed a treasure trove of artifacts from Bible times uncovered here in 2011. They found a clay vessel filled with valuable jewelry: Several large pieces of gold were inside, and more than a thousand small beads of gold, silver and carnelian. Experts believe the treasure was hidden about three thousand years ago by Canaanites on the eve of the Israelite conquest of Megiddo.

Whoever buried this treasure wanted to make sure it was safely hidden—and indeed, it eluded discovery for a very long time. But it never enriched its owners again.

There are probably more treasures buried here. Wealth was the reason for Megiddo's existence. The city perches on the side of the Jezreel Valley, a very narrow space between two mountain ranges through which that ancient highway, the Via Maris, was funneled—any caravan journeying between Europe and Africa had to go right through here.

Megiddo was built as a fortress city surrounded by high walls and strong gates. It offered protection, shelter, food and supplies to weary travellers—and also exacted heavy tolls from them in return. If you could control this spot, you could control much of the trade of the whole known world.

Consequently, it became fabulously rich. Of course, the richest man in Bible history was Solomon, the third king of Israel, and he had his eyes on Megiddo from the start. According to Scripture, after his Israelite army conquered it, this became one of the border outposts of his kingdom.

Our group climbs into the archaeological digs here, through the ancient Solomon-era gates. They once stood twenty feet tall, two-story structures with six chambers, three rooms on each side, filled with soldiers and toll collectors.

Once through the gates, we walk on a paved road Solomon himself probably travelled. The Bible says in 1 Kings 9:15 that he was the one who captured Megiddo from the Canaanites and designed advanced new defenses. So it's very likely he was here, on this very street.

I imagine him surveying the scene as workers constructed the walls above him.

But was it all ultimately satisfying? Maybe Solomon was thinking partly of his work here at Megiddo when he wrote:

> "I undertook great projects: I built houses for myself
> and planted vineyards. I made reservoirs ... My heart
> took delight in all my labor... Yet when I surveyed
> all that my hands had done and what I had toiled to

achieve, everything was meaningless, a chasing after the wind; nothing was gained — because I must leave them to the one who comes after me. And who knows whether that person will be wise or foolish? Yet they will have control over all the fruit of my toil into which I have poured my effort and skill under the sun...."

ECCLESIASTES 2:4–6; 10–11,18–20

In fact, that's exactly what happened. Solomon's own son was foolish and instantly caused a civil war that split the kingdom — and then this very city was later ruled by the evil King Ahab, after which the Babylonians wiped it all out, permanently. In the process of the destruction, who knows how many treasures were buried that may never be unearthed.

So what's it all *for?*

In Christ's day, Solomon's fortifications at Megiddo had already been in ruins for six centuries. The pile of debris that marked this once-great city would have been clearly visible across the valley from the cliffs around Jesus' hometown of Nazareth, giving silent testimony to the truth of his words:

"Do not store up for yourselves treasures on earth, where moths and vermin destroy, and where thieves break in and steal. But store up for yourselves treasures in heaven, where moths and vermin do not destroy, and where thieves do not break in and steal." MATTHEW 6:19–20

How do you store up treasure in heaven? Jesus says every act of kindness here will find its reward there. God saves us by his grace — and then, because of his grace, chooses to reward our smallest efforts as well!

If we all focused on storing up wealth *there* — by practicing grace and kindness and love — not only do we get a nicer *there*, someday, we get a nicer *here*, now.

SAFE TO THE END

Intriguingly, Megiddo is also the location of something in the biblical future: *Armageddon*. That's just another word for "Hill of Megiddo." In the Book of Revelation, this place is the site of one of the last battles in world history (REVELATION 16:16). After the battle, *"the cities of the nations collapsed"* (REVELATION 16:19).

That scene seems incredible to us, but from God's viewpoint, this has been happening for thousands of years already. All the lavish, luxurious, and powerful cities of the nations, like Megiddo, have collapsed.

Think of what Jesus knew when he said those words in Matthew.

From his divine perspective, Jesus had seen the rise and fall of so many kingdoms. Imagine witnessing history in fast-forward, strongholds on hills all around the Holy Land rising and falling as different civilizations rush in and then recede like ocean tides.

Egypt. Babylon. Persia. Rome. Us. For Jesus, each glorious empire eventually becomes just another layer in a tel. All human wealth and power fades.

And so he was saying, focus on the kingdom of God. That is what is real, that is what lasts. Store treasure where no thief—or archaeologist—will ever break in!

PRAYER: Thank God today for the opportunity to build treasure that lasts! Pray that your value system will focus on treasure that can never spoil, perish or fade.

AN AMAZING FIND AT MEGIDDO

In 2005, Israeli archaeologists discovered the remains of a church believed to be from the third century, a few hundred yards south of Tel Megiddo on the grounds of the Megiddo Prison.

They found a large (580 sq. ft.) mosaic celebrating the dedication of an altar that was consecrated to "the God Jesus Christ."

Apparently a Roman centurion built this as a chapel for his Christian soldiers, indicating that at least some Roman leaders were tolerant of the faith that was rapidly gaining adherents. These are the oldest remains of a building originally constructed as a church ever found in the Holy Land.

18 OF WINDMILLS AND FIGS

READ MARK 11:12-18

Minarets. Domed churches. Palm trees.

I'd expected to see those shapes silhouetted against the Jerusalem sky, but not what I'm seeing now.

A giant windmill. It looks like it was transported directly from Holland.

Our guide Kenny sees my confusion and explains. It's no mirage. It was built in 1857 to be a real, working mill. European Jews like the noted British philanthropist Sir Moses Montefiore were just beginning to take an interest in the plight of their impoverished brethren in Jerusalem in the 1800s, and often imported distinctly European solutions.

In this case, Montefiore decided to improve the outdated, donkey-and-millstone method for milling grain by hiring the best industrial designers in Britain, the Holman Brothers of Canterbury, to build a modern windmill.

It was the tallest structure outside the old city, at five stories high. It used the latest technology of the time, four patent sails. The entire top portion could actually be turned to face the wind. Each piece was laboriously imported from England, transported from the harbor at Jaffa by camel.

It was probably the most advanced windmill on earth when it was built.

But it never worked. Why? The builders had thought of everything, sparing no expense.

There was only one more little thing they needed.

Wind.

Small oversight: There are rarely windy conditions in this part of town.

So it stands tall and proud, looking great. It's still a landmark for tourists navigating Jerusalem's streets. But it never produced grain.

It reminds me of a confusing episode in the life of Christ.

I'll admit it: Jesus' cursing of the fig tree is one of those events that has made me feel awkward about him.

The Bible says Jesus is hungry and sees a fig tree in the distance in full leaf (MARK 11:13). Then he seems to get upset when there's nothing on the tree to eat and pronounces judgment on it, even though Mark points out that it wasn't even fig season yet.

On the surface this seems petulant. But this isn't about Jesus wanting a snack. It's about Jesus memorably showing what was wrong with the temple system. Looked great. No fruit.

See, even before fig season, the trees produce little knobs. I noticed them all over the fig trees when I was there. Arabs call these *taqsh*.

Passers-by can snap off *taqsh* to eat if they've got the munchies. But if leaves appear in the spring without any *taqsh*, that's an indication there will be no figs on that tree that year. As famous New Testament scholar F. F. Bruce put it, "For all its fair foliage, it is a fruitless tree." [28]

ALL LEAVES, NO FRUIT

Context: This happens just outside Jerusalem during the week before Christ's crucifixion. He's on his way into town, walking toward the Temple, which looms impressively in front of him.

During his time there, the disciples will point out to him the beauty of the Temple and its buildings — and they *were* beautiful.

The first temple had been built by Solomon about one thousand years before Christ. Then in 586 BC that building was destroyed by the Babylonians. After seventy years, the Jews in Jerusalem began rebuilding a temple, but their rather meager construction was completely remodeled on an awesome, grand scale by King Herod.

His goal? For the Temple to outshine any other building in the world. It would be bigger, more lavish, more colorful, and more spectacular than anything in Egypt, Greece, Babylon or Rome.

His mission was accomplished. In Jesus' day, primary construction was finished, and only a few details were still to be completed. After decades of work, the glorious Temple complex was sparkling and impressive.

The Roman historian Tacitus describes the Temple as "possessing enormous riches" and the first-century writer Josephus said the marble, tile, and limestone Temple Mount was "like a snowy mountain glittering in the sun." It was massive, capable of holding one million people during their religious pilgrimages. [29]

But, Jesus is saying, it's all leaves, no fruit.

He is echoing a theme from the earlier Hebrew prophets. In Hosea, God says that Israel showed so much promise early on — but then abandoned God for false religion. And look at the metaphor:

> *When I found Israel, it was like finding grapes in the desert; when I saw your fathers, **it was like seeing the early fruit on the fig tree**. But when they came to Baal Peor, they consecrated themselves to that shameful idol and became as vile as the thing they loved... Ephraim is blighted, their root is withered, **they yield no fruit**...*
> HOSEA 9:10,16

The fig tree Jesus found on the way into town was the perfect visual metaphor. Jesus wasn't being impulsive. He wasn't upset that he didn't get a snack. He was giving a memorable warning.

The Temple had a great design. The religious system was meticulously precise. But it was form without function.

Fig tree without figs.

Windmill without wind.

Same problem.

A great look holds great promise. However the essential component is missing. It's big and beautiful and broken.

And this isn't a topic he's just now introducing. Back in the Sermon on the Mount, Jesus gave a gauge to measure Bible teachers and preachers. Most of us judge teachers by their abilities, their gifts and charisma. But Jesus recommends a different measure: *"By their fruit you will know them."* (MATTHEW 7:16)

They may be trees in full glorious leaf. But show me the fruit! Are they producing love, joy, peace — in their own lives and the lives of their followers?

And ask yourself: What about me? I may be leafy with activity, or words. But where's the fruit?

As he continues to attack the strict yet shallow spirituality of the Pharisees, Jesus will soon use what may be his most stunning and offensive metaphor.

PONDER: What does the "fruit" of your life over the last few days tell you about your relationship with Jesus?

19 BEAUTIFUL TOMBS

READ LUKE 11:47-51; MATTHEW 23:27-36

One of the biggest industries in Jesus' day was making mansions. For the dead.

Like cars or jewelry today, having an elaborate tomb became a statement about how rich and important you were. It was the ultimate "keeping up with the Joneses" — everyone wanted a tomb nicer than the next guy.

How does a fad like this get started?

When primary construction on the huge Jerusalem Temple slowed, Josephus says about ten thousand skilled builders became unemployed. So what kind of work was there for a bunch of guys specializing in temple building, when there was only one temple to build, and it was finished?

Well, they built hundreds and hundreds of temple-like tombs for wealthy Jerusalem families — who probably found it prestigious to have a grave built by a Temple construction crew!

Most of these tombs are found in the Kidron Valley, a narrow gorge that runs between the Mount of Olives and the eastern wall of the old city of Jerusalem.

I'm standing there now, pointing out some of the tombs to friends. A lot of visitors to this area stand very near the tombs and never notice them, because the even more elaborate Temple Mount and golden Dome of the Rock grab their attention.

Looking from left to right, I see:

The Tomb of Absalom, which really has nothing to do with David's son Absalom, but was built for a now unknown person during the lifetime of Jesus. It's as high as a five-story building, with decorative pillars along the sides and a hat-shaped stone roof.

The Tomb of Benei Hezir is next door; it's carved out of solid rock and reminds me of the Lincoln Memorial. It was built before Christ, but in his lifetime it was still being used as a tomb by the priestly family for whom it was named. It's an indication of the vast wealth of the priestly class that they could afford elaborate monuments like this.

Next to that: *The Tomb of Zechariah*, a monolith carved from solid rock and capped with a small Egyptian pyramid. This was also built in the first century — although local custom holds that it was dedicated to the memory of the priest Zechariah mentioned in 2 Chronicles 24.

These are just the most obvious; eight hundred of these large tombs from the time of Christ have been discovered within a three-mile radius around the city! In many ways, first-century Jerusalem became a city of tombs.

Of course, many of these have been damaged or destroyed in the centuries of violence that have battered Jerusalem. The best place to get a feel for what this valley might have looked like in its tomb-building glory? The famous lost city of Petra.

In its heyday right at the time of Jesus, Petra still has hundreds of these monumental tombs. Many are even larger than the ones in Jerusalem, but with a similar design sensibility. Just as in Jerusalem, Petra's architects mixed exotic elements of Egyptian, Greek, and Babylonian graves and temples to create their impressive facades.

The most famous is the so-called Treasury building, which starred as the cave of the Holy Grail in the movie *Indiana Jones and the Last Crusade.*

PAINTED TOMBS

Today the tombs of Jerusalem and Petra have no color except their natural stone pigment, which tourists find beautiful, but in those days the tombs (and the other stone buildings like temples) were painted, sometimes in bright colors, but always at least with white paint.

So when Jesus talks about whitewashed tombs, he's not talking about the kind of stuff you see in your local cemetery. He's talking about these massive, elaborate monuments.

The Kidron Valley runs across the road Jesus took many times from Bethany, where Mary, Martha and Lazarus lived, to Jerusalem, so Jesus would have crossed in front of these very tombs very often. I imagine him pointing to them as he says,

> "Woe to you, teachers of the law and Pharisees, you hypocrites! You are like whitewashed tombs, which look beautiful on the outside but on the inside are full of the bones of the dead and everything unclean. In the same way, on the outside you appear to people as righteous but on the inside you are full of hypocrisy and wickedness." MATTHEW 23:27–28

The comparison between the tombs and the temple would have been obvious and scathing. The very same builders worked on both the temple and the tombs, and Jesus is implying there's not much difference. They're very beautifully designed and completed by the best craftsmen, but all they contain are rotting bones. There's no life. Only disease and death.

For the Pharisees, this would have been the ultimate insult. Their whole lives were about staying ceremonially clean. Even brushing up against a dead body was considered to be the worst kind of uncleanliness possible, requiring days of ritual cleansing. And now Jesus is saying that, on the inside, they're that dirty.

I NEED LIFE, NOT PAINT.

You might have noticed how Jesus continually rips into superficial religious leaders. From God's perspective, there is nothing worse — *nothing* — than a temple that's really a tomb, a religion that promises life but offers only death, a road to God that's just a dead end.

So Jesus skewers bad religion and its often abusive leadership with a sharpness he uses on no one else. As Martin Luther said, "With the weak sheep you cannot be too gentle. With the wolves you cannot be too severe."

Here's why I need to hear this: The same exact thing can — and does — happen to my own faith.

I can even get so busy with good "Christian" activities that my schedule is the equivalent of one of those tombs. Lots to look at, but not much spiritual life there.

In fact the emptier I feel, the more elaborate the architecture of my religious activity often becomes. I schedule more things to do, more rules to keep. Let's whitewash the tomb again.

But I don't need a renovation. I need a resurrection. The good news: that's exactly what God can provide.

The solution to your spiritual doldrums is not more paint on the grave. It's asking God to give life to the corpse.

Speaking of which, a world-changing event was about to take place in a Jerusalem tomb. Not the decorated tombs of the privileged and honored, but a newly carved tomb that would briefly hold the body of man abandoned and condemned.

PONDER: How have you lately been "decorating your tomb"? How has that prevented you from living the abundant life Jesus came to give you?

20 THE BIG PICTURE

READ MARK 12:15-34

Foreign visitors to Israel are often surprised that they're expected to observe some of the traditional Jewish kosher laws, especially as they travel closer to Jerusalem.

For example, in order to stay kosher, most hotels there will not serve meat and dairy products at the same meal. I watched at one dinner while a young rabbi—who had been strolling up and down our hotel dining room looking for violations—loudly upbraided a French tourist for smuggling in cream for her coffee.

Elevators and other electric appliances are often put on "Sabbath timers" so they automatically turn on and off without people having to risk breaking the Sabbath restriction against work by pushing a button.

Some tourists get frustrated. But I tell our church group that I *hope* they encounter some minor inconveniences like this. It helps them appreciate that they're not in an American colony, but in a different country with different rules.

It also helps them relate, at least just a little bit, to one aspect of the first-century religious culture of Jesus.

RULES ABOUT RULES

Back in those days, there were rules about everything.

When you think of the Bible's rules, you can probably think of about ten. The Ten Commandments.

But in Jesus' time they thought of *thousands*.

The Pharisees decided that, since there were 613 letters in the Hebrew Ten Commandments, then there must be 613 sub-commandments that explained the Top Ten.

And since they counted 248 different parts of the human body, there must be 248 laws governing the human body.

Then all these laws had about 1,400 other "fence laws," as they were called, added to them. These were designed to keep you from even getting close to breaking any of the other laws — that's why they were "fence laws." They were the rules about the rules!

THE UNANSWERABLE QUESTION

A popular activity in those days was for men to sit around discussing their religious rules day after day. They would have arguments about which rules were most important, and what the rules meant. They talked about the rules as fervently as baseball fans today might talk about the batting order of their favorite baseball team.

One day, some of them figured, let's ask this Jesus guy a question about the rules that is impossible to answer.

"Of all the rules in our religion, what is the single most important rule?"

It's the unsolvable equation. Because no matter what Jesus says, he'll be seen as leaving some important rule out.

The gospels say this is one of a series of questions designed to trick Christ. See the trap? Whatever his answer is, it'll ensnare him in controversy and get him off-message.

Great plan. Except they didn't count on Jesus.

He replied:

> *"'Love the Lord your God with all your heart and with all your soul and with all your mind.' This is the first and greatest commandment. And the second is like it: 'Love your neighbor as yourself.'"* MATTHEW 22:37–39

Notice the order. You start with loving God. Then you love your neighbors.

People say we need to love our neighbors. Help people out. Do social justice. Feed the poor. Spread the gospel. And they're right. Jesus said to.

But if you start there, without loving God first, eventually all that gets to be a burden. It becomes dry duty. *Because it's not the good news.*

Start with God. Remember his love for you — the love of the God who made the universe and came to earth to rescue you! *That's* the good news. It's when you overflow with this, with a sense of his grace, that it spills onto other people.

THE LARGER STORY

Just give me the Cliff Notes on the Bible, Jesus. What does God really want from me?

A lot of people would summarize it this way: .

Try harder!

Be a good boy or girl!

Behave, or you'll make God mad!

Not Jesus.

He says, here it is: *Love God. Love people.*

Here's how huge this is, Jesus says:

"All the Law and the Prophets hang on these two commandments."

John Eldredge wrote a book called *The Sacred Romance: Drawing Closer to the Heart of God* that has helped many people rediscover these priorities.

He points out that many Christians, who want so badly to live a righteous life, instead end up burned out, spiritually stale, lax and lukewarm. They try real hard to do the right things. But they forget what it's like to be in love with God.

They live in the "smaller story" of dos and don'ts instead of the "larger story" of the sacred romance.

See, if your summary of your religion is basically that God rewards me for my good behavior and punishes me for bad behavior, then you quickly move to a desire for an accurate scoring system — and the more precise the scoring system, the better. *Exactly how do I earn brownie points with God? Exactly how many points is this worth? Exactly how do I get demerits?*

In this answer to his critics, Jesus deftly points them away from their concerns with this smaller story and back to the larger story of God's love.

What story are you focused on?

PRAYER: Talk to God today about your "sacred romance" with him. Talk to him about the joys and struggles you have with that. Ask him for the courage to leave behind the "small story" and live in the grace of the "large story."

LOVING THE BIBLE TO DEATH

I've descended a little-noticed staircase into the basement of the Shrine of the Book museum in Jerusalem to see the legendary Aleppo Codex. Or, more accurately, to see what's left of it.

The Aleppo Codex (a codex is a large bound book) was compiled over a thousand years ago and remained for centuries the oldest, most complete manuscript of the Hebrew Bible (what Christians call the Old Testament) in the world.

IS IT SECRET? IS IT SAFE?

But there were many enemies of the Jews and their Scriptures. Fearing for the manuscript's safety, Jewish scholars in the 14th century smuggled the codex to a group of devout Jews in Aleppo, Syria. The rabbis there were told that this book was ancient and precious, and that they were to guard it with their lives. This they did for centuries.

The Crown was kept in a locked safe behind the walls of a secret room. Intended to be a reference work for scholars to regularly study so they could communicate the Bible's message to the whole human race, the Aleppo Codex instead became such an object of veneration that no one was ever allowed to read it.

When the Jewish state of Israel was endorsed by the United Nations in 1947, Arab riots tore through the Middle East. An angry mob descended on the synagogue in Aleppo, set it on fire, found the secret room, broke open the safe, and scattered the pages of the Codex. Amazingly, most of it survived. The next morning, synagogue members found their prized book in pieces — but still virtually complete.

TREASURING IT TO PIECES

However, the Jews of Aleppo had been taught for so long that The Crown was a sacred book that it had taken on mystical powers for them. Once it was out in the open, many of the separated pages were stolen—not by Arabs, but by Jews, who often cut them into tiny squares used as talismans, kept in wallets and worn around necks, to ward off evil and bring good luck.

They respected it not for the story it told or the principles it taught, but for the mystical power they thought it held. Scholars searching for the book's missing and irreplaceable pieces have found scraps worn as charms as far away as New York. [30]

What remained of the Aleppo Bible was smuggled to Israel, where it sits almost unnoticed in the museum, one floor under the Dead Sea Scrolls.

LOVED AND CHERISHED AND IGNORED

The sad story of the Aleppo Codex is a parable for all those who claim to hold the Bible's teaching sacred.

Jesus pointed out the same tendency in the Pharisees, the tendency to almost idolize the Bible into irrelevance. They missed the big picture the Bible was painting. Of him.

> *"You study the Scriptures diligently because you think that in them you have eternal life. These are the very Scriptures that testify about me, yet you refuse to come to me to have life."* JOHN 5:39–40

The Bible isn't meant to be worshipped. It's certainly not meant to be treated as some sort of magical charm. It's meant to lead you to abundant life, on your lifelong journey with Jesus.

21 DECISION TIME

READ JOHN 6:28-40; 66-69

Our group gathers on the ridge of Mount Carmel to see the breathtaking view 1,800 feet down into the Jezreel Valley. We try to imagine the scene that took place here nearly three millennia ago.

It was on this mountain that Elijah had his famous showdown with the priests of Baal (1 KINGS 18).

Elijah is quite a dramatic and charismatic figure in the Old Testament, daring, sarcastic, emotional—and divisive.

In fact, that's his primary mission. Probably his best-known statement is in 1 Kings 18:21:

> *"How much longer will you waver, hobbling between two opinions? If the Lord is God, follow him! But if Baal is God, then follow him!"* NLT

He's saying, *It's decision time.*

This is what prophets do: Call people back to God. Challenge them to make a choice. Left to ourselves, most of us *"waver, hobbling between two opinions."* I know I do.

Jesus said that John the Baptist fulfilled the role of Elijah for his generation (MATTHEW 17:11–12, LUKE 7:26–27). Like Elijah, John is piercing, emotional, powerful, and is calling people to a choice: *"Repent of your sins and turn to God, for the Kingdom of Heaven is near."* (MATTHEW 3:2 NLT). It's decision time again.

Then it's Christ's turn to point at the fork in the road. With increasing frequency as his ministry nears its conclusion, he tells people it's time to choose.

FOR JESUS, IT'S ALWAYS PERSONAL

Look how often Jesus challenges individuals to make a choice:

21 DECISION TIME

*"Who do **you** say I am?'* MATTHEW 16:15; MARK 8:27; LUKE 9:20

*"I am the resurrection and the life... Do **you** believe this?"*
JOHN 11:25–26

*"Do **you** believe that I am able to do this?"* MATTHEW 9:29

And when some of his followers begin to leave, he asks his closest disciples, *"What about **you**? Do you want to leave too?"*

You might sit inside a church with lots of other worshippers, or you might sit in a classroom with an atheist teacher, or you might sit in a break room eating hummus with rat-racing coworkers, but Jesus won't ask you about what they believe. He'll say: What about *you*? Do *you* believe this?

If I had x-ray vision of everyone's soul at those moments of choice, I suspect I'd see this: A lot of us don't want to have to answer that question. It's awkward. We want to say we believe in Jesus — and everything else, too. We don't want to seem to be putting down anyone's beliefs. We actually prefer to "waver between two opinions."

But at some point, indecision, as Elijah said on this mountain, *hobbles* us. Conviction produces forward momentum.

If Jesus is God, then follow him. If the way of the world is right, if pleasure and profit is what it's all about, then follow that.

Choose whom you will serve.

THE POWER OF A SLIGHT SHIFT

There's a famous mountain ridge in Switzerland that forms the line between continental watersheds.

On top of the ridge there's an old hotel, and next to the hotel there's a stable, and on the stable there's a sloping roof. When a drop of rain falls on one side of the roof, it goes into the gutter, down a spout, into a brook, which leads to a waterfall, which goes to a river, and eventually that drop of water ends up in the Mediterranean Sea. If a drop falls on the other side, it ends up in the Atlantic Ocean. One-eighth of an inch difference on either side of the roofline, and the drops end up oceans apart.

This the power of choice: One small decision today can eventually make a difference in your life the size of a continent.

And if you're thinking, *I'd love to make a choice, but my faith's a little shaky* — just look at the responses Jesus gets to some of his challenges:

> *Simon Peter answered him, "Lord, to whom would we go? You have the words of eternal life."* JOHN 6:68

I love Peter's response, I really do. It's almost like he's saying, "You know, we've thought about it — I don't want to lie to you, Jesus. You're not always easy to live with. You're always telling these riddles. We don't always get you. But — where else are we going to go that's better?"

Faith is hard sometimes. But consider the alternatives.

Peter and the other disciples still had questions. You see them come up throughout Christ's long march to the cross. But they chose to see if some of those questions would be answered as they followed — instead of as they stayed on the sidelines.

Peter finally says:

> *"We have come to believe and know that you are the Christ, the Son of the living God."* JOHN 6:69 WEB

"Come to believe and know." Interesting progression there.

They followed him first. They watched and listened and observed and served. And then they *came to believe*. And, later, *know*. They developed faith in Jesus because of what they had seen and heard — and this eventually resulted in an intellectual conviction.

21 DECISION TIME

I BELIEVE; HELP MY UNBELIEF

After church one day, someone confessed to me, "René, I am an unbeliever."

I said, "Define that for me." And he answered, "Well, I feel like I do believe in Jesus, but I also have all these doubts."

I turned to a verse in Mark where a man says to Jesus, *"I do believe; help my unbelief!"* (MARK 9:24). And Jesus *commends* him for his faith. I asked the man in front of me, "Can you pray that prayer? 'Lord, I believe — but help me in my unbelief?'" He said, "That describes me exactly!" I told him, "Then you have the faith that Jesus commended!" Because that's real life faith right there. "I believe — but I have questions."

Jesus says, "Great, follow me. You're just the kind of person I'm looking for."

Faith isn't about absolute certainty. It's about believing something's worth the risk. As John Lennox, a professor of mathematics at Oxford University and a Christian, says, "Pure proof is only found in mathematics. In all other fields of knowledge, it's about the weight of the evidence." If you wait for absolute certainty, you'll find yourself suffering from paralysis by analysis.

Maybe you hear echoes of Elijah today. *"How long will you waver between two opinions?"* Sooner or later, it's decision time.

PONDER: Do you tend to be decisive or indecisive? How has this tendency impacted the practice of your faith? In what area of your life do you need to "stop wavering between two opinions"?

PART 4
MIRACLES

22 FIRST MIRACLE

READ JOHN 2:1-11

Our bus rumbles into Kafr Kanna, the small town that's long been associated with Jesus' first miracle.

It's uncertain if this village was the precise location of first-century Cana, though there's been a church here dedicated to the "wedding miracle" since the fourth century. As I watch it slide past the window, my mind drifts to the scene described in the Bible.

Maybe it's because I'm thirsty.

You have to admit, it's a funny story. Jesus, his mother, and his disciples are at a wedding celebration in the Galilean village of Cana. The wine runs out. Maybe all they have left are crackers (and perhaps hummus). Major party stopper.

After his mom asks him to do something about it, Jesus tells the servants to set six "very large stone water-jars" on the floor, each holding twenty gallons, and fill them "to the brim" with water.

FROM STONE JARS TO WINE BOTTLES

Stop for a second. There was only one reason to have stone water-jars in a house in the first century.

Jars carved out of stone, instead of made from clay, were used only for religious ritual purposes. Pottery could be ceremonially unclean. It was porous and soaked up whatever was placed inside and so it was hard to wash thoroughly. But water in stone vessels was seen as pure.

These stone jars were presumably used to hold "holy water" used for ceremonial washing — a symbolic act of cleansing from sin, not for cleaning off the dust of the road or other dirt.

So Jesus doesn't just fill some wine glasses. He takes the large jars *used for religious ritual* and instead makes them *useful for a party*—specifically, a *wedding* party. Does anyone else see the poetry here?

Jesus then says, take some to the MC. They do, he tastes it, and it's all good. The man says to the groom, "Everybody I know puts his good wine out first and then when the guests have had plenty to drink, he brings out the swill. But you have kept back your good wine till now!" (SEE JOHN 2:10)

The writer of John's telling us, it wasn't just wine. It was *great* wine.

120 *gallons* of great wine.

Of all the things Jesus could have done as his first miracle, he helps a party go on a little longer.

What does this mean? Why did he do *this?* And why did he do it *this way?*

What if he had turned the water into mediocre wine—you know, like 120 gallons of Two-Buck Chuck? Wouldn't it still have been a miracle?

What if he had simply filled up their *wineskins* instead of using jars meant for *religious* purposes?

And why did he wait until they were *out* of wine—why didn't he quietly refill each glass as it emptied?

What is he teaching here? And he *is* teaching something. John says that the disciples became more than just students on this day. He says they "put their faith in him" because of this miracle, which John calls a "sign."

WHERE'S THE SIGN POINTING?
In fact, John calls all Christ's miracles "signs." I think it's because, writing his gospel later, as an older man, John sees that Jesus was an artist with miracles the way a poet is an artist with words, or a painter is an artist with a brush.

This is true even when the miracle is done at the request of his mom—it appears that Jesus hadn't set the stage. He hadn't stretched the canvas. He was an artist scratching out a sketch on a cocktail napkin at a party after a loved one said, "Please?"

But you can always see the hand of a master. Even in a doodle.

And in the lines of this miracle you can see so much.

Jesus is here to welcome us to a wedding feast. A party.

Jesus is here to put a new wine on the beverage table. Something brand new—yet something that has all the flavor of something vintage, something that had fermented and aged for years until it was uncorked.

Jesus is here because God saved the best for last. When all our human efforts were insufficient, he came to the rescue.

And Jesus is here to change the people's notion of their religion. They were only able to see it as a vessel for *ritual*. But Jesus turns it into a *gourmet experience*, something special, into a *relationship that produces joy and fellowship.*

And if you think this miracle was something, wait until you see the nature-bending miracles yet to come.

PONDER: How has Jesus taken the stone jars and filled them with wine in your life?

23   MAGIC OR MIRACLE?

READ MATTHEW 8:5-13

My wife, 13-year-old son, and I are enjoying a stroll through the winding streets of the ancient port city of Jaffa.

The sun sets over the Mediterranean on a beautiful warm spring night. The amber glow of street lights washes over narrow alleys made of white limestone. Streets converge crookedly at the small harbor, still filled with sailing vessels as it has been for thousands of years.

Historians believe that Jaffa (or Joppa, as it's referred to in the New Testament) is the only ancient port in the world that can boast uninterrupted habitation throughout its entire existence. And it plays an interesting role in the Bible.

The cedar logs Solomon used for the construction of the temple were sailed into Jaffa. The prophet Jonah hopped on a ship sailing for the far ends of the earth in Jaffa.

In Acts 9:36–42, a beloved Christian woman named Tabitha *("she was always doing good and helping the poor")* is raised from the dead by Peter in Jaffa.

In Acts 10, Peter is staying here at the house of Simon the tanner (there's an old house that still claims to be the actual place) when he has a vision endorsing non-kosher food.

And local tradition also holds that this is the site of a Greek myth.

SAVING ANDROMEDA

The legend tells of the chaining of Andromeda to the rocks facing Jaffa's shore. Her parents had bragged about her beauty. The gods were angered and sent Cetus, a sea monster, to ravage the coast. To stop this, her parents had to travel to a sacred spot and sacrifice Andromeda by chaining her to the rocks for Cetus to eat.

Perseus, on his way back from slaying the gorgon, swoops in invisibly on a flying horse to rescue Andromeda. Then he marries her — even though she's already pledged to be married to her uncle. At the wedding reception, they enjoy some hummus, and then a fight between Perseus and Andromeda's uncle breaks out. Perseus has, in a bag with him, Medusa's head (convenient!), which turns his rival into stone. And they live happily ever after.

Can you see some of the differences in tone between pagan myths and Bible stories?

By comparison the Bible stories sound very modern. They don't take place in a shadowy world of the fairy-tale past ("a long time ago in a galaxy far, far away") but are anchored firmly in real history. Many times the Bible writers, particularly in the New Testament, take pains to tie their story to a time and place that — to many of their original readers — was within their lifetimes and within a day's walk.

And while in Bible stories there are occasional miracles, they are miracles precisely because they are so special, so rare. They are surprise signs from God. In the Bible, hundreds of years might go by without a miracle. The miracles of Jesus astounded people precisely because these people did not live in a world of flying horses and demigods; they lived in a world of dirty dishes and daily chores where this sort of thing just did not happen.

MAGIC OR MIRACLE?

Let's keep comparing. There are two items in nearly every single pagan myth. There is a magic object — a magic sword or a magic robe or a magic Medusa head. And there are always impossible-to-please, mercurial gods.

These two things are not in the Bible narratives. Ever. You do not find magical tools. And you do not find easily angered, tricky gods.

In the Bible, miracles are seen as coming directly from God — not rooted in a human's cleverness or occult knowledge, but in God's powerful grace.

Magic, by contrast, is about humans knowing the secret ways to tap into some mystical power. Magic is really about human resourcefulness, not God's grace.

This is exactly why the Old Testament prophets like Isaiah—and then Jesus and Paul in the New Testament—criticized not only pagan religions but their own religious structures because of a drift back into these two pagan elements: (1) religious magical thinking, and (2) impossible-to-please gods.

DRIFTING INTO MAGICAL THINKING

Ironically, many of the Jewish religious people of Christ's day, in their obsession with pleasing God through precise rule-keeping and lengthy memorized prayers, were becoming more pagan, not less.

Jesus points this out:

> *"When you pray, do not keep on babbling like pagans, for they think they will be heard because of their many words."* MATTHEW 6:7

Religion—including Christianity—can easily drift back into pagan magical thinking. Divine intervention is seen as something earned by my acts: "I have to go to church or the temple and keep these rules, and maybe pray these prayers, and then I'll have done my ritual guaranteeing fertility"—or whatever it is I'm praying for.

One serious problem with religious systems that devolve into superstitious, magical thinking is that, in practical terms, the power is not really held by God anymore, but by the master magicians, the priests who peddle their petty charms and spells, often in the form of legalistic religious behaviors that are prescribed to earn a desired result. This kind of perceived power corrupts completely because the religious leaders gain too much unquestioned authority—and the grace of God is masked behind a veil of manufactured mystery, a veil Christ came to tear open.

But we don't really need priestly pushers to fall into this trap. We gravitate toward magical thinking all on our own. Daily devotions, church attendance, ecstatic experiences, missions trips, volunteer service, Bible reading, tithing, special religious diets, and even religious jewelry can all be twisted in our minds to the point where they cease to be expressions of worship and become instead acts of religious magic: "If I'm not getting what I want from the deity, then it must be because I'm not performing the magic rituals sufficiently."

This became the main thrust of Christ's critique of the religion of his day: Magical thinking (in their case, peddled by so-called priests) had infiltrated it so thoroughly that it had become almost pagan in practice, a hollow idolatrous shell of the simple love relationship God desires with all people.

That's is why Jesus is astounded at the Roman centurion in Matthew 8 and Luke 7. Here's a guy from a pagan culture, yet his faith is clearly not in his own strength or his ability to earn a miracle from Jesus. In fact, he admits he does not deserve even the presence of Christ. But he trusts totally in Jesus' gracious power.

FREE GRACE, NOT EARNED PRIZE

Jesus' miracles are never a result of strong individuals earning God's favor because they've gone on a heroic quest, or shown amazing strength. They are always acts of God on behalf of the weak — or even the dead.

Just think of a few miracles. Healing the official's son (JOHN 4:43–54). Healing the lame man (JOHN 5:1–9). Feeding the five thousand (JOHN 6). Healing the man born blind (JOHN 9). Raising Lazarus from the dead (JOHN 11). These are acts of God's grace, pure and simple.

And remember how, in John's gospel, the miracles are always called *signs?* Christ's miracles are all signs showing the *greater* miracle of salvation in your life and mine. You are not saved because you earned it somehow — like a hero in a pagan myth. It comes out of the blue, a direct intervention by God, an act of rescue precisely because you were not able to do anything to save yourself.

So watch your own tendency toward magical thinking. Faith is not about trying harder, or about external magical rituals to please a tricky god. It's about a personal relationship with a gracious God.

You're not Perseus, cleverly manipulating the gods' powers. You're Lazarus, dead until Jesus raises you to life.

Salvation is a miracle, not magic.

PRAYER: Thank God today for the miracle of your salvation. Thank him for his immense love for you. Pray that his love will impact your heart and actions today.

24 MADE WHOLE

READ JOHN 5:2-16

We stare down into something that resembles an abandoned subway construction project cutting through the middle of the old city of Jerusalem.

I explain to our group that when we peer into this gully we're diving down through two thousand years of time, past the modern era, through the remains of Crusader and Byzantine era churches, past a Roman temple and finally into ruins from the time of Christ.

At the bottom of the trench, as our eyes learn to discern the various layers of ruins, we can see a colonnaded walkway cutting from top to bottom across what looks like a massive rectangular concrete swimming pool.

This is the fifth of the five colonnades referred to by the author of John's gospel in today's Scripture reading.

AMAZING DISCOVERY

Just a few years ago, some scholars said the Gospel of John was in error when it described the five colonnades of Bethesda.

Commentators pointed out that clearly there were not five colonnades around a four-sided pool. They used this as an example of how the author of John apparently only wrote symbolically, and not literally, and that the number five must have meant something mysterious.

Then, in the 1960s, this small area was excavated. Now we know why John said there were five colonnades. It's because there were five!

Four covered sidewalks bordered with columns ran around the pool, one on each side. Then there was a fifth colonnade that split the pool in half.

This area may have been a *"mikvah"* or ceremonial bath, with the northern side containing ritually "unclean" water, and the southern side, closest to the Temple, being ritually "clean," the two pools separated by the fifth colonnade.

That helps explain the origin of the name *Bethesda*, which literally means "The house of two pools." Thanks to the excavations, we now understand that the fifth colonnade turned one large pool into two.

These days you can only see about one-tenth of the pool (the rest is under active shops and residences in the city) but the small part that was unearthed contains that fifth colonnade. It's as if God wanted the archaeologists to find the one bit that confirmed John's description!

After the time of Christ, anti-Christian Romans took over this location. What they did with it is intriguing. They turned it into a temple to Asclepius, their god of healing. They asserted that these waters were magical and that if you were sick, you might get healed. Sounds to me like they were continuing the folk tradition John describes—and maybe they were also trying to squelch early Christian worship of Jesus by claiming they had their own healing deity.

John's gospel does not claim the legend was true; it only describes what folklore claimed happened around the pool.

People were waiting for magic. Then Jesus brought a miracle.

CRUEL POOL

The pathetic scene in John 5 is easy to imagine. Poor, despairing, disabled people stare in misery at the "magic" water hoping to see some ripples, perhaps caused by an underwater spring.

Then someone shouts *"Bubbles!"* and everyone hobbles into the pool, shoving each other aside, trying to be first.

So who do you think gets in first, every time? The really needy? Not a chance. It's the guy with a headache, or an ingrown toenail.

As R. Wayne Stacy writes,

> It's a cruel pool. It taunts them. The whole fly-swarming, foul-smelling scene is a judgment on the kind of religion that has everything to offer to those who don't really need it — and nothing for those who do. [31]

It's all a race, a competition, all about coming in first, all about performance.

And Jesus walks into the scene and immediately goes to the guy who has *never* come in first. Not for thirty-eight long years.

DO YOU WANT WHOLENESS?

I love that Jesus asks him, "Do you *want* to get well?"

Jesus understood the psychology of victimization. Sometimes we get so used to living as a victim we don't realize that we really can be healed.

Or we don't want to be. As someone said, the problem is often not just that we are diseased. It's that we are *addicted* to our disease.

Of course this does not mean that the conclusion to which people often leap necessarily follows, that those who are sick must be so because they don't truly long for wholeness. Please don't say "You must not really want to be well!" to the next disabled person you meet. That's just bad theology.

The question is meant for you and for me. Do you want to get *well*?

The word translated "well" is the Greek *hygies*, from which we get our English word hygiene. It can be used for physical health — or health in the larger sense. To be made *whole*.

Jesus doesn't just heal this man outwardly. He makes him *whole*.

24 MADE WHOLE

THE INSIDE FIX

The posters for the obscure indie film *Sympathy for Delicious* (Haven't seen it, so I can't recommend it) had a great tag line: "You get the healing you need, but not always the healing you want."

That fits what Jesus does. Because Jesus isn't just interested in body work. He's about soul work.

People today tend to want an outside fix. "My life would be so much better if only my nose was fixed, or my teeth, or my hair, or my finances, or..."

But Jesus goes deeper. He makes you *whole*.

This is always the offer Jesus makes to anyone sick and dying inside, anyone trapped by a performance-oriented religious system that has prizes for those who come in first and has little for those who can't make it into the magic pool.

He comes straight to you and stretches out his hand and makes his offer. Do *you* want to be made *whole?*

Not because of anything you do to make it happen. Not because you were first into the water. But because Jesus comes to you in your disability and makes you an offer.

See, from Christ's perspective, he was surrounded by spiritually sick people locked into a performance-oriented folk religion. The Pool of Bethesda was just a microcosm for their whole system.

I received this email recently from a man who escaped just such a system: " I was caught up in the long and tedious practice of trying to work my way to heaven. Grace was something I was taught only kicked in after you died: If you worked hard enough, grace would bridge the gap, so to speak. Now that I have accepted Christ, I understand how grace works. Grace comes first, and then out of your total gratitude to God you will naturally do good works."

That's exactly right. Grace gives you the power to walk.

RELIGIOUS POLICE

This story does not end with the healing, of course. Able to walk for the first time in years, this man immediately bumps into the religious police, who place him under arrest for carrying his mat — not astounded that this disabled man is now walking, but outraged that he is breaking their laws against carrying stuff on the Sabbath!

For thirty-eight years this man had been trying to become whole by being first into the pool. Thirty-eight years of human effort. Then he gets healed by God's grace — and the religious police tell him it's the wrong day of the week.

It would not be the last time the theology of grace conflicted with the restrictions of legalism.

Legalism keeps people crippled with its rules. Grace empowers them to move forward.

PONDER: In what area of your life are you feeling broken? What prevents you from embracing the desire to be "whole" in that area?

25 GIVE HIM YOUR LUNCH

READ JOHN 6:1-21

As I amble down the pilgrim path toward an ancient church about two miles west of Capernaum, I notice the vegetation becoming increasingly lush.

In California I'd suspect sprinklers. Here there's a natural cause.

Several springs water the landscape, creating an oasis of trees and flowers on the lakeshore. This small hollow set between linen-colored hills stands out like a bright green emerald when viewed from a boat on the lake.

I'm walking toward Tabgha. Its ancient Greek name was Heptapegon, or "seven springs." These days there are only six springs — the seventh was apparently closed by earthquake activity at some point in the past two thousand years.

The springs do more than refresh the plants; they produce water warmer than the Sea of Galilee. The water flows into the lake, and algae grows abundantly in the higher temperature just offshore. The algae attracts fish.

And the fish attract fishermen.

That's why this has been a local favorite fishing spot for thousands of years.

Recently, two ancient curved breakwaters that created a first-century harbor were discovered along the shore here. That, plus the fact that it's so close to Capernaum, makes it likely that the disciples of Jesus did a lot of their fishing right in this spot. People have been coming here to relive the calling of the first disciples for as long as anyone can remember.

It's also the place where Christians have celebrated the miracle of the loaves and fishes since the fourth century AD. In the church here you can find a famous ancient mosaic commemorating it.

That miracle actually happened in a more remote spot the Bible calls Bethsaida. After all, between the fish and the water and the nearby towns, there would have been more than ample food for the crowds in this location. But this is a good place to consider the meaning of the miracle.

This was apparently the most famous miracle Jesus did in his lifetime — it's the only one recorded in all four gospels. We call it "The Feeding of the Five Thousand," but there were many more people than that; the Bible says there were five thousand *men,* so there were likely thousands of women and children here too. And there was no food to feed them.

So Jesus feeds them all. With one lunch.

I love the set-up for this in the Gospel of John.

COUNTING THE CROWD INSTEAD OF COUNTING ON CHRIST

Jesus asks Philip, *"Where shall we buy bread for these people to eat?"* (JOHN 6:5).

25 GIVE HIM YOUR LUNCH

The Bible says he already knew what he was going to do, so why seek advice from Philip? He asked this to test Philip. Jesus is teaching his disciples something here, in this open-air lab class.

Philip's reply? *"Eight months' wages would not buy enough bread for each one to have a bite!"* (JOHN 6:7)

Do you see what happened there? Jesus asked one question, and Philip answered another. Jesus asked, *"Where..."* and Philip answered *"How..."*

"Where can we get the food?" became *"How will we pay for the food?"*

Important switch. Philip could have answered, "I saw what you did at the wedding, Jesus. You already catered the beverage table. Now it's time for lunch counter. Where? Well, with you, that's where."

But instead of starting with the *where*, Philip starts with the *how* and immediately anxiety kicks in.

I often find myself doing the same thing when I see a need. I don't go first to Jesus. I go right to the *how*. And then I get so thoroughly discouraged that I never even try.

Ask yourself: Am I stalled out at "how"? Maybe you need to overcome an addiction. Or change a habit. Or make a life change. Or get through grief. The first question to ask is not, *"How* will I do it?" It's, *"Where* will I go for strength?" Go to Jesus.

LOOKING AT THE LOAVES INSTEAD OF THE LORD

Then Andrew shows up. And his problem is, he goes on for one sentence too long. He says, "Here's a boy with five small barley loaves and two small fish." (Just stop right there, Andrew!) "But (imagine an Eeyore voice here) how far will they go among so many?"

Like I do a lot of times, Andrew gives Jesus an excuse. "Hey, what about — dumb idea. Never mind."

I find that usually I'm either Philip or Andrew.

Like Philip, I can be overwhelmed: "The problem's too big!" Looking at the crowd instead of Christ.

Like Andrew, I can be discouraged: "Our resources are too small!" Looking at the loaves instead of the Lord.

Then Jesus shows them how it's done. He says, "Have the people sit down." The word he uses here means to recline, and that's important, because that was the dining posture in those days. Their dining tables were low to the ground, and they reclined on their left side when they ate. What he's saying is, *Get them ready to eat. Hand out napkins. Set the table.* He is ringing Pavlov's bell. So now you've got five thousand hungry, salivating men. They're looking around for the hummus appetizer. There is no going back.

Jesus prays, he distributes the loaves and fishes… and the disciples are amazed that there is more than enough. In fact, Jesus tells his disciples to clean up the food so that nothing is wasted — and there are twelve basketfuls left over. One for each disciple!

So where in your life have you been thinking that there's just too little for God to work with?

I DON'T HAVE ENOUGH, BUT HE IS ENOUGH

The lesson of this story is not that you have enough resources, or that the need is not great. In fact, often you do *not* have enough resources. And sometimes the needs really *are* too big for you to handle. But through Christ, the work gets done. Because he is the one who miraculously multiplies.

We experienced one small example of this at our church last fall. I call it the Feeding of the One Million.

It all started when one small six-year-old boy named Travis told me he was going door-to-door selling paper kites he made to raise money for the food bank. The next weekend, I interviewed Travis in front of the church.

And we all got motivated to do something we never thought we could do before. Something that, to my knowledge, no church has ever done before: We raised over 1.2 million pounds of food for a food bank in a single food drive.

Was it a miracle? You might be thinking that our food and funds were not miraculously multiplied, but our resources, which most of us had assumed were too meager to make a difference, were gathered and used by God in a mighty way.

If you are overwhelmed by the need, you may be looking at the crowd instead of Christ. Like Philip.

If you are discouraged by the resources, you may be looking at the loaves instead of the Lord. Like Andrew.

Instead, just give Jesus your lunch. And watch him cater a banquet.

> When I start to worry, I go to the mirror and say to myself, "This tremendous thing which is worrying me is beyond a solution. It is especially too hard for Jesus Christ to handle." After I have said that, I smile…
> —Corrie Ten Boom [32]

PONDER: Where in your life do you feel like you have too little for God to work with? How can you "give God your lunch" today?

26 WIND AND WAVES

READ JOHN 6:16-25; MARK 4:35-41 & MARK 6:46-51

We're on a boat in the middle of the Sea of Galilee, the very lake Jesus often sailed with his disciples. It's early in the morning and we're enjoying the sunrise from a wooden ship built as a near-replica of those first-century vessels.

My 13-year-old son tells me this is his favorite thing so far about his trip to Israel.

Of course he loves it. He grew up on the ocean, in Santa Cruz, California. Waves and water mean one thing to him: Fun. Whether it's sailing, surfing, boogie-boarding, stand-up paddleboarding, body surfing, or just swimming, there's no shortage of water sports in our culture. You can see the same recreational opportunities in Israel. *Today.* But in Jesus' time, water was looked at a lot differently.

The seas, whether the ocean, or smaller bodies of water like lakes, were *not* usually places of enjoyment for the people of ancient Israel. Generally speaking, the seas were *feared.*

SINISTER SEAS

Ancient Israel was not a seafaring society. It never developed a lot of technology for water navigation. The seas were seen — accurately — as uncontrollable.

I've often thought the Hebrew Scriptures sound like they were written by a culture that was carrying a corporate memory of some great trauma from water. Oceans and lakes are often referred to in violent terms — great floods and storms.

Very few Israelites in the Bible — maybe only the professional fishermen — voluntarily go on water. No one seems to go sailing or swimming for fun, even though the country is right on the ocean and has two large lakes (and even though other ancient peoples who lived here did have swimming pools and pleasure boats). When the Israelites have to go out on the ocean in the Bible, they always use some other country's sailors and marine technology.

The very word for "sea" in Hebrew is apparently derived from the name of the evil god in the Babylonian creation myth, and carries connotations of a mysterious, malign, and threatening force opposed to God's order. [33]

Almost every time the sea is mentioned in the Old Testament, it's a place of chaos and terror.

When it first appears in Genesis, the "surface of the deep" is empty and dark.

Of course there's Noah's destructive flood. Job even compares the sea to a monster (JOB 7:12).

Psalm 65:7 speaks of God as the only one with the power to *"still the roaring of the seas, the roaring of their waves...."*

The people knew: The surface of the water may look calm now, but in the next moment a rogue wave or tide might change everything.

WILD WAVES

And there were plenty of waves on the Sea of Galilee. Just thirteen miles long and seven miles wide, it's still very dangerous.

Cold air descending from the often snow-covered Mount Hermon range, just twenty miles away but almost ten thousand feet higher than the surface of the lake, collides over Galilee with warm air from the below-sea-level Jordan Valley, creating volatile weather systems. As recently as 1992, ten-foot-high waves crashed into downtown Tiberius, flooding the city and destroying millions of dollars of property.

With all that in mind, I picture this scene as I look at the lake from our wooden boat....

> *... a fierce storm came up. High waves were breaking into
> the boat, and it began to fill with water. Jesus was sleeping
> at the back of the boat with his head on a cushion. The
> disciples woke him up, shouting, "Teacher, don't you care
> that we're going to drown?" When Jesus woke up, he
> rebuked the wind and said to the waves, "Silence! Be still!"
> Suddenly the wind stopped, and there was a great calm.*
> MARK 4:37–39

Did you notice? No magical incantation. Jesus adds no drama to the situation. He doesn't raise his hands and strike a pose and invoke the mighty powers of the spirits of nature. As someone said, "Jesus quickly rebukes the storm as if it's a misbehaving child" — almost off-handedly.

And note the disciples' reaction: They were afraid before. Now they're absolutely terrified.

> *"Who is this man?" they asked each other. "Even the wind
> and waves obey him!"* MARK 4:41 NLT

The disciples were astonished at Christ' control over the frightening force of water, even more than the other miracles they had seen to this point. If they were vulnerable to the vicissitudes of water, then what about this man, who, it is dawning on them here, they had obviously been vastly underestimating to this point?

"Who is this man?"

He can *"calm the roaring seas, the roaring of their waves."* Which Psalm 65 said only *God* can do. Jesus has an almost casual power over a force of nature that represented primal chaos to their culture.

And Jesus made this point more than once. In John 6, for example, he appears to the disciples when they are trying to row out of a storm:

> *A strong wind was blowing and the waters grew rough...
> they saw Jesus approaching the boat, walking on the
> water; and they were frightened. But he said to them, "It
> is I; don't be afraid."* JOHN 6:18–20

26 WIND AND WAVES

As John Ortberg points out, in the original Greek, that last phrase is just four words. Literally it reads:

"I am; no fear."

The take-away for me? Jesus is Lord over all the things you and I fear, too; over all that represents chaos to us. He is ultimately in charge. He is God with us, in all our storms.

He doesn't always calm the storm exactly when and how I want him to; but he is always willing and able to calm *me*.

WHAT ARE YOU SO AFRAID OF?
Where in your life is Jesus saying, *"I am; no fear"*?

If the ocean and lakes represented the deepest, darkest fears of the ancient Israelites, what is the primal fear for you? What storm terrifies you? What is fiercely roaring in your heart?

Is it death? Flying? Finances? Public speaking? Jesus can calm your fear. He is Lord even over that. Make no mistake: The storm doesn't always pass. But you can learn to always see Jesus there.

Matthew makes an interesting comment in his account about what happened after they were so terrified: *"And those in the boat worshipped him, saying, 'Truly you are the Son of God.'"* (MATTHEW 14:33)

This is a first. Their respect and enthusiasm for this man is turning into worship. The disciples are beginning to believe there is far more to this man than they can see. There are depths and dimensions to this Messiah that they never anticipated.

And they have another surprise waiting on the waves.

PROJECT: Write down one thing you're worried or fearful about right now. Each time that worry/fear crosses your mind today say (out loud if you need to), "I choose to trust Jesus who says, 'I am. No fear.'"

I AM

I love to visit Tel Dan, in the beautiful nature preserve north of Galilee. Recently archaeologists discovered the oldest arched gate in the world here. Before this unexpected discovery, college textbooks taught that the arch was an architectural innovation by Romans a few hundred years before Christ. Now we have an amazing example of a massive, triple-arched city gate more than four thousand years old — it was old when Abraham walked through it looking for Lot.

That reminds me of one of Jesus' most controversial statements: *"Before Abraham was born, I am!"* (JOHN 8:58) Before this tripled-arched gate was made, Jesus said, *"I am."*

Notice Jesus did not say, "Before Abraham was born, I was." That would have been strange enough. Abraham existed nearly two thousand years before Christ. But Jesus used the present tense: *"Before Abraham... I am."*

This enraged some of his listeners because his use of the phrase *"I am"* was in reference to a famous verse from their Scriptures:

> *God said to Moses, "I AM WHO I AM"; and he said, "Tell the sons of Israel, 'I AM has sent me to you."*
> EXODUS 3:14

Jesus didn't just use this phrase once: In the Gospel of John alone he said:

"I am the bread of life." JOHN 6:48

"I am the light of the world." JOHN 8:12

"I am the gate." JOHN 10:9

"I am the good shepherd." JOHN 10:11

"I am God's son." JOHN 10:36

"I am the resurrection and the life." JOHN 11:25

Some of his opponents understood Jesus quite correctly:

"You, being a man, make yourself out to be God!"
JOHN 10:33

But—what if it's all true? What if he is the *"I am,"* the ever-present God? That is someone worth following!

27 FULL-BODY FLOATATION

READ MATTHEW 14:22-33

I am literally standing upright in water—bobbing along like a cork, waist-high—without my feet touching the ground.

Swimming in the Dead Sea is a surreal experience. No matter what you do, you just can't sink.

But that doesn't keep me from trying.

I lay flat on the surface of the water like some kind of water-bug. My body barely slips beneath the surface of the waves.

Then I sit on the water like a chair, using its surface like a seat. Still floating.

Now I face forward and do the breast stroke, so buoyant that it's less like swimming and more like crawling.

Our whole group plunges in, most of us far into our adult years, but giggling like little kids as we try out new float strategies. "Check this out!" "Look at this one!"

The Dead Sea is the lowest place on the surface of the earth, at nearly 1,400 feet below sea level. It's about 33% saline, making it one of the saltiest bodies of water on the planet (it has about 8.6 times more salt than the ocean). The saline concentration makes you amazingly buoyant.

While I float here a thought crosses my mind: I wonder if Peter might have felt something like this that night he walked on water. Maybe during those few moments that he cruised along on the H_2O highway, he had that same sense of near weightlessness I feel in the Dead Sea—only he was in the fresh water of Galilee. And he was buoyed all the way up—he walked by faith, not by salt.

27 FULL-BODY FLOATATION

LOOK BEFORE YOU LEAP

The story in Matthew 14 has been seen for centuries as a great example of the kind of faith-in-action God wants us to have. And it is inspiring. But I've also seen people use this story as an excuse for all kinds of hare-brained ideas.

Someone came up to me after church one day and announced, "Well, tomorrow I'm moving to Phoenix!" I asked if they had a job there, or relatives, or were going to college, or had some ministry hopes. "Nope! But I've been thinking and thinking about it, and now I'm just gonna get out of the boat and walk on that water!"

Well... that could have been God's will. And I am confident God can work in Phoenix as well as any other place in that person's life.

But what do you notice about the faith of Peter in this story?

First, he asks, and *waits*, for Jesus to call him out of the boat. He doesn't just plop into the water because he feels like it.

I'm a preacher, so I'll admit that we preachers love to use this story as an illustration of *action*. "Do you have faith? Then get out of the boat!" It's a great one for a building campaign or a mission trip recruitment drive.

But are we guilty of adapting this to our initiative-taking, outward-focused modern American mentality when we emphasize that part of the story? Peter didn't shout "Cowabunga!" and leap out. He *waited* until he was sure it was the Lord. And this is exactly where some Christians go wrong. They leap forward without waiting patiently on God's direction — and then they wonder why God didn't bless their move. Their focus is more on their awesome faith than on the compelling call of Christ.

After all, Satan asked Jesus to take a leap of faith too. Remember? A leap right off the top of the temple. He even quoted Scripture. Very motivational! And yet Jesus flatly *refused*. Certainly not because he lacked faith. But because it wasn't God's will. Not every leap is a leap of faith. It's OK to stay in the boat if God's not asking you to get out.

You can always cherry-pick Bible verses to support some audacious risk (following you-know-who's example) but true God-honoring leaps of faith need to take into consideration what wise Christians call "the whole counsel of God," the big picture of the Bible and the historic Christian faith. The goal of faith-in-action is to do God's will, not for me to fulfill some agenda of mine. The purpose of following Jesus is not to have adventures or thrills, but to do God's will. Believe me, adventure will follow.

GO FOR IT

So some Christians err by justifying any scheme of theirs as a leap of faith God is obligated to honor. Others, on the other hand, don't appreciate the *second* part of Peter's example: When Peter is convinced it's Christ calling, he goes for it.

He doesn't focus on his fear. He doesn't focus on his circumstance. He doesn't think about the opinion of the other guys. And he is able to walk across the water toward Jesus.

The point: You can do *whatever* Jesus asks you to do.

So Jesus is asking you to stay holy in an impure world. To stop a habit. To say you're sorry. To forgive an enemy. To stop worrying. To share your faith. And it seems impossible. Walking-on-water-level impossible.

But it's *Jesus* asking you. And that means if you keep your eyes on him, it will get done.

This story is about what it's *like* to believe in Christ.

We're all sinking in the sea of our sin and shame and sorrows. Then Jesus calls us to himself.

Is it really him? Is he really there, in your stormy world? You wonder if it's real or just a mirage.

27 FULL-BODY FLOATATION

But if you listen, you will hear his gentle call: *"Come to me."*

It seems foolish in the middle of life's storms, surrounded by "real life," to believe that you can actually connect to Jesus, to the Christ you are seeing through the mist.

Then you see his face with the eyes of faith and take that first tentative step. You don't understand it. You simply try it.

And you find that by *his grace* it happens — when you simply look to him. Suddenly you realize you're floating over all kinds of barriers that you thought separated you from Jesus: Barriers of peer pressure, emotional baggage, sexual issues, a checkered past, intellectual obstacles....

When your eyes are on Jesus and not the obstacles, you move toward him — no matter what is underfoot.

You'll hear lots of motivational speakers using this story to challenge listeners to be more like Peter. But from start to finish, this story is not really about Peter. It's about Jesus; the strength that flows from Jesus when you listen to him, respond to him, and stay focused on him. This is all about the grace of God.

In a sense, anyone who trusts in Christ has taken exactly these steps.

STAY FOCUSED

Of course, you know how the story ends: When Peter's attention drifts to the troubled waters around him, he sinks. I've been there.

When you're distracted from this simple focus on Christ, and turn your eyes again to the dangers and pressures of the world, or to your own self and your progress or lack thereof, you lose that forward momentum and sink again into inaction.

But *even then* Jesus has grace and lifts Peter out of his troubles.

This reminds me of one of my favorite obscure verses written by the Apostle Paul to the Corinthian church. They'd been getting distracted by all kinds of extra teachings that false teachers told them they needed to know. Paul says:

> *I fear that somehow your minds may be seduced away*
> *from your simple and pure devotion to the Messiah.*
> 2 CORINTHIANS 11:3 CJB

Keep it pure and simple. Focus on Jesus.

Will you get distracted from Christ even after you decide to follow him, and begin to sink again? Of course. Peter did. But when you do, you can count on the arms of Jesus to lift you up and gently turn your eyes back to him. He will not let you drown.

Next: Any assurance the disciples felt when Jesus calmed the storm is tested when he immediately has another showdown with the dark side.

PRAYER: Thank God today for his amazing power. Talk to him about your struggles to keep your eyes on him. Pray that you'll trust him and focus on him as you journey through life.

28 THE DARK SIDE

READ MARK 5:1-20

I race my son across the Byzantine ruins, through a thicket of trees, and up weathered stairs to the top of the hill at Kursi, an archaeological site right on the shore of the Sea of Galilee.

Crumbling ancient arches made of black basalt—instead of the nearly ubiquitous white limestone—lend a sinister air to the scene here, more so when we realize where we're standing: The probable site of the tombs of the Gerasene region, where Jesus encountered a demon-possessed man.

I tell my son the story as we sit down to catch our breath.

Jesus was exhausted. He'd had a very busy day, and he tells the disciples he needs some rest, so please let's sail to the other side of the lake.

Night falls. That famous storm hits. Jesus is so tired he sleeps through the waves swamping the ship until the disciples wake him up in alarm. He frightens them even further by calming the wind, and there seems to have been a very awkward silence as the rattled fishermen skim over the suddenly calm surface of the lake until their boat bumps the shore.

Owls screech. Insects whir and click in the dark. Something rustles in the distance. And then rapid footsteps approach.

"And guess what's waiting for them right here, in the blackness of the night?" I ask my son. He's leaning forward, half-waiting for the bogeyman to jump out of the ruins.

I tell him to imagine the hair standing up on the neck of every single disciple as the night is shattered by a sudden shrieking and rattling of chains—and then they see him in the moonlight: A madman, naked except for some useless shackles, rushing down the hillside toward them, screaming at the top of his lungs as he points to Jesus.

To complete the creepiness, note where this takes place: The boat apparently went a little off course in the storm, and it seems they landed right here, in a *cemetery*, at *night*.

It's like a horror movie. After all they've been through, the disciples' nerves must have been stretched to the breaking point. Their adrenalin is pumping. They're probably grabbing oars, ready to defend themselves.

But not Jesus.

He calmly and firmly orders the demons out of the man, and, strangely, into some pigs, which rush down the hillside and are drowned. Maybe he does this because the people there were Jews who shouldn't have been raising pigs anyway, or maybe there was another reason now known only to Jesus; in any case, the man is instantly cured. There's no tension, no complicated ritual exorcism. Jesus just gives orders. And they are obeyed.

The people from the village gingerly approach when they hear the weird old guy in the cemetery isn't running around wailing anymore. And when they see how well he's doing, but mostly how all their pigs are dead, they don't exactly rejoice; they beg Jesus to leave! They aren't inspired. They're freaked.

So is my son. And you know what? This story kind of freaks me out too. In modern Western cultures, most people feel pretty uncomfortable with stories of Jesus driving out demons.

How are we supposed to understand these verses? Again, it's important to see what is happening here in historical context.

BACKGROUND TO AN EXORCISM

In those days, the more orthodox Jews near Jerusalem were the least likely people to have detailed beliefs about evil spirits. The Sadducees, the leaders of the Temple, didn't believe in any spirit beings at all, angels or demons.

But here in the north near Galilee, especially on the east side of the lake, people were more likely to believe in demons, possibly because they were influenced by the pagan religions of the surrounding countries.

Remember how the Sea of Galilee was politically and culturally divided in half, with the west side being the more religiously observant Jewish side, and the right side consisting of much more pagan, Greco-Roman culture? Temples to all sorts of pagan deities dotted the landscape there: Greek, Persian, Roman, and Egyptian cults devoted to all sorts of gods and demigods.

If you look on a map, you'll notice that the area where this particular story takes place — Kursi — is on "the other side of the lake," as the gospel writers call it. The eastern side. The dark side.

The large, Greek-inspired Decapolis cities of Hippo and Jerash were near Kursi; in fact, we travelled into Jordan and walked through the astoundingly impressive ruins of Jerash (or *Gerasa* in Greek; it gives its name to the "region of the Gerasenes" in the Bible). The streets there are still lined with amazing columns and stunning architecture dating from the time of Christ. But on every corner, and on every hilltop, there's something that would have made an observant Jew wince: A pagan temple.

How was a first-century Jew going to make sense of all these religions, when Judaism taught there was but one God? One alternative: To assume that these were not temples to gods but "spirits," some of them malevolent.

Of course, not all Jews made this assumption; some considered the pagan cultic sites as shrines to nothing at all. But for the semi-religious Jew who saw the temples to the gods as potentially enshrining demons, fear and superstition were a part of daily life.

This may help explain why Jesus is not described in the gospels as delivering anyone from demons near Jerusalem, or anywhere far into the west side of Galilee. The demon exorcisms all happen on the east side — or right on the border, at Capernaum. This is where people were the most afraid of demons; this is where their daily lives were ruled and ruined by the evil spirits. Jesus meets them where they are.

Demons to them represented the uncontrollable side of the spirit world. And in their religious culture, the only way to gain some control over demons was through learning more about the arcane occult arts. In other words, *magic*.

Descriptions from the first century show exorcists relying on elaborate rituals using magic words, magic gestures, and special magic tools. Josephus, the first-century Jewish historian, described one exorcism (obviously with some skepticism) performed by a Jew named Eleazor before the Roman emperor Vespasian:

> The manner of cure was this: He put a ring that had
> a root of one of those sorts mentioned by Solomon to
> the nostrils of the demoniac, after which he drew out
> the demon through his nostrils; and when the man fell
> down immediately, he adjured him to return unto him no
> more... reciting the incantations which he composed. And
> when Eleazor wanted to persuade and demonstrate to the
> spectators that he had such power, he set a little way off a
> cup or basin full of water, and commanded the demon, as
> he went out of the man, to overturn it, and thereby to let
> the spectators know that he had left the man. [34]

My point: The freaky thing for us in our culture is to read stories about evil spirits. The striking thing about these stories for people in the first century would not be that there were demonic spirits. The unusual element here, the plot twist, is just how easily Jesus is able to dispatch them. He has instant, permanent authority. He does not need to use any mumbo-jumbo, no incantations or posturing or rings or cups. He says, *"Out!"* and they're gone. It's not a magic show.

Jesus wasn't the only exorcist the people had seen. But he was the only one who didn't make a theater of it, and the only one with this kind of authority, the only one with immediate, 100% success. He was something else, something entirely new and unique in terms of his spiritual power.

HE HAS THE POWER

The inclusion of these episodes in the gospels is clearly meant to demonstrate that Jesus has power—if he wishes to use it—over *every* realm of and every aspect of human experience:

In the gospels he is shown as *intellectually* superior to the wisest men in the country, who repeatedly try to trick him with no success.

He is shown to have power over *physical* human needs when he multiples food.

He is shown to have authority over the realm of *nature* as storms and sickness flee at a word from him.

And here the Messiah demonstrates that he has ultimate authority even over the *spiritual* realm, over powers of darkness—the most frightening, evil, unpredictable, nightmarish side of life.

Between Jesus and any other power, it's just not an even match.

Later, when Pontius Pilate shouts at him, *"Don't you realize I have the authority to release you or kill you?!"* Jesus basically laughs and says, Authority?! If you realized who I am, you would not talk about authority. You would have no authority over me at all unless it had been given you from above. (JOHN 19:11)

One caveat: These stories are meant to inspire you about the *Messiah*; they are not meant to teach you *methodology* about demons. This is the difference between *prescriptive* and *descriptive* passages of the Bible. The prescriptive passages explicitly *prescribe* behavior; that is, they *teach*. The descriptive passages relate *descriptions* of events as they were witnessed and remembered.

When the Apostle Paul wants to *prescribe* to the early church how to win in spiritual warfare, he talks about weapons such as truth, peace, the Word of God, and the gospel of grace (EPHESIANS 6:10–18). There are never any prescriptive passages with instructions on exorcism — beyond the words of Christ to fast and pray, which is always good advice.

Of course I am not saying that I don't believe in a spiritual realm; I do. Definitely.

But I suspect that when Paul was writing to the developing church, he saw the error of gnosticism begin to creep in. The Gnostics believed that there were many spirit beings ("emanations," they called them) and to communicate with God you needed to learn mystical secrets to getting through these layers of good and evil spirits. A generation after Jesus, Christianity under the influence of the Gnostics was slipping away from a simple emphasis on grace, and back to magic.

That's why Paul says, essentially, keep it simple. Stay focused on Jesus. Remember, it's about grace, not your knowledge of occult spiritual secrets.

THE MAN OF THE TOMBS GETS A LIFE

Back to the story: After the man is "in his right mind" as the gospel writer describes him, he wants so badly to travel with Jesus and leave his pagan-influenced area. Hey, Jesus, I see you've got twelve disciples — let's make it a baker's dozen!

But Jesus wants him to stay right there, and tell his friends and neighbors, who knew him *when*, what happened to him.

I have heard so many people tell me Jesus "freed me from my demons."

Sometimes they're speaking metaphorically, other times literally, and most of the time, it's a mix: In physical, psychological, and spiritual ways, these people were oppressed and out of control. But Jesus came into their lives, and set them free. With a *word*.

Were you once living in the tombs, among the dead and dying, but now you're alive and free?

It's tempting to want to just cluster with the other delivered people, to huddle with the healed and holy. But don't forget to tell those who knew you *before.* Jesus says to you:

> "Go *home to your own people and tell them how much the Lord has **done for you**, and how he has **had mercy on you**.*"

But Jesus is not done with the dark side. He is about to go from the man of the tombs to the Gates of Hades. To tell us not to panic.

PONDER: How does believing that Jesus has mastery over the spiritual realm impact your confidence?

PART 5

TENSION

29 ON THIS ROCK

READ MATTHEW 16:13-23

Ever been panicked about the future, filled with anxiety and dread? Today I'm at Panic World Headquarters, reading words of peace.

As our group hikes today in Caesarea Philippi, I enjoy its raw natural beauty, its forests and waterfalls. And I think about how, toward the end of his earthly ministry, Jesus journeyed here, to the extreme northern reaches of his country, as far away from Jerusalem as he could get without heading across the border.

In Jesus' era this was a resort town with a spa and impressive Greco-Roman temples. Pagan shrines were carved into an enormous cliff face with a yawning cavern from which a spring-fed waterfall gushed.

Earthquakes have since diverted the water flow from the cave mouth to fissures at the bottom of the cliff, but the spring here is still one of the primary sources of the Jordan River.

In a land often in desperate need of precipitation, the water pouring out of the dark cave must have seemed to ancient people like a supernatural source of fertility. Maybe that's why, from prehistoric times, this was a place of pagan worship.

TEMPLE OF PANIC

By the time of Christ, the cavern here was venerated as one home of the god Pan. I wonder if Jesus' disciples thought Pan looked like the devil, with his goat-like horns, and his tongue always stuck out in a suggestive leer like some eighties heavy metal star.

Pan was the god of *panic*. In fact, we get our word "panic" from his name. Romans prayed at this temple for their enemies to be filled with dread and confusion.

In 70 AD, the Roman general Vespasian rested his troops here for twenty days before they went on to destroy Jerusalem and tear down Herod's temple. Every day, he sought the blessing of Pan on his soldiers, that they might foment panic in their enemies.

But why are Jesus and his disciples way up here in this pagan area, about as distant from Jerusalem as possible?

I think it's an escape from the pressure they're feeling further south.

It's now been three years since Jesus started his ministry, and the Jerusalem religious leaders are becoming more and more extreme in their opposition to Christ. Any trip toward Jerusalem by Jesus would ignite the political powder-keg there. And he knows it's not quite time for that yet.

Many of Christ's early followers have become impatient and disillusioned. If he's the Messiah, they ask, why doesn't he make it clear? And now his closest disciples are starting to feel anxious too. They're probably wondering why, if Jesus is the Messiah, they're on the run, he's speaking in riddles, and they have so much opposition from fellow Jews.

I imagine they looked around at all these intimidating big beautiful rock-carved temples. Then they think of Jerusalem with *its* beautiful temple.

And for all their sacrifices, they have *nothing* to show. They have no beautiful buildings. Fewer followers. They don't even really have momentum anymore. Nothing seems to be going right.

They're discouraged, dreading what's next. That's where their heads are at when Jesus asks them:

*"So. Who do **you** say I am?"*

And Simon Peter answers, *"You are the Christ, the Son of the living God."*

Jesus seems astounded that Peter says this, endorses this as a revelation from above (after all, every other time Peter opens his mouth he seems to stick his foot in it), and then says, *"You are Peter, and on this rock I will build my church...."* (MATTHEW 16:15–18)

Stop right there. Do you see how he's talking about building on rock — right here in the very place where there's a temple built out of a huge rock?

And there's more. He makes a pun on two different words for *rock* here. Peter's name — from *petros* — means "little stone." Then the word used in the phrase "upon this rock," *petra*, from the same root, means a *giant rock*.

Jesus is saying: From you, a little pebble, I will build my massive community, a kingdom stronger than any of these stone temples. And not just Peter. Anyone who answers Jesus' question the same way is one of the "living stones," as Peter himself later points out (SEE 1 PETER 2:5).

Remember how Jesus was probably raised to be a *tekton*, working in stone, as Joseph was before him? Well, he is the master stonemason still, shaping Simon Peter and you and me into the church he is building.

Note: *He* builds it. Not us. We're the stones. But he's got the plan. He's in control.

FROM TINY PEBBLES TO ROCKING THE WORLD

Now remember again where they are standing. Roman power is in full flower. Looks like Pan and his disciples are here to stay. In fact, Pan's worshippers will literally destroy the glorious Jerusalem Temple in a few short years.

Yet I can picture Christ's next words right here as I look at the ruin: Perhaps Jesus gestures to Pan's shrine, which literally looked like massive gates leading into the cavern here, when he says, *"Even the Gates of Hades will not withstand what I am building."*

And, in fact, this place crumbled into ruin after about 600 AD, while Christ's movement has grown for centuries and centuries.

DON'T PANIC

Jesus' assurance to the disciples goes for you, too. You may feel dread, panic, a feeling that life is purposeless. Like you're just a little pebble. Unimportant. Surrounded by the trappings of true power. The ways of the world may seem to you to be looming large, far greater than the mild efforts of Christ-followers.

I went through a time in my life when I felt exactly that way too. Filled with a continual sense that something horrible was always just around the corner, I couldn't sleep, couldn't focus, had no appetite — and ended up in the hospital with anxiety attacks. I wondered if all my meager efforts for God were meaningless.

I am so thankful for a godly doctor who helped me through that time. And who led me to the words of Christ in this very passage, words which became my anchor.

There will be times you will feel like the disciples. *Don't panic*. The Prince of Peace is right here. He has a greater plan than the Prince of Panic. And he uses little pebbles like you and me for his purpose, building a kingdom that will last forever.

If the disciples were discouraged and doubt-filled, in need of a vision readjustment, they were about to get one beyond their wildest dreams.

PONDER: How have you been feeling like a pebble lately? How are you encouraged by today's devotional?

30 THREE MOUNTAINS

READ MARK 9:2-8 & MATTHEW 17:1-6

From the bus windows we suddenly catch a glimpse of something few of us imagined we'd see in the Holy Land: A snow-capped mountain with a ski resort!

We're looking at Mount Hermon, a volcano-shaped summit looming more than nine thousand feet high on the extreme northern end of Israel, right on its border with Syria. In the morning you could ski on one of the fourteen runs at the resort here, then hop in your car and by lunchtime be in the middle of the desert sliding down sand dunes — and then after another short drive you could be surfing while the sun sets over the ocean! Not exactly the vacation most people imagine in Israel!

It may have been on this mountain that Jesus was transfigured before three of his disciples (the event is usually called "the Transfiguration").

Although there is a different, traditional site for the transfiguration closer to Galilee, I think this mountain more closely fits the gospel descriptions of a high, remote place near Caesarea Philippi.

What happens here is pure poetry. I don't mean to say the transfiguration is *only* poetry, that it didn't actually happen; I'm convinced it did.

But once again, God shows himself to be an artist, as the sight the disciples experience here is literally a revelation — it reveals, makes clear, in visual terms, what Jesus is all about.

Can you perceive the poetry? Listen first to the echoes from other mountains.

First mountain: Mount Sinai.

About 1,400 years before Christ, the Bible says God showed his glory to Moses in a cloud referred to as the *"shekinah glory."* The *shekinah* was the shining, unfiltered glory of the Holy One. But it was too intense, too pure, for humans to bear. Even Moses was told to hide in a cave as the *shekinah* passed nearby. "No one can see my face and live," God tells him.

The *shekinah* makes a reappearance in the tabernacle, which was sort of a temporary temple, hovering over the ark of the covenant. Here (and later in the temple) the high priest atoned for the sins of the people of Israel behind a thick veil of separation, a curtain separating the Holy of Holies from the rest of the world. This curtain was a visible reminder that the *shekinah* could not dwell with sinful man. Only the high priest can be near God's *shekinah*, and only when making atonement for sin.

Moses' mountaintop experience teaches us that God is holy. And the people were afraid.

Second mountain: Mount Carmel.

Several centuries after Sinai, Elijah has his famous showdown with the priests of Baal. He challenges them to something like a god-contest. They build an altar to Baal, Elijah builds an altar to Yahweh, and a crowd gathers to see which one will accept the sacrifice. The Baal priests pray and get no answer. Then Elijah prays and the mountain is lit up as with lightning — fire comes down from heaven — Elijah's sacrifice is consumed in a bright instant, proving God's existence and might.

Elijah's mountaintop experience teaches us that God is powerful. And the people were afraid.

Third mountain: The Transfiguration.

Fast-forward several centuries more. We're on a mountain again. There's Moses again. There's Elijah again. And it's as bright as lightning again.

As I squint at Mount Hermon's snow-capped slopes, it's easy to picture the white light the gospels describe. Ever leave a dimly lit cabin to emerge in the brightness of a snow-covered landscape at midday? The brightness actually has *power.*

The disciples had been seeing through a glass, darkly. Now they see reality unobscured, for just an instant. Their eyes hurt in the brightness. Mark says the light was so intense that it made Jesus' clothes appear whiter than anything on earth.

But this time there's a twist. The glory comes *from* Jesus. The *shekinah* is *not* shining from above, *onto* him. It's shining from *inside* him.

Jesus doesn't *behold* the glory of God. He *is* the glory of God.

SHELTER FROM THE LIGHT

But wait, Peter seems to remember: The last two times there was a mountaintop lit up by God, the lessons were that God is holy and powerful—and scary. Maybe this is the reason for Peter's otherwise hard-to-understand suggestion that they build three shelters. *The word used there for "shelter" is also the Greek word for "tabernacle."*

Peter was appropriately overwhelmed with awe and terror at the *shekinah.* So he responds the way humans have responded in all their religions for thousands of years: Let's built a tabernacle, a temple, a system for mediating this achingly vast distance between God's glorious brightness and man's sinful darkness.

He doesn't just want to house Jesus, Moses, and Elijah.

He wants to shield himself from the brightness.

He is afraid of the light. So his solution is religion.

It's an understandable reaction. But God the Father says he just needs Christ. As soon as Peter says those words, a cloud envelops them and from within comes the voice of the Father: "This is my Beloved Son. Listen to him!"

30 THREE MOUNTAINS

The cloud lifts. And Moses and Elijah are gone.

THE LAW, THE PROPHETS, AND SOMETHING NEW
The two great divisions of the Hebrew Scriptures were called the Law and the Prophets. Moses represented the Law, and Elijah the Prophets. They both endorse Jesus. And then they leave. The Law and Prophets are no longer needed as a protective mediator between God and people.

Because something new is here. Law and Prophets, meet Gospel.

The very *shekinah* of God is now with humans. *God with us.* Jesus is the ultimate priest to end all priests, the prophet of all prophets.

The veil keeps tearing.

INVITED INTO THE GLORY
Jesus sees the disciples cowering in fear and he touches them and says, "Get up. Don't be afraid."

That right there, that's the message and mission of Jesus, always. He comes to bring us the very presence of God. He touches us. And he says, 'Don't be afraid."

Maybe you've been afraid of God. Maybe you've been so aware of the difference between your dingy darkness and God's beautiful brightness that you've almost given up—if there is a God, how could you ever approach him? All your religion has done is remind you of the distance.

The point of Christ is, he bridges that gap. He touches you. And he sends fear fleeing.

THE SON SHINES
At the mountain, Peter, James, and John get an inspiring preview of what Jesus will do when his mission as Messiah nears completion.

He will not always be the Lamb. One day he will return as the Lion. And they get a glimpse of this glory.

When he's an old man, John sees Jesus again in a vision. And it's this transfigured Christ. And look at what Jesus says to John. Again.

> *His face was like the sun shining in all its brilliance. When I saw him, I fell at his feet as though dead. Then he placed his right hand on me and said: "Do not be afraid. I am the First and the Last. I am the Living One; I was dead, and now look, I am alive for ever and ever!"* REVELATION 1:16–17

The *shekinah* glory of God appears again. And God speaks. And says the thing he always has to say, because no one is ever ready for him to show up. *Fear not.*

PRAYER: Thank God today for the truth that Jesus is the exact representation of God – that he is the glory of God. Pray that you will grow in your understanding of this truth and be comforted by the power and peace of God in Jesus Christ.

DID JESUS CLAIM TO BE GOD?

I used to wonder why Jesus never quite comes out and says, "Point (1:) I'm God. Point (2:) Worship me. Thank you for listening." Yet any honest reading of the gospels shows that he is clearly making these points. Although his claims are veiled at first, he is eventually understood to be claiming divinity even by his opponents (JOHN 10:33). He accepts worship (JOHN 20:28). He says he and the Father are one (JOHN 10:30, 14:7–10). So why all the riddles and parables at first?

Well, he had to stay alive for a while! Jesus needed to serve, teach and then publicly die on a cross in order to accomplish his mission (MARK 10:45). It wouldn't have been a very strategic idea to step into his rather fundamentalist culture and announce he was God. He would have been instantly derided as a lunatic, would never have had a single follower, and would likely have been stoned for blasphemy. The truth of his identity had to be gradually and subtly revealed, through his teaching, his miracles, and ultimately his resurrection.

But the claim to divinity is there all through the gospels, if you look. There's a lot more to say about this, but just as a start, consider the acronym HANDS:

HONORS

Jesus is given all the *honors* due to God alone, like worship (MATTHEW 14:33), or obedience (JOHN 14:15).

ATTRIBUTES

Jesus claims all the ***attributes*** of God, although veiled in his humanity, like knowing man's thoughts (MATTHEW 9:4); pre-existence (LUKE 20:41–44; JOHN 17:5); everlasting words (LUKE 21:33; SEE ISAIAH 40:8).

NAMES

Jesus accepts the ***names*** of God, like *Lord* (MATTHEW 3:3); *"I Am"* (JOHN 8:58); *God* (JOHN 20:28)

DEEDS

Jesus does the ***deeds*** of God, such as forgiving sins (LUKE 5:17–26); granting eternal life (JOHN 10:27–28); controlling nature (MARK 4:35–41).

SEAT

Jesus sits in the ***seat*** of God as Lord over God's Law (MATTHEW 12:8); and judge of mankind (MATTHEW 25:31–32).

*See *Putting Jesus in His Place: The Case for the Deity of Christ* by Robert M Bowman, Jr., and J. Ed. Komoszewski for a more complete study.

31 | THE PALM SUNDAY MYSTERY

READ JOHN 12:12-19

We're walking with a crowd of Christians from all over the world, just two weeks after Easter, down the road that slopes westward from the Mount of Olives to Jerusalem. The Palm Sunday Road.

We can see the Temple Mount across the valley in front of us. This very route, or one close to it, was the one taken by Jesus when he rode on a donkey into the city on that famous spring day.

Then it was lined with his fans. They yelled their support and waved palm branches to welcome him to the city. Less than a week later, he was killed.

You could call it *The Palm Sunday Mystery.*

How could a crowd welcome Jesus with such enthusiasm — and then rally for his execution a week later? Why did the cheers turn to jeers?

Let's try to solve the puzzle. Put aside any of your preconceived ideas. And look at these verses through the lens of history. Examine the clues in the words of the text.

GREAT CROWD

John says there was a *"great crowd that had come for the feast."* Who were these people, and how big was this crowd?

They were in town for the feast of _Passover,_ when the Jews remembered their deliverance from Egypt with the ritual sacrifice of a lamb.

The ancient Jewish writer Josephus reported that at one Passover in the mid-first century there was an official tally kept of sacrificial lambs slain in Jerusalem, and it added up to 256,500. From this figure he estimated there were 2,565,000 people in the city for the feast, based on an average of about ten people per lamb — and since

169

Jerusalem had no more than a few hundred thousand residents, about two million of those must have been pilgrims who came from other cities or countries. [35]

Think of the pictures you've seen of the Hajj, the Muslim pilgrimage to Mecca, and you'll get an idea of the crowd size — and of the fervor that can be quickly produced in such a massive gathering! [36]

Bible scholar D. A. Carson describes the emotion this crowd would have been experiencing:

> The Passover Feast was to Jews what the fourth of July is to Americans… It was a rallying point for intense, nationalistic zeal. This goes some way to explaining their fervor that tried to force Jesus to become king. [37]

PALM BRANCHES

Why were they waving palm branches? The palm was a symbol of national independence for Jews at the time. Almost exactly two hundred years before Palm Sunday, there had been a successful revolution against foreign oppressors led by a man named Judas Maccabeus. He minted coins with the symbol of a palm tree.

This became the icon of Israel's freedom. Waving the palm branch was like waving the stars and stripes: It was a patriotic statement, a fond memorial of the Maccabean revolution. In the Israel Museum in Jerusalem, I saw several Jewish coins from the first and second century stamped with palm trees and the slogan, "For the freedom of Jerusalem!"

SHOUTING HOSANNA

And this patriotic sentiment goes perfectly with what the crowds were yelling: "*Hosanna*," which simply means, "save us now!" Note: Not just, "Save us," but, "Save us — *now!*"

31 THE PALM SUNDAY MYSTERY

The Messiah-mania sweeping the country had to have been intensified by a kind of bicentennial fever because, again, Judas Maccabeus had ridden in from Galilee about two centuries before this. And now here comes Jesus, riding in from Galilee, too. The people surely hoped for another Maccabean-like revolution — right away! Perhaps they thought Jesus had been toying with them through his riddles and stories. But now his intent was clear: To throw the Romans out!

READY FOR A RUMBLE

You could say the dry kindling was all arranged. The bases were loaded. The bullets were in the barrel. All Jesus had to do was light the fire, swing the bat, pull the trigger — just make the slightest move to revolt — and he would have had massive popular support. The expectation level must have created a palpable buzz. The people were ready for a rumble.

Then what is Jesus' *very next move* in Jerusalem?

It takes every single observer by surprise, including all of his disciples. And it seems like a colossal miscalculation that not only costs him popular support but leads to his death.

ROOM FOR MORE GENTILES

He strides into the city *(the tension mounts!)* goes up to the Temple *(so far so good!)*, and instead of going to the barracks of the soldiers and palace of the Roman governor, he turns left *(what's he doing?)*. He heads for a plaza known as the Court of the Gentiles. And instead of kicking the *Gentiles* out of the temple area, he... *makes more room for the Gentiles!*

The Court of the Gentiles was originally designed to be a "place for prayer for all nations" as Jesus points out, but it had turned into a bazaar for religious merchandise, a "den of thieves."

Here's the background: The Temple authorities had to approve all the lambs people brought for sacrifice during the Passover. They had to be "unblemished." Apparently, it was typical for the priests to find some small flaw with the beasts the travellers brought in. The pilgrims were so far from home they couldn't easily go back and get another animal. So they had to buy the handy "pre-approved" lambs from the stalls on the Temple Mount — at an inflated price, of course. Where did the priests find room for these extra stalls? The Court of the Gentiles.

What's more, people couldn't purchase these lambs with just any old money. They had to exchange their Roman Empire coins for temple money, good only with temple merchants (Roman coins were engraved with images of Caesar, and since "graven images" were forbidden in Jewish law, the priests said they couldn't be used to buy temple animals). Of course, this money exchange turned into a scam too.

So the Court of the Gentiles became a place where Gentiles were squeezed out by all this activity — activity which was also ripping off the Jewish people.

And Jesus is upset, to put it mildly. He clears the plaza of this racket, setting the animals free and overturning the tables of the money-changers.

Again he shows his mission as Messiah: To bring people to God. That means all people. Jew and Gentile alike. *Any obstacle must be removed.*

Now he really has the undivided attention of the leaders of the Temple system. He is endangering their livelihood. They want him silenced. And the crowd is confused and enraged because it looks to them like Jesus has just given them a major head-fake. He slips out of town, and they're left holding the palm branches, shouting for a revolution that never happens, vulnerable to Romans who quickly punish insurrection with death.

31 THE PALM SUNDAY MYSTERY

QUICK CONSPIRACY

The Roman presence on the Temple Mount was always beefed up during Passover because of the potential for riots. These Romans had just seen the people hail Jesus as their king. A few years earlier, thousands of Jews had been slaughtered in Jerusalem on the merest suspicion of treason.

The corrupt members of the high priest's council see an opportunity to get rid of this annoying Galilean threat. They encourage the frightened mob to do the math: It was them or Jesus. As one priest says, *"Don't you realize that it's better for one man to die ...than for the whole nation to die for the actions of one man?"* (JOHN 11:50)

It should be made crystal clear that very few Jews were involved in the leadership that conspired against Christ. Plus, only the Romans had the actual authority to sentence someone to capital punishment. And of course, ultimately, this was not about human power play, anyway—it was all God's plan. So any bigoted portrayal of Jews as Christ-killers is at best inaccurate and at worst viciously harmful.

But from a human perspective, a small group of corrupt politicians and religious leaders instigated the call for Christ to go on trial, seeding the mob with agitators and false witnesses. All they had to do next was to produce Jesus. Quick. While emotions ran high.

And that problem was unexpectedly solved by one of Jesus' own disciples—the one named for the national hero.

DISAPPOINTED DISCIPLE

It wasn't just the corrupt elements of the religious leadership who had a beef with Jesus. One of his own disciples was bitterly alienated by this time.

It's easy to see why. I imagine Judas had been raised on stories of his namesake, Judas Maccabeus. He'd seen Jesus as the next liberator, and had been so excited to be part of a new rebellion, and perhaps to gain some power for himself in the bargain. And then when Jesus, right on the verge of a hitting a grand-slam home run, instead insults the crowd—and leaves the city? Judas feels angry and confused. His country has been *endangered* by Jesus, not liberated by him. He has had it with Christ's riddles and mysterious behavior. And so Judas betrays him.

Agitators in the mob yell, *"We have no king but Caesar!"* as they send to Pilate the man some had cheered as Messiah—but who had disappointed them so severely.

And the palm trees turn into Calvary's tree.

MOVES LIKE JESUS

From a human perspective, Jesus made all the wrong moves between Palm Sunday and Good Friday. But from his perspective, it was all part of the plan.

All the details had to be the right ones, fulfilling prophecy.

The place had to be the right place: Jerusalem.

The timing had to be right: Passover, when the sacrificial lambs were slain, completing the amazing symbolism.

Even the method of execution had to be right: Crucifixion, so that *"the Son of Man is lifted up"* as Christ prophesied to Nicodemus.

FORCING JESUS INTO MY AGENDA

Palm Sunday shows me an example of something that keeps happening all through the gospels:

People give Jesus an *identity* that isn't his (human soldier, in this case).

An *agenda* that isn't his (human soldier, overthrow Romans!).

And a *schedule* that isn't his (human soldier, overthrow Romans *now!*).

And then they get upset when *his* plan isn't *their* plan.

Do people still today force Jesus into their political agendas? Uh, yeah. And social agendas, and personal agendas....

I look at these people and I see myself.

I try to fit Jesus into my own mold. I imagine my top priorities must also be his. I praise God enthusiastically when I think my prayers will be answered the way I want them answered. *Now.* Then I get impatient when God won't make everything turn out the way I envisioned.

But the Messiah is his own person, with his own agenda and schedule.

CONNECTING THE DOTS

Sometimes I think we look at life like one of those connect-the-dot books. Remember those from when you were a kid? As a child they seemed mysterious, but as adults it seems so obvious how the dots are supposed to connect. We can practically see the picture!

We can feel that way about life sometimes. It's so obvious to us how the dots should connect.

But God sees dots we don't see. He sees dots way off our page. And his dots form a bigger picture. A masterpiece.

The people were connecting dots that went back to the Maccabean revolt.

But Jesus was connecting dots that went all the way back to the first Passover, all the way back to the first sin, and all the way forward to the recreation of heaven and earth.

Here's what his big picture looked like when the dots were connected. Did you know there is one other time in the Bible that people wave palm branches and cheer Jesus? It's in heaven....

> *After this I looked, and there before me was a great*
> *multitude that no one could count, from every nation,*
> *tribe, people and language, standing before the throne and*

*before the Lamb. They were wearing white robes and were holding **palm branches** in their hands. And they cried out in a loud voice: "Salvation belongs to our God, who sits on the throne, and to the Lamb."* REVELATION 7:9–10

That's the ultimate Palm Sunday.

That's the day we stop singing the blues. Forever.

But in the days immediately following Palm Sunday, the tension between Jesus and the Temple authorities gets cranked up to a new level of tension—and usually it's Jesus doing the cranking.

PONDER: How in your past have you seen Jesus connect dots you couldn't see to make a bigger picture?

32 NOT ONE STONE

⌐ *READ MARK 13:1-2; LUKE 21:5-24*

We stop in the cool, dark tunnel beneath the Arab quarter of Jerusalem.

The noisy bustle of the Old City has receded entirely and we hear only the steady drip of water from the tunnel ceiling into an ancient water cistern.

The bearded rabbi leading us through the dimly lit subterranean passage points to the two-thousand-year old retaining wall built by King Herod, and whispers, "We are now as close to the spot of the Holy of Holies as it is possible for any Jew to be."

He figures we're about sixty feet from the place on the Temple Mount where the Ark of the Covenant once stood as the seat of the *shekinah* glory of God.

In this same tunnel, the rabbi points out the largest stone yet discovered in the Temple wall. He says it's bigger than any building block in any Egyptian or Roman monument, measuring about forty-five yards across and weighing hundreds of tons.

I'm blown away by what's left of Herod's Temple, especially when I realize I'm just seeing the remnants of the retaining wall; Jesus' disciples saw the whole thing near the height of its glory! The Temple was *"adorned with beautiful stones and with gifts dedicated to God"* (LUKE 21:5). The disciples were impressed with the splendor: *"Look, Teacher!"* they said to Jesus. *"What massive stones! What magnificent buildings!"* (MARK 13:2)

THE MOST BEAUTIFUL BUILDING

By Jesus' day, the spectacular temple site was nearing completion after forty-six consecutive years of construction. The retaining walls for the platform alone were about 140 feet tall, the height of a modern fourteen-story building; then the porches and other Temple buildings on top were higher still.

It was all covered with gleaming white marble. Gold leaf was layered on the interior — and possibly exterior — Temple walls. Josephus reports that the Temple contained vast wealth, much of it used as decoration, as Jews from all around the world sent money for the construction. In a preview of modern Holy Land tourism, in Jesus' day vendors sold souvenirs and guides gave tours! [38]

Beyond all its beauty, though, it's difficult for modern Christians to accurately imagine the cultural and theological importance of the Temple to first-century Judaism.

The Temple represented:

The bridge between heaven and earth. God's presence in the Holy of Holies was not just a metaphor; it was the literal spot where God connected to humanity. He is omnipresent, but this was the place of holy encounter.

The place of God's presence. Inside the Holy of Holies, the shekinah glory of God appeared.

The visual representation of the character qualities of the invisible God. There were no idols, of course, but the Temple represented the perfection and majesty of God with its impressive decorations and white-robed priests.

The means of atonement. Once a year, the high priest would sacrifice a lamb and then release a scapegoat for the forgiveness of the people's sins.

The symbol that bound the people together. The traditions and common rituals that connected the followers of the One God from all over the world found their root here. The Temple was the center of life and worship. [39]

And then Jesus says, *"The day is coming when not one single Temple stone will be left in place."*

32 NOT ONE STONE

Not one stone.

Pretty disconcerting! The Messiah was supposed to purify the Temple, not destroy it — or prophesy its destruction.

The people really do not like this. In fact, this prophecy is misquoted at Christ's trial as evidence against him:

> *"We heard him say, 'I will destroy this temple made with human hands and in three days will build another, not made with hands.'"* MARK 14:58

And it was not only offensive talk; it was crazy talk.

By this point, Jerusalem is a big city, it's on a hill, it's fortified by thick walls and surrounded by steep ravines — so it's very defensible. And even if the city was sacked — the idea of the Temple being torn down? Its foundation stones were the size of boxcars. No, what Jesus said was proof he was one sheep short of a flock.

Then of course, Christ's prophecy is precisely fulfilled about forty years later, on July 9, 70 AD, when Roman soldiers begin to systematically destroy Jerusalem.

Josephus describes the Romans razing the Temple building down past its foundations, all the way to bedrock, literally prying every single stone loose and tossing it to the streets below so that no evidence of it remained.

I saw remnants of this destruction when I walked through archaeological digs around the Temple Mount. It almost looks as though the destruction happened yesterday. Massive pillars and blocks thrown down from the Temple buildings still remain where they crashed into streets below, left as a warning to all who would oppose Rome.

Even before the rebellion, though, Herod's lavish Temple was beginning to fall apart: Josephus says its foundation had begun to sink dramatically, causing the Temple to crumble. Herod the Great's grandson Agrippa imported huge timbers from Lebanon, hoping to underpin the sanctuary and raise it up twenty cubits, but the war with Rome stopped his restoration. [40] To me, that's a metaphor for any legalistic system: Eventually, it sinks under its own weight, sucked under by its own thick fortress walls.

NO MORE TEMPLE

Jesus wasn't just prophesying the temple's destruction. He fulfills the role of the temple, in every way:

The bridge between heaven and earth.

The place of God's presence.

The visual representation of the character qualities of the invisible God. As Jesus said, "If you have seen me, you have seen the Father." Want to know what God the Father would do in any situation? Look at Jesus.

The means of atonement.

The symbol that bound the people together.

We no longer need a temple. Not one stone. Except the cornerstone.

> *Jesus said to them, "Have you never read in the Scriptures: The stone the builders rejected has become the cornerstone; the Lord has done this, and it is marvelous in our eyes"?*
> MATTHEW 21:42

IMAGINE THERE'S A HEAVEN WITH NO TEMPLE

Cut to the future: In John's vision of the perfect Jerusalem in the new heaven and the new earth, there is no temple:

> *I did not see a temple in the city, because the Lord God Almighty and the Lamb are its temple.* REVELATION 21:22

This is history coming full circle, the culmination of the story that began at Genesis. In the beginning, we lived in paradise and walked with God. Then there was a separation between God and humanity because of our sin.

We have been longing for reunion with God ever since, a reunion only imperfectly achieved through temples and sacrifices which foreshadow the ultimate solution: the day God himself gives us his *shekinah* glory permanently, on earth as it is in heaven.

> Our lifelong nostalgia, our longing to be reunited with something in the universe from which we now feel cut off …is the truest index of our real situation… The longing to bridge some chasm that yawns between us and reality is part of our inconsolable secret. And surely from this point of view the promise of glory becomes highly relevant to our deepest desire… The door on which we have been knocking all our lives will open at last… At present we are on the outside, on the wrong side of the door… but all the leaves of the New Testament are rustling with the rumor that it will not always be so. —C. S. Lewis [41]

PONDER: Jesus fulfills the role of the Temple. What implications does this have for your daily life?

TREASURE HUNT

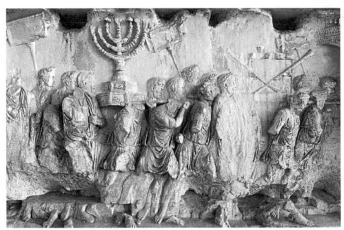

ROMANS PILLAGE THE TEMPLE, AS DEPICTED ON THE ARCH OF TITUS

The Holy Land has been the exotic background for treasure hunts throughout the centuries. Here's the story of one of the most colorful. Early in the 20th century, a Finnish scholar and poet named Walter Juvelius claimed he had broken a code hidden in the Bible that revealed the location of the Ark of the Covenant and other Temple treasures.

The British aristocrat Captain Montague Parker was mesmerized by his ideas, and financed an expedition to Jerusalem. In 1908, the two of them, with a friend, set out on their quest.

Juvelius believed there were secret underground tunnels which led from the area of Hezekiah's Tunnel, south of the Old City, to a secret cave underneath the Temple Mount, so they began digging there.

When no subterranean passageways were found at the end of Hezekiah's Tunnel, they decided to make their own, creating mine-like timbered shafts.

Frustrated at their slow pace, they bribed the sheikh in charge of the Temple Mount to let them sneak in nightly and dig there, under the Dome of the Rock. They were soon discovered by someone who had not been cut in on the deal, and the whole crew had to flee at night to the port of Joppa.

Of course, rumors followed. People claimed to have seen them leave with large crates containing the staff of Moses, the Ark of the Covenant, King Solomon's crown, and ancient texts predicting the return of Jesus Christ.

Their adventure was only one of many such hunts in Holy Land history.

One of the Dead Sea Scrolls, the Copper Scroll, claims to describe the hiding places of vast amount of treasure. For decades, no one's been able to decode it, although many have tried.

Treasure hunts like this are romantic but ultimately tragic examples of missing the whole point. Jesus spoke of the treasure of the kingdom of heaven in several parables:

> *"The kingdom of heaven is like treasure hidden in a field...."* MATTHEW 13:44

But this treasure is not found in a coded book or underground vault. It's right here, right now. It's the treasure of living with the kingdom values of peace and love and gentleness.

Jesus offers you this abundant life now and forever. Live it!

33 SQUEEZED

READ MARK 14:32-42

I'll admit, I feel a chill. And it's not just because it's a cool morning. Our group is standing on the actual Mount of Olives, a ridge of hills that rises to the east of the city of Jerusalem.

ANCIENT OLIVE TREES IN THE GARDEN OF GETHSEMANE ON THE MOUNT OF OLIVES

And I'm in awe as I think of all the important things that happened here. Zoom into the gospels for glimpses of the Mount of Olives throughout Christ's life.

Several times he walked to Jerusalem from Bethany, which was on the other side of the ridge from Jerusalem. The road cuts right across the Mount of Olives.

When Jesus was in Jerusalem he liked to spend time up here. In those days the whole ridge was covered with olive trees, so it must have been shady and cool during hot summer days.

The Bible also says that Jesus entered Jerusalem from the Mount of Olives on what we know as Palm Sunday.

And this is the place he prayed on the night he was betrayed.

Now zoom out a little and ask — why a Mount of *Olives?* Why was there a whole area full of olive trees next to a big city like Jerusalem?

Because olives were an important commodity.

33 SQUEEZED

ALL ABOUT OLIVES

Olive oil was fuel for lamps, a base for cosmetics, a liquid for cooking — olive oil was a staple (you even need it to make hummus — really!).

For oil extraction, olives are placed in something called the "sea," a round bathtub-like container, where a millstone crushes them over and over again. Next, the crushed olives are put in a reed basket, under a heavy stone called the olive press. And the weight of the stone slowly squeezes out the oil.

Oh, and there's one more thing olive oil was used for in Bible times. *To anoint the Messiah.* In fact, the word Messiah means "Anointed One."

So picture the scene. The night before he dies, Jesus goes to the Garden of Gethsemane on the Mount of Olives.

Guess what *"Gethsemane"* means? Olive press.

THE WEIGHT OF THE WORLD

As Bible scholar Ray Vander Laan suggests, in the Garden of Gethsemane the night he was betrayed, Jesus began to feel the burden that was laid on him. The pressure. Laid on him was the sin of the entire world. He was burdened in the place of the olive press.

This reminds me that Jesus' message was not merely, "Be loving, be meek, go and change the world." It was: Your sin is laid upon him. He bore the weight of the world. And the pressure began that night here at Gethsemane.

What happened next must have seemed like a fast-forward nightmare to Jesus' followers.

WHY DID THIS HAVE TO HAPPEN?

You may be wondering what the disciples themselves asked: Why did Jesus have to die?

Well, we all sin. And we all sense that there is a sin-debt that we must somehow work off, or atone for. But the Bible says it's way too big. No one can bear the weight.

So God came to us. And he bore the burden. Felt the weight of the world. So you and I can have a relationship with him based on his love — not our fear and guilt.

Imagine trying to have a close personal friendship with someone who owes you a million dollars, and hasn't paid you a penny on his debt for a decade.

Even if you were generous enough to give him all the time in the world to repay the loan, he would constantly be thinking of his debt to you. Any friendship would be overwhelmed by feelings of shame and guilt — unless you yourself wrote out a contract declaring the entire debt paid in full, and showed it to your friend.

Now your friend can have a relationship with you based on nothing but love — love intensified with his deep gratitude toward you!

This is why Jesus went to the cross, where he fulfilled John the Baptist's words spoken three years earlier: *"Behold, the Lamb of God, who takes away the sins of the world."*

A week after he entered the city in triumph, *on the very night the Passover lambs were being sacrificed* — the Lamb of God paid for the sins of us all.

And that long night began here, in Gethsemane, where the Messiah was anointed at the place of the olive press — anointed not with oil but with his own precious blood.

PONDER: Jesus bore the weight of the world so you don't have to. See the burden of your sin carried by his strong shoulders. Worship him for carrying that weight!

34 IN THE PITS

READ MATTHEW 26:56-74

Our group bunches together in a cold, dark dungeon believed to have been part of the High Priest Caiaphas' house. It's here, or very near to this place, that Jesus was held overnight before being taken to Pilate for sentencing.

Excavations at this site, now known as the Church of St. Peter in Gallicantu, have unearthed the remains of a large mansion apparently connected to the Jerusalem priesthood: There are servants' quarters, indicating the house was owned by a wealthy family, and a complete set of weights and measures used by the priests in the Temple, along with a door lintel inscribed with the word *"Korban"* (sacrificial offering), showing this was a priest's residence.

It's a little creepy to realize that, in addition to implements used in religious ritual, this priest's mansion also contained a *dungeon*. Clearly the priestly families of the time had a lot of status, and the power to protect it.

There's a guardroom one floor above us, with wall fixtures to which prisoners were chained. In the middle of the room are pillars with holes to fasten prisoners' hands and feet for flogging.

On one side of the guardroom there's a pit into which captives were lowered with rope. Originally this vertical shaft was the only way in or out of the dungeon; today we walked down narrow steps to get to the place Christ may have been held for questioning.

THE DARKEST DEPTHS

In the dungeon I ask the group to stand in silence and imagine the feelings of Jesus, here in a dark pit, abandoned by even his closest companions.

I notice that the Christian priests who now own this site have left a Bible in the pit, opened to Psalm 88. On that night, in this place, Jesus may have remembered the very words I now read aloud to our group:

> *I am overwhelmed with troubles*
> *and my life draws near to death.*
> *I am counted among those who go down to the pit;*
> *I am like one without strength.*
> *You have put me in the lowest pit,*
> *in the darkest depths.*
> *You have taken from me my closest friends*
> *and have made me repulsive to them.*
> *I am confined and cannot escape;*
> *my eyes are dim with grief.*
> *Why, Lord, do you reject me*
> *and hide your face from me?* PSALM 88:3,4,6,8,9,14

Can you relate?

Every night this prayer is prayed. From lonely apartments or hospital beds or jail cells or street corners.

> *I am confined and cannot escape;*
> *my eyes are dim with grief.*

And Jesus felt the same way.

IN THE PITS WITH JESUS

We often make the mistake of thinking Christ was detached and serene during his trial and crucifixion. Maybe we'd rather imagine him that way, but the Bible describes Jesus experiencing pain and rejection and loneliness just as intensely as any other human being. He was the Son of God, but he was also 100% human. He was in the pits, in every way.

That means when you're in the pit, you'll find Jesus there. He gets it. He knows the ache of betrayal, the agony of loneliness.

And above him, in the courtyard, his own disciple Peter was about to inflict more pain.

BETRAYED BY A FRIEND

Jerusalem nights can be cold. The city sits 2,400 feet above sea level and gets cool breezes at night. There are snow flurries every year. So the high priest's servants make a charcoal fire to warm themselves.

Peter probably figures he'll be safe from detection in the dim firelight, but even there his appearance and northern accent give him away, and a servant girl accuses him of being a Galilean Christ-follower.

And this rough, tough fisherman who once swore he would never, ever leave Jesus sees his resolve crumble — not before the expert tortures of the Roman soldiers but the simple taunts of a servant.

He vows with an oath that he never knew Christ (and he's a fisherman, so he knows his oaths!). And maybe he is telling the truth in a way, revealing exactly how he felt: *"I never really knew him."*

It must have seemed like his world was crumbling all around him, that it was all over now, that Jesus was just like any other bug squashed by the jackboots of the Roman bureaucracy. And Peter's betrayal adds to Christ's despair.

> *You have taken from me my closest friends*
> *and have made me repulsive to them.*

HE GETS IT

The Messiah, Jesus taught, had to suffer and die — and be resurrected (LUKE 24:46). Not just die. But *suffer* and die.

Why? While the resurrection reveals God's triumph, the sufferings of Christ show that he can truly sympathize with your pain.

Remember what the angel said Jesus would be called? *God with us.*

In Jesus we see God with us *all the way*, all the way through the experiences of injustice and suffering and death.

> *We do not have a high priest who is unable to sympathize with us in our weakness, but he has been tempted in every way as we are, yet without sin.* HEBREWS 4:15

Jesus is a high priest who can *sympathize*. He was born in obscurity. He was poor, misunderstood, tempted, lied to, lied about, betrayed, beaten, spat upon, slandered, disowned, despised, abandoned, tortured, killed.

No matter what your circumstances, Jesus relates to you. There is sympathy. Aren't you glad?

He was not a Messiah who rode into town as an invulnerable superhero, a Man of Steel who felt no pain. He was something better: *He was one of us*, one of the very *least* of us, all the way from his birth in a manger to his unjust suffering to his unfair death sentence.

If you're going through tough, confusing, unfair, painful times, remember the very symbol of faith in Christ.

It's not a sword. It's not a treasure chest. It's not a dollar sign. It's not a flag.

It's a *cross*.

Jesus gets it. And while he promises you will not stay in the pit, that there is a resurrection on the other end, in the meantime, he will be *God with you* through it all.

PRAYER: Thank God today that Jesus gets it. Share with him a dark struggle, knowing he will sympathize.

35 VERDICT

READ JOHN 18:28–19:16

Our group walks through a crumbling palace as waves crash on the beach below. It's a beautiful, blue-sky day, a scene reminiscent of our California home. Except that beaches in the Monterey Bay don't have elaborate Roman ruins.

We're about seventy miles northwest of Jerusalem at the formerly luxurious seaside home of Pontius Pilate: Caesarea Maritime.

Forty years before the crucifixion of Christ, Herod the Great built a gleaming new city and state-of-the-art harbor here that served as the headquarters of the Roman presence in Israel. Underwater archaeologists are still figuring out how Herod's builders used hydraulic cement to create two massive breakwaters in order to shelter the harbor. In Jesus' day, this city featured spectacular palaces, a marble temple to Caesar, a racetrack with seating for twenty thousand spectators, an elaborate aqueduct system which piped in fresh water from the mountains many miles away, and a beautiful theater which faced the Mediterranean Sea.

It's at this theater that archaeologists discovered the first physical evidence of the Roman governor Pontius Pilate. His name was inscribed on a stone in the theater, on a dedication to his boss, the Caesar Tiberius.

And it was from this city that Pilate set out for Jerusalem's Passover Feast around 30 AD.

CAUGHT IN THE MIDDLE OF HISTORY

He was surely hoping that his mere presence there would dissuade any troublemakers from starting a revolt.

Pilate went to Jerusalem every year at the same time, just to establish a reminder of Roman authority during the pilgrimage.

And every year he went back to his coastal headquarters without many incidents to report. Except for one year, the year he wrote himself into the most famous story in history by sentencing Jesus to death.

Three other ancient historians also mention Pilate: Josephus, Philo, and Tacitus. Philo describes him as possessing "vindictiveness and furious temper... [he was] naturally inflexible, a blend of self-will and relentlessness." Philo characterizes Pilate's reign as full of "briberies, insults, robberies, outrages and wanton injuries, executions without trial constantly repeated, (and) ceaseless and supremely grievous cruelty." [42]

So why would a guy this cruel have hesitated for one second to crucify Christ?

Well, Pilate was apparently on thin ice with his Roman supervisors several times during his administration.

According to Josephus, Pilate was officially rebuked by Rome for antagonizing the Jews in Jerusalem on at least one, and possibly two occasions.

Philo reported that Caesar Tiberius had even written Pilate, criticizing him "with a host of reproaches and rebukes for his audacious violation of precedent" and for insensitivity to Jewish customs. [43]

This may help explain why Pilate seems so indecisive about what to do regarding Jesus. He was really in a conundrum.

On the one hand, his role, as Roman prefect, is to prevent insurrection. He'll get into trouble with Caesar if he allows the political situation to get out of control. If Jesus is claiming to be a king, then he must clearly be treated as a traitor to the government, punishable by death.

On the other hand, Pilate's under pressure from Rome to stop approving executions without adequate trial. So should he use capital punishment against a possible rebel, or should he demonstrate to Rome that he has stopped the trend of hasty executions?

But then what if a hasty execution is being demanded by the very people Rome has told him not to offend?

Throughout this account, he seems to be asking himself which course of action is less likely to get him into career trouble, not what is the right thing to do.

Finally he approves the crucifixion — yet attempts to avoid legal responsibility by "washing his hands" of the situation (MATTHEW 27:24). Hand washing was a Jewish custom originating in Deuteronomy 21 and amplified in the Mishnah. Pilate is using the Pharisees' own symbolism in a desperate, falsely pious attempt to justify what he felt uncomfortable doing. He was performing a religious ritual in advance of a sin to try and escape the consequences, like a man going to confession before meeting his mistress. This is not a man sincerely seeking truth. This is a politician just trying to cover his you-know-what.

CALCULATING THE SOCIAL COST

When I look over the beautiful vista of the Mediterranean from Pilate's home base in Caesarea Maritime, I understand some of his motivation. It's really nice here. Pilate wants to leave Jerusalem without any career-threatening incident and get back home. Back to his palatial beachfront estate. Back to his Roman culture and entertainment and luxuries. He sees the Jews, including Jesus, as bothersome irritants, threats to his comfortable status quo.

To me, Pilate is emblematic of the way many people treat the claims of Christ. They don't really listen to what Jesus is saying as much as they calculate the social cost of their response.

Maybe you've been considering the claims of Christ, and are hesitating for some of the same reasons as Pilate:

Misunderstanding. Pilate seems eager to interpret Jesus' kingdom language as something merely political, earthly — even when Christ corrects him. Similarly, people today seem to want to reinterpret the message of Jesus as primarily social or political to escape his personal, spiritual claims on their lives. Of course, his spiritual message does have social implications. But the kingdom of God starts in the heart.

Social position. Pilate has heavy equity in his political world, and so he's stuck in that paradigm. He can't seem to take seriously Christ's claims that there is an invisible kingdom *not* of this world that is far more important than the visible empire. Or maybe he just finds such claims a little unsettling. Because if Jesus is right, Pilate's whole value system must change.

Relativism. Pilate's dodge is still used today: *"What is truth anyway?"* (JOHN 18:38)

There are so many alternative belief systems in the modern world (as there were in the first century, incidentally!) that it's easier to shrug and say, "What is truth — It's all relative!" than commit to a decision. But of course, in not deciding, you're still making a choice.

You can try to wash your hands, try to say you want nothing to do with him, but in the end we're all judged by what we do with Jesus.

Was Jesus who he claimed to be? In a way, Jesus is still on trial in every heart today. What's your verdict?

PONDER: What have you decided about Jesus? How has that decision impacted you?

PART 6
CULMINATION

36 THE MYSTERY OF JESUS' DEATH CRY

READ MATTHEW 27:1-2; 27-50

Ancient stone steps wind down into Jerusalem from the ruins of the high priest's mansion on the slopes of Mount Zion. While archaeologists argue over the exact location of Annas and Caiaphas' first century homes, on this they agree: Jesus likely walked down these very steps as he was led to face Pontius Pilate for his final trial. Ultimately, these steps took Jesus to the cross.

As I stand here, our guide Kenny tells me how Neil Armstrong, the first man to walk on the moon, visited Jerusalem in 1988. He had become a devout believer, and asked his guide to take him to a place where it was certain Jesus had walked.

Armstrong stood on these very steps and seemed to go into deep prayer. His guide asked him what he was feeling, and the former astronaut said: "This is the greatest moment of my life. It means more to me to walk on these steps than to walk on the moon."

As I place my hand on the weathered stone steps, I close my eyes and think of what Jesus must have been feeling. Down this slope Christ walked to his final trial before Pilate, and from there to the cross.

Surely he felt a deepening dread of the death he knew awaited him at Golgotha.

THE CRY OF THE CROSS

My mind goes to Calvary. One sentence Christ spoke there has confused many Christians over the centuries:

"My God, my God, why have you forsaken me?"

When I was in college, I had an atheist professor who had been a Jesuit priest. He told me one of the things that rocked his faith was his belief that, at this moment, Jesus himself lost his faith.

Is that what was happening?

I'm convinced Jesus was directing the few followers who had returned to be near the cross to an amazing prophecy he wanted them to remember.

SONG OF THE CROSS

The national songbook of Israel was the Psalms. They were all written hundreds of years before Christ. Every Jew knew them. But in those days, the Psalms were not numbered. They were known by their first line — that served as their title.

The first line of Psalm 22?

> *"My God, my God, why have you forsaken me?"*

Why would Jesus, hanging on a cross in agony, be quoting the first line to a song?

Because often, when someone quotes you the opening lyrics to a song, you instantly remember the rest of it, right?

"In the town... where I was born...." ("Lived a man who sailed the sea" you are probably thinking)

"Oh, say can you see..." ("By the dawn's early light...")

Christ was calling out the title to a song that he wanted his followers to recall.

But again, why would he do that? Read it for yourself. It's eerie. Psalm 22 sounds like it was written by an eyewitness of the crucifixion — until you realize it was composed ten centuries before Christ was born!

Just a few verses from Psalm 22:

> *All who see me mock me;*
> *they hurl insults, shaking their heads.*

"He trusts in the Lord," they say,
"let the Lord rescue him." PSALM 22:7–8

(See Matthew 27:41–44)

I am poured out like water,
and all my bones are out of joint.
My heart has turned to wax;
it has melted within me. PSALM 22:14

(See John 19:33–34)

My mouth is dried up like a potsherd,
and my tongue sticks to the roof of my mouth. PSALM 22:15

(See John 19:28)

…a pack of villains encircles me;
they pierce my hands and my feet. PSALM 22:16

(See John 19:36–37)

They divide my clothes among them
and cast lots for my garment. PSALM 22:18

(See John 19:23–24)

And it goes on. Psalm 22 predicts about a dozen details of Jesus' crucifixion *about a thousand years before they happened.* David (the author of Psalm 22) lived about 1043–973 BC.

And get this: These details were written in Psalm 22 *about seven hundred years before crucifixion was developed.* That's all strong evidence for me that the Bible was literally inspired by God. And that Jesus really was the promised Messiah.

PAID IN FULL

Psalm 22 starts grimly, but ends with hope, with a prophecy that the furthest reaches of the earth will turn back to the Lord. And then here's the last line of the psalm. Ready for some more goose bumps?

36 THE MYSTERY OF JESUS' DEATH CRY

"He has done it!" (PSALM 22:31). Another way to translate that phrase? *"It is finished!"* It's the last thing Jesus shouts from the cross, according to John 19:30. The Greek word John used for "finished," *tetelestai,* is an interesting word. It's an accounting term that people in the first century would put on their bills to indicate "paid in full!"

Jesus wasn't saying, *"I* am finished!" He was saying, "My act on your behalf is finished. Your debt has been paid."

Picture your sin. The sin that still haunts you with guilt. The one you're trying to atone for.

Now picture next to it the phrase: *paid in full.* Do you grasp the grace?

It's not up to you to prove your worth or earn God's favor. You just receive what Jesus paid in full through his death on the cross.

PURPOSEFUL PAIN

Don't get me wrong. I think Jesus was experiencing devastating emotions on the cross. In crying out loudly to God, "Why have you forsaken me?" he was sending a message to us: *I know how much life can hurt.*

That's so good to hear. Because at times of great sorrow I have cried out, *God, what are you doing? Where are you? Why have you left me?* When I feel like that, Jesus is not unsympathetic.

He gets it. He's been there himself.

But in the midst of his pain, he was also reaching out to those he loves, wanting to show them a prophecy about the very events that were unfolding before their eyes!

In doing so he was also sending another message to them, and to us: *I did this on purpose!*

He went to the cross because that is why he came. God came to pay your debt. *In full.*

199

THE FINAL BARRIER DESTROYED

And in a bookend to his description of the heavens being *"torn open"* at Christ's baptism, the gospel writer Mark now repeats that word at the culmination of Christ's ministry.

> *The curtain of the temple was torn in two from top to bottom.* MARK 15:38

From top to bottom. From God to us. Listen to the first-century writer Josephus' description of that veil:

> It was a Babylonian curtain, embroidered with blue, and fine linen, and scarlet, and purple, and of a texture that was truly wonderful. Nor was this mixture of colors was not without its mystical interpretation, but was a kind of image of the universe... [44]

So the veil being torn was an image of the heavens being opened.

This is why he came: The separating veil between a holy God and sinful man is ripped apart, through the sacrifice of Christ Jesus, in whom the two came together, the God-man.

> *When I survey the wondrous cross*
> *On which the Prince of Glory died,*
> *My richest gain I count but loss,*
> *And pour contempt on all my pride.*
> *Were the whole realm of nature mine,*
> *That were a present far too small;*
> *Love so amazing, so divine,*
> *Demands my soul, my life, my all.* — Isaac Watts

PROJECT: Write down on a piece of paper – being as creative as you want to be – the phrase "paid in full." Place the paper somewhere you'll see it daily and be reminded that's the truth about you because of Jesus.

37 EXCAVATING THE EMPTY TOMB

READ LUKE 24:13-53 & JOHN 20:10-17

A beautiful shaft of light beams down through the domed roof.

Hundreds of voices speaking different languages and dialects mingle and echo in the stone-surfaced church creating a beautiful noise. I imagine it's how God might hear all our prayers.

We've returned with a great crowd of pilgrims swirling into the center of the Church of the Holy Sepulcher in the old city of Jerusalem.

As unlikely as it seems to modern visitors, most church historians think this is likely to have been the actual location of the crucifixion and tomb of Christ.

And ironically, it was a vehemently pagan Roman emperor who preserved our knowledge of the site.

BURYING CHRISTIANITY

Hadrian, a Caesar who despised Jews and Christians, decided to crush both faiths once and for all.

He made Jerusalem off limits to Jews.

Changed the name of the city to Aelia Capitolina.

Remade it in the Roman style, with colonnaded sidewalks.

And he placed pagan temples over the sites Christians venerated most: the place where Christ was crucified, and the nearby tomb.

This was in 135 AD, about one hundred years after Christ was crucified. Hadrian built a huge retaining wall on all four sides of these neighboring sites and filled it in with dirt, and then on top of the dirt he built shrines to Jupiter and Venus.

JOURNEY OF REDISCOVERY

Two hundred years later, Christianity became legal. Constantine was the famous emperor of the time, and his Christian mother Helena journeyed to the Holy Land to uncover some of the sites that had been suppressed or buried by previous Roman administrations.

Some of the relics she found and sites she discovered were apparently merely the products of tradition and superstition, and not founded in any real preserved historical knowledge. However, she and her entourage did stumble upon some astounding discoveries. I've already told you about Bethlehem. Here's the Jerusalem story.

Because local legend insisted that Hadrian's temple to Venus was built over the actual tomb of Christ, Helena supervised its removal. The Jerusalem-based bishop Eusebius wrote that he was skeptical she would find anything under the tons of dirt. But he was there when workers found, much to his surprise, empty tombs from the first century.

One tomb in particular showed signs of early veneration. This was apparently the tomb that, at least in 135 AD when Hadrian buried it, Christians believed had once held the body of Christ.

To Eusebius, the unearthing of this tomb was reminiscent of the Easter miracle:

> As soon as the original surface of the ground, beneath the
> covering of fill dirt, appeared, contrary to all expectation,
> the monument of our Savior's resurrection was discovered.
> Then indeed the rediscovery of this most holy cave
> was like his return to life, in that, after lying buried in
> darkness, it again emerged to light, and afforded all who
> came to see the site a testimony to the resurrection clearer
> than any voice could give.... [45]

Of course, we can't know for certain whether this was the precise tomb of Christ, but it is indeed an actual, empty first-century tomb in the right location in the right city — and it encouraged Christians at the time, who had been oppressed for so long, to begin telling their story freely once more.

Other first-century tombs were discovered here, too. They were largely left intact, but the tomb venerated as Christ's was cut away from the hillside and a chapel was built around it.

This whole episode reminds me that God can take even the most violently anti-god movement and turn it around and use it for his glory — and this is true in your life, too!

TRACES OF THE PAST

Constantine's beautiful church surrounding the tomb was destroyed — then rebuilt — then destroyed again — and then rebuilt by the Crusaders in about 1000 AD. That is the church we're visiting today. Some find it uninspiring, layered with centuries of odd decorations and confusing architecture, not to mention the pressing crowds.

But — if you know where to look — you can see traces of what was here before. I'm excited to show some of our group where to discover these treasures.

We slip past the crowds in the dome,

> then through an old burned-out chapel,

> then under a small doorway,

> and there we see actual old tombs from the time of Christ.

They're ignored by the vast majority of visitors to the church. But it's in looking at these very humble, nearly hidden stone tombs that I get a sense of the holiness of the place — not in the busy, confusing attempts at splendor in the rest of the ancient structure.

And just as the church here has layers of construction and destruction that have obscured the first-century tombs, the story of the risen Christ can get encrusted with generations of decoration. We can forget the impact of that moment, the instant of shocking recognition, when people who had just been grieving the gruesome death of their Lord realized he had truly come back to life.

SURPRISE!

I had a chance, the first time I was in Israel, to go inside another first-century tomb that had been discovered when road crews were widening a highway near Megiddo. This one even had a rolling stone near the entrance, just like the tomb described in the Bible.

I grabbed my camera, went inside, and took some shots. It was so quiet.

I laid down on the cool stone slab. With eyes closed, I quietly thought about what Jesus might have felt and smelled and seen, in a tomb much like this, at the moment of resurrection.

Then I heard a tourist bus pull up. And some people walking toward the cave entrance. And, well—I couldn't resist.

I waited until they were just inside the door, before their eyes adjusted to the darkness, and then I jumped up, waving my arms, shouting:

"I'M ALIVE!!"

And after they beat me up, I was so glad I had that experience. I had the rare chance to sense a little of the shock of the disciples—and the playfulness of the risen Christ—when he pops right into gardens of grief and locked rooms and slow shuffling walks home, and gives people the thrill of a lifetime!

GOOD NEWS ANNOUNCED TO OUTCASTS – AGAIN

This is the climax of the whole Gospel story, the moment everything in Christ's ministry has been pointing toward.

And just as the birth announcement of Christ was given to outcast shepherds, the resurrection news is given first to an outcast woman.

A recent PBS documentary on the Roman Empire confirmed that women in the first century were oppressed. Women were not allowed to be active in politics, so nobody wrote about them. Neither were they taught how to write, so they could not tell their own stories. [46] Women were usually uneducated, and were denied legal status equal to men.

But Jesus had always included women in his circle of followers. And now he appears first to a woman — and not just any woman.

Mary Magdalene had been a very troubled person, cured by Christ of "seven demons" (LUKE 8:2, MARK 16:9). Her name is intriguing: People in those days were usually known by their family heritage, referred to as "son of Joseph" or "daughter of Jacob" or "wife of Abram" and so on. But this Mary was referred to merely as "Magdalene" meaning "of Magdala," which was a very rough fishing village on the shore of the Sea of Galilee.

The ancient town of Magdala, or *Migdal* in Hebrew, is currently being excavated. Archaeologists have discovered the foundations of a tower there — it was apparently used to help fishermen spot schools of fish. This corresponds with the literal meaning of the word Magdala: "tower" or "fortress."

That Mary was referred to only in reference to this town probably indicates that she had no family to call her own. Some have suggested that because of the strange actions she displayed while under the influence of the demons — extra-biblical traditions throughout the ages describe her as mentally ill or sexually promiscuous before Jesus healed her — she was considered *persona non grata*.

But should it surprise anyone that Jesus would want the greatest news scoop of all time to be given to her, an outcast? It's the way he rolls.

CAST ASIDE FOR THE CASTAWAYS

And speaking of the way he rolls, John 20:1 says the stone had been *"removed"* or *"rolled away"* from the tomb. The word John uses there literally means "cast aside," as in: flung, thrown, tossed.

It wasn't tossed aside so that Jesus could get out. You see later that he can pass right through walls in his resurrected body. It was cast aside so the castaways could get in. So that his ragtag band of followers could see that the tomb was empty.

But Mary's first reaction is not hope. She thinks someone has taken Jesus' corpse. She lingers there, weeping. The one person who had given her dignity in life had apparently been desecrated in death. And she is alone again.

Then Jesus appears. And says a word that means the world to her: *"Mary."*

Not "Mary of Magdala," the place she'd been before he found her.

Simply *"Mary."*

The label that stretched into her past was gone.

And, whether it's the grief-stricken Mary or the anxiety-riddled disciples in the upper room, that moment, when they met the risen Jesus, electrifies them. Sets them free. Starts them talking. And no one can ever shut them up again.

RADICAL AND REAL

That's because Jesus Christ's resurrection is his validation and vindication.

Anyone can say anything about God that they want to. But how do you know it's true? If you're going to look for God's stamp of approval on someone, resurrection from the dead would be a pretty significant stamp.

Jesus Christ's resurrection means that all the stuff he's been teaching — about God's love, God's care for the outcasts, God's willingness to forgive sins, God's disdain for "religion" and eagerness to lavish grace on the repentant sinner — all of that is *true.*

And it means that no matter what people do to you, there is certain hope even beyond the grave. It means there is *always* hope. Because you can be resurrected too.

HE SURPRISES US STILL

In the centuries since, the risen Christ has popped into other dark gardens and locked rooms, coming to people afraid and people ashamed and people grieving. They're often surprised, and, like these first witnesses, similarly set free.

> You called, you cried, you shattered my deafness.
> You sparkled, you blazed, you drove off my blindness.
> You shed your fragrance, and I drew in my breath,
>   and I pant for you.
> I tasted and now I hunger and thirst.
> You touched me,
>   and now I burn with longing for your peace.
> — St. Augustine of Hippo

PONDER: How does it change your life and attitude to know that Jesus rose from the dead and lives today, interceding for you, walking with you, and giving you strength?

THE HISTORICAL CASE FOR THE RESURRECTION OF JESUS

N. T. Wright has taught at Cambridge, Oxford, and Duke. He's published 40 books. He has two doctorates from Oxford. And he is a strong believer in the bodily resurrection of Jesus Christ.

In the journal *Gregorianum*, Wright wrote an influential article titled "Jesus' Resurrection and Christian Origins." You can find it here:

http://ntwrightpage.com/Wright_Jesus_Resurrection.htm

Wright also did a lecture at the prestigious University of St. Andrews called *"Can a Scientist Believe in the Resurrection?"* Here's the link:

http://www.st-andrews.ac.uk/~jglectures/tom_wright.php

His case for the resurrection has three main points:

1. The idea of the Messiah dying and being bodily resurrected to eternal life was completely unexpected in Jewish theology, and so is very unlikely to have been a myth invented by Christ's disciples in their grief. It was not an idea that would have given them any credibility or authority.

2. The tomb was empty, a fact never denied by any of Jesus Christ's enemies. This fact must be explained in a way that explains all the other facts of the case as well.

3. The post-mortem appearances of Jesus do not have the characteristics of hallucinations or myths.

He elaborates on these points in his book *The Resurrection of the Son of God* (Minneapolis: Fortress, 2003)

38 HOW DO YOU SEE IT?

READ JOHN 20:1-10

I sit on a cool bench inside an underground stone hollow that was probably used as a water cistern in first-century Jerusalem. Our group walks down a staircase to join me after they poke their heads into an ancient, empty tomb.

It's a tomb that resembles the one which once held the body of Christ.

We're in a beautiful area known as the Garden Tomb complex, just outside the old city.

In 1883, a man named Charles George Gordon noticed a cliff face just outside the city walls that, from some angles, resembled a skull. Since the Bible says Jesus was crucified at the "Place of the Skull," his interest was piqued.

Like many visitors to the old city, Gordon found it hard to relate to the stuffy Church of the Holy Sepulcher. After centuries of reconstruction, it just didn't look like a garden anymore. Gordon thought the area he discovered looked more like the place Jesus was crucified than the traditional site. When he learned several ancient tombs had also been found nearby, Gordon became convinced one of them must have been the tomb of Jesus.

While most biblical archaeologists still favor the Church of Holy Sepulcher as the more likely historical location for the biblical events, the Garden Tomb is nevertheless a great pilgrimage site. It's much easier here to imagine the scene of the resurrection as described in the Bible, easy to picture Peter and John running to this tomb.

A RACE TO THE TOMB
The Gospel of John describes their footrace.

Along with most other pastors, I assume John the disciple was the anonymous person who wrote this gospel, and that adds some real humor to details like *"the other disciple outran Peter and reached the tomb first."*

It's as if John decided, when he began writing his gospel, to remain humble and refer to himself simply as "the other disciple" — but at a few points he still wants to give himself a shout-out!

John says that although Peter lost the race to the tomb, he actually went in first — and something in particular caught his eye: The cloth that had been wrapped around Jesus' head was folded up neatly, while the other grave clothes were still in their place.

In other words: This is not what a grave robber would do. Or could do.

Peter was working the scene out in his mind like a forensic detective: Either the body would have been stolen with the grave clothes still on it, or, if they were desecrating the body, they might have removed the grave clothes — but then the funeral linens would have looked like unspooled toilet paper, littered across the floor of the sepulcher.

But this? It's almost as if the body had just faded right through the cloth without disturbing it — and then the head covering was neatly folded up.

What did this mean?

Then the gospel writer says, *"Finally the other disciple ('who had reached the tomb first,' he is quick to reassert!) also went inside. He saw and believed."*

THREE WAYS TO SEE
There are three different words used for "see" in this passage.

The first word, in verse 5, when the first disciple to the tomb bends over and looks in, is a word meaning "to quickly glance at something."

38 HOW DO YOU SEE IT?

Then in verse 6, when Peter goes in and sees the strips of linen, it's a different word, the one from which we get our English word "theorize." He was trying to come up with a theory to explain the weird things he was seeing.

Finally in verse 8, when the other disciple goes in and believes, the word used there means "to perceive, to understand, to intelligently comprehend the truth." He got it. There was only one possible explanation.

Peter saw the same stuff as the second disciple. The physical things. The evidence. But he just looked and theorized. Maybe he just couldn't believe what his eyes were telling him.

The other disciple *saw* — and *believed.*

Someone said he had Easter eyes.

I read this story to our group and I ask them , "So after all our days here in the Holy Land do you *see?* Or do you see *and believe?*

"After all this time, you can still just see the *stuff.* The archaeology. The sites. Make theories. Or — you can see and believe. That is your choice."

Then we take communion right there in this ancient garden.

The body of Christ, broken for you.

The blood of Christ, shed for you.

What do you see?

Why *didn't* Peter see and believe right away?

For one thing, I suspect he was hampered by guilt. And fear. If what he was seeing meant that Jesus was alive again, then he, Peter, surely felt he was in big trouble. He had denied Christ in his hour of need!

And Jesus is about to take care of that shame on the shores of Galilee.

JESUS JOURNEY

Make no mistake; if He rose at all
It was as His body;

If the cells' dissolution did not reverse,
    the molecules reknit, the amino acids rekindle,
The Church will fall.

Let us not mock God with metaphor,
Analogy, sidestepping transcendence;
Making of the event a parable,
    a sign painted in the faded credulity of earlier ages:

Let us walk through the door. — John Updike [47]

PONDER: How do you see it? Have you been merely glancing at the evidence? Have you stalled out at "making theories"? Or do you choose to see and believe?

39   FROM DOUBT TO DECISION

READ JOHN 20:24-31

We're thoughtful as we walk to the next site in Israel, the Cenacle, the traditional location of the Upper Room just outside the walls of Jerusalem.

A member of our group tells me how she once loved to mock her own daughter for having faith in Jesus. Yet on this very trip this woman was baptized as a believer in the Jordan River.

It happens to the best of us.

My new friend is just joining the ranks that started with Thomas in the upper room. He too was skeptical. In fact, he announces, *"I will not believe—unless I myself put my fingers in the nail holes."* He is adamant.

Then Jesus shows up.

THE UPPER ROOM

I think about Thomas as we visit the Cenacle. Although this is the area Christian pilgrims have visited for about 1,700 years to remember what happened in the "upper room" mentioned in Scripture, it's unknown whether this is the actual spot where those events took place.

The building itself has changed, of course. The current structure was probably part of a Crusader church built about a thousand years ago. It's been remodeled since, but it gives us a quiet place to remember that, somewhere in this city, the risen Christ appeared to Thomas and changed his mind.

Later, Jesus walks with two disciples on the road to Emmaus. "We had hoped…" they say, the sad sentence of believers who have lost their faith.

Then Jesus changes their minds too. Even before they knew for sure who he was, they later recall, "Were not our hearts burning within us while he talked with us?"

You might wonder how any such skeptics ever come to faith today — after all, they can't meet the risen Christ anymore. Or can they?

Doubters meet Christ still. Skeptics meet Jesus in the compassion of his Body, the Church. They meet the Word in the word of God, the Bible. They meet Christ in his creation. And they meet him one-on-one, spiritually, in his supernatural presence.

Latter-day Thomas-types. Like these:

ANNE LAMOTT

Bestselling author Anne Lamott was an agnostic who began finding herself strangely attracted to church — for the music only. She'd leave before each sermon, steadfast in her determination never to even consider believing in such religious nonsense.

But Christ met her during her grief following an abortion:

> I turned off the light. As I laid there, I became aware of someone with me... the feeling was so strong that I actually turned on the light... to make sure no one was with me — of course, there wasn't. In the dark again, I knew beyond any doubt that it was Jesus.

> ...And I was appalled. I thought about my life and my brilliant hilarious progressive friends, I thought about what everyone would think of me if I became a Christian.... I turned to the wall and said out loud, "I would rather die."

> I felt him... watching me with patience and love, and I squinched my eyes shut, but that didn't help, because that's not what I was seeing him with.... This experience spooked me badly, but I thought it was just born of fear and self-loathing and booze and loss of blood. But then

everywhere I went, I had the feeling that a little cat was following me, wanting me to... pick it up ...to open the door and let it in. But I knew what would happen: you let a cat in one time, give it a little milk, and then it stays forever.

And one week later, when I went back to church... I felt like *something* was rocking me in its bosom, holding me like a scared kid, and I opened up to it... and it washed over me.

I began to cry and left, and I raced home and felt the little cat running along at my heels, and I opened the door... and I stood there a minute, and then I hung my head and said "[expletive]! I quit!" I took a long deep breath and said out loud, "All right. You can come in." So this was the beautiful moment of my conversion. [48]

C. S. LEWIS

The well-known author of *The Chronicles of Narnia*, C. S. Lewis, was an avowed atheist and an Oxford professor at prestigious Magdalen College when he found himself reluctantly converting.

You must picture me alone in that room at Magdalen, night after night, feeling, whenever my mind lifted even for a second from my work, the steady, unrelenting approach of Him whom I so earnestly desired not to meet. That which I greatly feared had at last come upon me. In the Trinity Term of 1929 I gave in, and admitted that God was God, and knelt and prayed: perhaps, that night, the most dejected and reluctant convert in all England. [49]

What happened that led to that moment? He met, through his reading and conversations at Oxford, Christians like *Lord of the Rings* author J. R. R. Tolkien. It was his friendship with Tolkien that brought him to Christ. After one late-night conversation with him, Lewis wrote a letter to a friend revealing, "I have just passed on… to definitely believing in Christ, in Christianity." [50] It changed his whole life and career.

MALCOLM MUGGERIDGE

After a long and distinguished career as an atheist, British communist, journalist, and magazine editor Malcolm Muggeridge had a conversion experience.

One day, in a flash, he suddenly saw a bridge reconciling God and Man:

> And this bridge, this reconciliation between the black despair of lying bound and gagged in the tiny dungeon of ego, and soaring upwards into the white radiance of God's universal love — this bridge was the Incarnation, whose truth expresses the desperate need it meets. Because of our physical hunger we know there is bread; because of our spiritual hunger we know there is Christ. [51]

FRANCIS COLLINS

Geneticist Francis Collins, director of the National Human Genome Research Institute, began re-examining his own atheism in grad school. His doubts about the historicity of Christ began to fall, one by one, until, he realized he had a choice to make: Did he, personally, believe or not?

He finally converted quite suddenly during a hike on a beautiful fall afternoon. He describes himself now as a "serious Christian — That is, someone who believes in the reality of Christ's death and resurrection, and who tries to integrate that into daily life." [52]

BRIAN WELCH

Brian "Head" Welch, former guitarist and founding member of the multi-platinum rock band Korn, was baptized in the Jordan River in 2005, at the same Kibbutz Kinneret where our church group was baptized.

39 FROM DOUBT TO DECISION

Condemned by the *Chicago Tribune* as being "perverts, psycho-paths, and paranoiacs," Korn was a popular heavy metal group that saw its greatest popularity in the 1990s—and the last place you'd expect to find an enthusiastic convert to Christ.

But Welch told *MTV News*:

> It's not about religion, I'm saved by grace only. I didn't do anything except just ask Jesus. I even prayed a doubting Thomas prayer: "Jesus, show me you're real." And he did. [53]

A liberal author. An Oxford professor. A leading scientist. A rock star.

All unbelievers. Then the risen Christ showed up.

What about you? Maybe you were raised with Christianity, but recently the spiritual fire's been burning a little low.

The risen Christ is here, now, with you. Wherever you are, reading this book. Ask for the gift of faith. Ask him to open your eyes to the evidence of his presence and work in the world around you.

THE GAP

Did Jesus live? And did He really say
The burning words that banish mortal fear?
And are they true? Just this is central, here
The Church must stand or fall. It's *Christ* we weigh

All else is off the point: The Flood, the Day
Of Eden, or the Virgin Birth — Have done!
The Question is, did God send us the Son
Incarnate crying Love! Love is the Way!

Between the probable and proved there yawns
A gap. Afraid to jump, we stand absurd
Then see *behind* us sink the ground and, worse
Our very standpoint crumbling. Desperate dawns
Our only Hope: to leap into the Word
That opens up the shuttered universe
—Sheldon Vanauken [54]

PROJECT: Jot down your own testimony. It may not be as dramatic as those in this chapter. But in one to two pages, write how your own faith developed.

40　FOR EVERY TIME

READ JOHN 21

Waves wash pebbles on the Galilean shore. Early morning fishing boats scud quietly past. They set the scene perfectly for the scripture I'm reading our travel group.

It's a touching story, one of my favorites in the whole Bible. And I'm reading it in the very spot Christian pilgrims have been remembering this awesome encounter for at least 1,700 years.

I'm back at Tabgha, the spot with the seven springs. There's a church built here in honor of the events in John 21, the Church of St. Peter's Primacy.

But we sneak behind the building, to a beach on the lakeside where fishermen have been washing out their nets for centuries. The story in John 21 may not have happened in this precise place — the Bible doesn't specify a location — but it was at a place like this, on this lake.

I love this story because, here's the risen Jesus, with disguise power, disappearing power, walking-through-walls power... I mean, he could have literally done anything, gone anywhere. But what he *chooses* to do is find his disciples, and specifically his ashamed sheep.

Because that's his *agenda*. That's how he *always* uses his power. He came to seek and save the lost.

And today it's Peter who is lost.

HE IS RISEN, OH NO
Peter's already seen Jesus alive, in the upper room on the previous Sunday.

But if you read the gospels carefully, you'll notice Peter doesn't say much then. For once! My guess is he felt stupid and guilty. He

219

had denied even knowing Christ in his hour of greatest need. And now — Jesus is risen? Peter probably said, "He is risen? Oh, no!" Not, "He is risen indeed!"

A few days after Resurrection Sunday, Peter says to the other disciples, "I'm going fishing."

In other words, "I quit."

Peter's obviously disgusted with himself. He feels he's disqualified. So he's cutting himself from the squad. He goes back to his old job, after three years away. Fishing. And it goes from bad to worse, because he's a failure even at that. Even though the others come along to help, he cannot catch a thing.

As if to rub it in, a typically playful post-resurrection Jesus appears on the shore in the misty morning and yells out to the boat before they recognize him: "Catch anything, boys?"

I imagine them a little irritated, yelling back, *"No!"* Then Jesus says, "Try the other side of the boat!" Brilliant. Some of the disciples might have muttered something like: "So who's the fishing genius?" but some may have already been suspecting who this was because they do flip the nets over to the other side — and instantly their ship is nearly swamped sideways with the weight of the catch as hundreds of fish rush into their net.

"It's the Lord!" says John and of course Peter, ever impulsive, bounds into the waves and on to shore, leaving John and the others to do most of the heavy lifting (a fact John may be rubbing in a little when he meticulously points out there were 153 fish in that net!).

THE CHARCOAL FIRE
The next verse contains a crucial word.

> *When they landed, they saw a fire of burning coals there with fish on it, and some bread.* JOHN 21:9

Don't miss the detail: A fire made of what? *Coals.* Intriguing. Why would the gospel writer specify that? And why didn't Jesus just use wood?

The Greek word *anthrakia* (from which we get the English word "anthracite," meaning a *charcoal* fire), is found only twice in the New Testament. The second time is here. The first time is in John 18:18. It's the word used for the courtyard fire where the servants of the high priest stood warming themselves through the chilly night of Jesus' trial. It was there that Peter denied Jesus. Three times.

You know how smells can bring back memories? For me?

Campfires = fun. Coffee = morning.
Pine trees = vacation. Popcorn = matinees.

For Peter, charcoal = failure.

I think Jesus is building a charcoal fire here as if to say, "Hey Peter, remember another charcoal fire a few days back? Let's wipe that memory away. Let's rebrand that experience."

Then, instead of lecturing him, Jesus says, *"Come and have breakfast."* (JOHN 21:12) I *love* that Jesus is making breakfast for them. "The Son of Man came eating and drinking" and he's still at it here. He makes them fish and bread (and hummus — well, not really).

> *When they had finished eating, Jesus said to Simon Peter, "Simon son of John, do you love me more than these?"*
> JOHN 21:15

More than what? Maybe he's asking, "...more than these fish?" As in, "Do you want to follow me more than you want to fish?" Or maybe he's reminding Peter of his boast, "Even if all *these* deny you, I never will!" As if to say, "So, how'd that work out for you, Peter?"

Peter says he does. Then Jesus asks Peter if he loves him, three times in a row.

"Do you love me?" Times three.

Not, "Will you try harder next time?"

Not, "Do you promise never to do that again?"

But, *"Do you love me?"*

He is asking what, to him, is the most important question of all. He said it was the most important command. He said our understanding of all the Law and the Prophets hinges on the answer to this question.

If you don't understand that this is the question Jesus is asking still, then you will assume that he evaluates you based on your performance. Peter is depressed precisely because he thought this way. He had bragged to Jesus that he, Peter, would prove himself worthy, that he would impress Jesus with his valor and faithfulness. His performance and his potential were the way he measured his spiritual life. Then when he fails, he assumes Jesus will reject him. But that's *his* measuring stick, not *Christ's*.

You have nothing to prove to Jesus. You don't have to impress Jesus. You don't have to earn anything from Jesus. You just have to love Jesus.

When Peter insists he does, then Jesus says "Feed my sheep." Three times. Again.

Once for every time Peter denied him.

In other words, get off the bench and back in the game!

I CHOOSE YOU, AGAIN

I think it's strategic that Jesus chooses a spot like this to reinstate Peter. Think about it: Why did Jesus wait? Why didn't he just do this in Jerusalem?

Because he was communicating, *Look, Peter, I called you when you were a fisherman right at this very lakeshore three years ago, and now — knowing everything I know about you — all your failures and your foot-in-mouth disease — I would do it again.*

I chose you. I choose you still. And I will never un-choose you.

I don't know about you, but when I fall into sin, or some stupid habit, I sometimes imagine Jesus saying — "You stupid idiot, why did I ever die for *your* sins? Why'd I choose you? How do I get out of this?"

But in fact, he's saying the same thing he said to Peter: *"Do you love me?"* Then don't waste time in self-pity. *"Feed my sheep!"*

Jesus will never un-choose you.

Aren't you glad?

> God uses broken things. It takes broken soil to produce a crop, broken clouds to produce rain, broken grain to give bread, broken bread to give strength. It is the broken alabaster box that gives forth perfume . . . and it is Peter, weeping bitterly, who returns to greater power than ever.
> —Vance Havner [55]

Do you ever feel like you've disqualified yourself from God's love, or from Christian service?

Spend some time listening to Jesus speaking to you. *What is he saying?*

Based on the authority of the Bible, I believe it's, *"Do you love me? Then feed my sheep."*

And he says it once for every time you deny him.

PONDER: Have you ever wondered if your failures disqualify you as a Christian? What does this story teach you? In what ways can you obey Christ's command to "feed my sheep"?

223

EPILOGUE: JOURNEYING ON

It's our last day in the Holy Land. Our bus is crossing the Jordan River via the Allenby Bridge from east to west, heading back to Tel Aviv airport for the long flight home.

We've seen so many sites, felt so many emotions, had so many adventures over the last several days. We walked where Jesus walked, sailed where he sailed, smelled smells, saw sights, stood on steps that were all part of his life experience.

But why did this time in this land hold such power? Really, the geography here is not much different than my California home. The small canyons remind me of San Diego, the desert is like Death Valley, Mount Hermon is like Mount Shasta, the rolling hills of Galilee similar to the Bay Area.

So why did it all make such an indelible impression?

FROM THE STARS TO THE STABLE

I remember how, as I peered through that telescope on the Dead Sea shore, I thought of the stars of the Milky Way far above me, and the stables of Bethlehem just beyond me.

And my mind goes back to a phrase I once heard about the incarnation of Christ:

"The scandal of particularity."

What gives believers goose bumps is the scandalous idea that the infinite creator of the vast universe came to a particular people, in a particular time and place.

Think of the Jesus we've met on this journey:

> *Time-and-space traveller.*
> *Kingdom builder.*
> *Lost-sheep finder*

EPILOGUE: JOURNEYING ON

Embracer of outcasts.
Critic of religion.
Lover of the unlovely.

Victor over human authorities, anxieties, and agendas.
Defeater of darkness, demons, and death.
Miracle worker, grace giver,
*   surprising Messiah, resurrected Redeemer, Lord of all.*

God with us.

The land here is beautiful, but it's not the land that inspires so deeply. It's the idea that such a God would choose to come to this land—the crossroads of three continents, a real land, not a fairy tale kingdom—to win us back to him.

God did not love humans philosophically. He is not with us abstractly. He came to us specifically.

Christians don't merely believe in a God who radiates love unthinkingly and impersonally in all directions like the sun beams its light. When we say "God is love" we mean he loves everyone like a laser beam. We mean he loves *you*. We mean he knows your name.

And we mean he *had* a name. He came, in the flesh, to pay for your particular sins once for all time. And he is with you personally until the end of the age.

CROSSING INTO HOLY GROUND

When Joshua and the Israelites first crossed the Jordan River about 3,400 years ago, very close to where the Allenby Bridge is now, they were coming home to a place they'd never been. With every new step they were reclaiming territory for God. Establishing a kingdom.

1,400 years later, in virtually the same spot, John baptized Jesus. In a sense, John and Jesus were crossing another border. Beginning another era. With each deliberate step he took after his baptism, Jesus was introducing a new kind of kingdom.

And now it's our turn. As we cross the Jordan on our way to the airport and out of the country, we continue his kingdom work.

The *Jesus Journey* is not just about what he has done, where he walked, two thousand years ago.

It's about what Jesus will do, and where he will go, in the years to come, through you and me.

He will be with you always. On your continuing *Jesus Journey*.

Leaving the Holy Land? No.

Through you and me, with each new step we take, Jesus is making the whole *world* into Holy Land.

PRAYER: Thank God for his amazing gift of love in Jesus. Thank him for the opportunity to grow and change over the last 40 days. Pray your journey with Jesus will continue to grow and you will become more like him.

Bonus Jesus Journey devotional readings are available for free at WWW.JESUSJOURNEYBOOK.COM

SMALL GROUP STUDY GUIDES

WEEK 1 PREPARING THE WAY

If you're starting a new group, or have new group members, take time for introductions.

Share with the group the format for each week. You'll begin with introductions and brief discussion starter questions. Then you'll watch a short video filmed in Israel. Following this, you'll read related Scriptures and discuss your responses to questions. Then you'll close with prayer requests and plans for group projects or meals.

If you're using the *Jesus Journey* book for daily devotions during this study, Day 0 is today. Day 1 begins for your group tomorrow!

TOUCH BASE

As a brief discussion starter today, share some of your travel dreams: If you were to take a journey anywhere in the world, where would it be and why?

How do you hope to grow during this *Jesus Journey* study? What are your expectations?

Open in a brief word of prayer, asking God to bless your time together.

PLAY WEEK 1 SMALL GROUP VIDEO

On DVD or on the web at WWW.JESUSJOURNEYBOOK.COM

TAKE IT IN

1. Have group members share insights they learned about Jesus or the context of his ministry from the video. How does this help you understand the ministry of Jesus better?

2. How do the Dead Sea Scrolls help build confidence that our Bibles accurately reflect the ancient manuscripts?

3. How do the Dead Sea Scrolls help us better understand the historical context of the ministry of Jesus Christ in the first century — what was happening then that helped prepare people for the ministry of Jesus?

TALK IT OUT:

Let's journey through some of the messianic prophecies in Isaiah.

1. *Have someone read Isaiah 29:13–14 out loud.* Jesus clearly loved the book of Isaiah; this is one of the many sections of Isaiah that Jesus quotes during his ministry (MATTHEW 15:7–9). How did these words become a theme of his ministry?

2. *Have someone read Isaiah 40:1–11 out loud.* This is another Isaiah prophecy about the Messiah. John the Baptist became the *"voice calling out in the wilderness"* in these verses. This is one of the prophecies that caused people to expect the Messiah to be a supernatural warrior who would level the Roman pagan temples with blasts of God's wrath and instantly restore the kingdom of Israel. What aspects of this prophecy would lead the people to expect such a warrior?

3. How did Jesus fulfill this Isaiah 40 prophecy in unexpected ways?

4. *Have someone read Isaiah 53 out loud* as the rest of the group follows along in their Bibles. Isaiah 53 is full of prophecies about Jesus. As a group, identify as many as you can, and have someone record your observations:

5. Which Isaiah 53 prophecy impacts you the most today — and why?

6. *Making it personal, have someone else reread Isaiah 53:4–5 out loud,* and replace the plural pronouns (our, us, we) with the personal (my, me, I). How does it encourage you to know God was willing to suffer so much for you and for me? Is this difficult for you to accept? Why?

7. *Read Isaiah 61:1–3.* Jesus reads this prophecy out loud — stopping in the middle of verse 2, before the "vengeance" section — in his hometown synagogue in Nazareth at the very beginning of his ministry, and announces that after all these years of waiting, the Messiah is here, and it's *him!* But the people do not like his announcement! In fact, they try to kill him. How would you explain their strange reaction?

TAKE IT WITH YOU

What have you learned during this week's lesson that has encouraged, enlightened or challenged you?

God prepared the way for the Messiah. How have you seen God preparing the way for Jesus to come into your life?

JESUS PROJECT

You can journey with Jesus each day as you reach out to the "least of these." How will you follow Jesus to people a little outside your comfort zone during this study?

Agree to begin thinking about a project your group could take on together during this 40-day journey with Jesus. Think of something that will give you the opportunity to grow closer to Jesus and reflect his character and love.

Some ideas: You could volunteer for a day or an evening with a nursing home ministry, a jail ministry, a ministry to physically or developmentally disabled people, a rescue mission, or a food bank. You could serve your city or school by cleaning up or painting where needed. Agree to collect ideas and share them with the group next week.

WEEK 1 PREPARING THE WAY

TALK TO GOD

Take some time to share personal prayer requests.

As you spend time in prayer together this week thank God for his willingness to send his son to suffer on your behalf.

Commit to making this 40-day journey with Jesus personal!

WEEK 2   A MESSIAH FOR ALL HUMANITY

TOUCH BASE

Open in a brief word of prayer, asking God to bless your time together.

Ask any new members to introduce themselves.

As a brief discussion starter, share how you prepare for a journey: Do you work from a plan — or do you just let life happen?

Has anything impacted your life in the daily devotions you've read so far this week? Share it with the group.

PLAY WEEK 2 SMALL GROUP VIDEO

On DVD or on the web at WWW.JESUSJOURNEYBOOK.COM

TAKE IT IN

1. Have group members share insights they learned about Jesus or the context of his ministry from the video. Did anything intrigue or surprise you? How does this help you understand the ministry or strategy of Jesus better?

2. Summarize why Capernaum was such a strategic spot for the ministry of Jesus.

3. René shared some lessons from Jesus' choice of Capernaum:

   - Jesus' message was always intended to spread beyond one ethnic group. God is a God for all humanity.

   - Jesus sees the purpose of a small, seemingly insignificant village — as he sees the purpose in the smallest, seemingly insignificant person.

   - Jesus sees the long-term, big picture strategy in his choice of a headquarters — as he sees the big picture in all of history, including my life.

• Jesus planned strategically. This reminds me there is nothing unspiritual about strategic planning. Just letting things happen is not necessarily more godly.

Which of these lessons hits home for you?

TALK IT OUT:

Read Matthew 4:12–25. There's another prophecy from Isaiah, which, as we saw last week, is filled with verses later quoted in the gospels. *Look up Isaiah 9:1–7* and read it out loud. This is the original passage quoted in Matthew.

1. What added significance does the phrase *"the way of the sea"* (ISAIAH 9:1) take on when you know the history of Capernaum?

1. Isaiah 9:4 says the Messiah will "shatter the yoke" that burdens the people. How did Jesus fulfill this prophecy in an unexpected way (SEE MATTHEW 11:28–29)?

1. What other prophecies about the Messiah are in this same passage in Isaiah (SEE VERSE 6)?

2. How does this verse help defeat the idea that Christians only later invented the idea that the Messiah would be divine?

3. How does this description of the Messiah encourage you?

4. Back to Matthew 4. What did Jesus ask Peter and Andrew to do? What do you think it cost them?

5. How do you think their lives would be different if they had chosen *not* to follow?

6. What sacrifices do you think are involved in following Jesus today?

7. How is your life different because you've followed Jesus?

TAKE IT WITH YOU

What have you learned during this week's lesson that has encouraged or enlightened or challenged you?

In what area of your life right now would it help to be confident that God sees the long-term, big picture and has a strategic plan?

JESUS PROJECT

Discuss plans for your group service project. Remember, journeying with Jesus is not just about study. It's about going in the same direction he went, to help the "least of these." Check with your church, local food bank or local government office if you're looking for ideas.

TALK TO GOD

Take some time to share personal prayer requests. As you spend time in prayer together this week thank God for his willingness to reach out and save everyone. Pray that you will be willing to follow Jesus wherever he calls you.

WEEK 3   BENEATH THE SURFACE

MOUNT OF BEATITUDES, SEPPHORIS

TOUCH BASE

Have any new group members introduce themselves.

As a brief discussion starter, share your answer to one of these questions:

- Who is your favorite actor and why?

- Have you ever acted in a play? When? Did you like it?

Open in a brief word of prayer, asking God to bless your time together.

Has anything impacted your life in the daily devotions you've read so far this week? Share it with the group.

PLAY WEEK 3 SMALL GROUP VIDEO

On DVD or on the web at WWW.JESUSJOURNEYBOOK.COM

TAKE IT IN

1. Have group members share insights they learned about Jesus or the context of his ministry from the video. Did anything intrigue or surprise you? How does this help you understand the ministry of Jesus better?

2. How would you summarize the theme of the Sermon on the Mount, in your own words?

3. How does the idea that the word "hypocrite" meant "actor" give you insight into Christ's message?

TALK IT OUT

1. *Read through Matthew 5:1–12.* As a group, list the type of people Jesus calls blessed.

2. What stands out to you — or surprises you — from this list?

3. How do you think this list would have been particularly surprising, and encouraging, to people in the first-century religious culture Jesus is originally speaking within?

4. If you could write one beatitude that summarizes it all, what would it be? "Blessed are the _____ for they will _____." How is this similar to the idea of "hitting bottom" so that you come to the realization that you need God?

5. *Read Matthew 6:2–8.* How does Jesus describe the behavior of a religious "actor"?

6. Do you think this still happens in churches today? How? Share examples of "religious acting" you have witnessed, or been a part of yourself (try not to name any specific people or groups so this doesn't turn into a complaining session). Does this get noticed by people outside church? What kind of an impact does this have on them?

7. Do you ever struggle with religious "acting"? In what ways?

8. I actually like the advice *"fake it 'till you make it"* from the drug and alcohol recovery community. It's a reminder to those recovering from addiction that they will not always *feel* like being sober is the best way to live. But they should continue in their sobriety even though they may *feel* more like partying than going to a meeting. How does the meaning of "fake it 'till you make it" differ from the kind of religious fakery Jesus is criticizing here?

TAKE IT WITH YOU

1. In what area in your life do you sense you are just playing a role?

2. What steps can you take this week to drop the mask and be more like Christ (i.e., attend a 12-Step recovery group; getting honest with an accountability partner; changing certain behaviors; prayer; Bible study)?

JESUS PROJECT

Finalize plans for your group outreach project. Be sure everyone knows what's expected and has the details. How do you hope this project will help you grow to be more like Jesus?

TALK TO GOD

Take some time to share personal prayer requests with the group.

As you spend time in prayer together this week thank God that his grace allows authenticity. Pray that your faith will be genuine and you will live in the grace of the beatitudes. Also pray that God will use your group to reflect the love and grace of Jesus to the people you serve together in your project.

WEEK 4 STORMY SEAS

TOUCH BASE

Have any new group members introduce themselves.

Open in a brief word of prayer, asking God to bless your time together.

If you're finished with your group project, take some time to talk about it. What did you learn about working together? What did you learn about Jesus through serving?

Did anything stand out to you from this week's daily devotions?

As a brief discussion starter, share a worry or fear you have...

PLAY WEEK 4 SMALL GROUP VIDEO

On DVD or on the web at WWW.JESUSJOURNEYBOOK.COM

TAKE IT IN

1. What did you learn — or what surprised you — about Jesus or the context of his ministry from the video?

2. How did the ancient Hebrews tend to look at the sea — positively or negatively?

3. The ancient Israelite culture's general dislike of the sea contributed to their relative lack of seafaring technology. When they needed to ship freight via the ocean, or to travel on the ocean, Israelites in the Bible always use sailors and ships from other neighboring cultures and not their own. What insight does this give you about the effect of deep-seated fears on our lives — in other words, how does fear limit us? What does it cost us?

4. Have everyone in the group open their Bibles and *skim through the first three chapters of Mark* to refresh your memory about

what miracles the disciples had already seen. Have group members call out the miracles as they notice them.

5. Why do you think the disciples were more "terrified" after this miracle than any that had come before?

TALK IT THROUGH
Read Mark 4:35–41 and 6:45–56.

1. What were the disciples' occupations prior to following Christ (name as many as you can)? What is the predominant occupation on that list? How does this bring added insight to the disciples' state of mind during the storms?

2. How are these storms described?

3. What fears were the disciples facing?

4. How did their view of Jesus affect their fears?

5. Why do you think it was important for Jesus to show the disciples his power over the seas?

6. Why do you think it was important for the gospel writers to include these stories? What is the point they are making about Jesus?

7. How could your view of Jesus affect the fear(s) that you mentioned earlier?

TAKE IT WITH YOU

1. Picture living life *without* those fears you mentioned earlier. How does it differ from the life you're living now?

2. How can seeing Jesus as Lord even over that fear help you out?

3. What is one practical step you take toward that life today?

4. How has this *Jesus Journey* contributed to your spiritual life so far?

JESUS PROJECT

If you've completed your group project, determine to raise some food for the poor as your second Jesus Project in this series. Work together as a group — or even get your entire church in on your plan — and find a way you can reflect Jesus' compassion and help feed people in your community this week!

TALK TO GOD

Take some time to share personal prayer requests.

As you spend time in prayer together this week thank God that he is bigger than all your fears. Pray that you will grow in your faith in God and leave behind your fears. Ask him to use your group to encourage people who need food in your community.

WEEK 5 SOLID ROCK

TOUCH BASE

Have any new group members introduce themselves.

Open in a brief word of prayer, asking God to bless your time together.

What stood out to you from this week's teaching (sermon and daily devotions)?

Since we're talking about panic and anxiety in today's lesson, do you think panic and anxiety are on the rise in our culture? Why?

How is your anxiety level these days? What do you tend to be anxious about?

PLAY WEEK 5 SMALL GROUP VIDEO

On DVD or on the web at WWW.JESUSJOURNEYBOOK.COM

TAKE IT IN

Share at least one thing you learned about Jesus or the context of his ministry from the DVD.

Why do you think Jesus took the disciples to Caesarea Philippi for this teaching? How did this location serve as a sort of visual aid?

TALK IT OUT:

Read Matthew 16:13–17:8. This is a good time to point out Jesus' use of the term "The Son of Man" in reference to himself. This is a phrase used in a prophecy from the Book of Daniel about the Messiah.

Daniel has a vision of the evil kings and terrible wars that will herald the end of this era on earth. Then he sees the final, eternal ruler over all the earth. *Read Daniel 7:13–14.* This prophecy was one of those in the Dead Sea Scrolls studied by the Essenes; in fact, the Essenes refer to these verses specifically in their studies about the Messiah.

On the other hand, the term "Son of Man" is also used extensively in the Book of Ezekiel to refer *not* to the Messiah, but to the prophet Ezekiel himself.

So perhaps Jesus is asking, "Which definition of the 'Son of Man'—Messiah or prophet—do people think applies to me?"

1. When Jesus asked, *"Who do people say the 'Son of Man' is?"* what were the disciples' initial answers? What do all these answers have in common—in other words, did most people at this point consider Jesus the Messiah or a prophet?

2. Who did Peter say Jesus was?

3. This was a very important point for Peter to make, and he is commended for it by Jesus himself. Peter distinguishes between the common idea that Jesus was a prophet like Elijah or Jeremiah, and his own belief that Jesus was the Messiah, the Son of the Living God, *not* just a prophet or teacher with wise sayings.

4. How do these same distinctions apply today: Who do people say Jesus is?

BACKGROUND NOTES

If you have a Catholic background, you know that verses 17–19 here are interpreted by the Roman Catholic church to refer specifically to Peter's leadership, and, by extension, the office of the Pope, since the popes are held to be Peter's successors.

On the other hand, Protestants believe that, while Peter was a leader of the early church, there is no explicit promise here of succession. Plus, they point out that Jesus doesn't seem to be commending Peter's *character* (see his rebuke of Peter in verse 23) as much as he was commending Peter's *confession*.

I don't mean to oversimplify either of these positions, and I don't want your Bible study to turn into a debate. I bring this up because, in my experience, the debate around these verses often overshadows the application that these verses can hold for all of us today: You and I can be confident, because *Jesus* builds his work, not us *("I will build my church...")*; he does so with the *least likely suspects* (Peter, for crying out loud!); and he builds it for *certain victory ("the gates of Hades will not stand...")*.

That's confidence-building!

The word "church" in verse 18 is the Greek word *ekklesia*, which at this point in history simply meant "assembly" or "gathering." It may help to think of similar words like "movement" or "group" to avoid the negative baggage that can sometimes accumulate around the word "church" (even though I do love the church!).

The point of these verses is, Jesus is starting something significant here, something that, though it may begin with a single follower voicing for the first time a truly Christian confession, will grow and endure until it conquers hell itself. He is using kingdom language to reinforce that he is indeed the Messiah who will build the everlasting kingdom, fulfilling those ancient prophecies.

So, with all that background... How can these verses encourage you today?

5. What does Jesus begin to explain to his disciples, according to Matthew 16:21?

6. Why do you think Peter rebukes Jesus? How do people still rebuke God's plans today?

7. Have you ever tried to tell God you have a better plan? How? How are you struggling with that right now?

8. OK, here's a bonus question for you: How do you explain the "whatever you bind on earth will be bound in heaven" phrase in your own words?

Again, some hold this to mean that Peter and his successors, or church leadership generally, have the authority to declare someone "saved or unsaved" in church discipline situations — in other words, in this verse Jesus gives the church leadership the authority to excommunicate.

I think it's much more likely that this means that the church (as in, anyone in Christ's movement) has the opportunity to bring people to heaven by presenting them with the gospel.

That is the key to the kingdom. And truly, whatever is bound here is bound in heaven, in the sense that the decision we make here on earth to receive the gospel impacts us for eternity.

TAKE IT WITH YOU

1. Look back to those times of panic or anxiety you mentioned earlier. What truth from the study this week can help you when you feel panicked or anxious?

2. What big idea will you take home from today's lesson?

3. How has the *Jesus Journey* been impacting your spiritual growth so far?

4. I've suggested that, as a group project, you set an ambitious goal to help a local food pantry. How could reaching out and providing food for people in need help your struggles with panic and anxiety?

JESUS PROJECT

If you already have completed your group projects, agree together that you will each individually look for a way to serve someone this week — someone who doesn't expect it. Next week, share with the group what you did!

TALK TO GOD

Take some time to share personal prayer requests. As you spend time in prayer together this week thank God for his willingness to reach out and save everyone. Pray that you will grow in your faith and assurance that Jesus truly is the Christ, the Son of God.

WEEK 6　UNDER PRESSURE

TOUCH BASE

Open in a brief word of prayer, asking God to bless your time together.

What stood out to you from this week's teaching (sermon and daily devotions)?

How have you been growing during this *Jesus Journey*?

As a brief discussion starter, share a time you felt overwhelmed... either by joy or stress!

PLAY WEEK 6 SMALL GROUP VIDEO

On DVD or on the web at WWW.JESUSJOURNEYBOOK.COM

TAKE IT IN

Share at least one thing you learned about Jesus or the context of his ministry from the video.

Why do you think Jesus felt he had a heavy weight on him, like the heavy olive presses that surrounded him on the Mount of Olives?

TALK IT THROUGH

1. *Read John 12:1–46.* This is a fascinating chapter, because you see Jesus' inner circle starting to fray (Judas' criticism, some doubters in the crowd) even as some of Christ's former opponents in the Temple leadership start to believe in him (verse 42). Groups of Christ's supporters are fracturing and realigning as Jesus presses his agenda. How does this happen even to this day?

2. *Look more closely at verses 13–15.* In what ways did the video's explanation of the historical context of Palm Sunday help you understand the people's response to Christ — both on Palm Sunday and later, when he was crucified?

3. What confused people then about Jesus' agenda? What confuses people today about Jesus' agenda? What confuses you?

4. What could help you keep an accurate perspective on Jesus and his agenda while living in today's world?

5. *Read John 14:1–14.* What does Jesus say here that encourages you during times of pressure?

TAKE IT WITH YOU

1. Jesus did not avoid the pain of the cross — because of his love for you and God's plan. In what area of your life are you stressed right now?

2. How could the truth of Jesus' own suffering help you stay the course when you are facing stress?

JESUS PROJECT

What did you do this week to show love to someone? Share your experience with the group. How do you think acts of love and kindness might help to spread the kingdom of God?

TALK TO GOD

Take some time to share personal prayer requests.

As you spend time in prayer together this week thank God for his willingness to fulfill his mission. Pray that your life will reflect his devotion to reaching others.

If you have been raising food for a food bank, pray for those who receive the food you give. Ask God to use that food to show people his love for them.

WEEK 7 GET BACK IN THE GAME

TOUCH BASE

Open in a brief word of prayer, asking God to bless your time together.

How has this journey with Jesus impacted you?

What devotions or small group lessons have particularly stood out for you during this study?

PLAY WEEK 7 SMALL GROUP VIDEO

On DVD or on the web at WWW.JESUSJOURNEYBOOK.COM

TAKE IT IN

Share at least one thing you learned about Jesus or the context of his ministry from the video.

Do you ever feel permanently disqualified from ministry when you fall?

What does this story have to say about how God wants us to handle the guilt and shame we feel when we fall away from Jesus?

TALK IT OUT:
Please read John 21.

1. What is Peter doing to handle the stress of Jesus' death and resurrection in verse 3? Why do you think he returns to his old habits? What old habits do you tend to return to when you're disappointed or stressed?

2. What was Jesus' advice (verse 6) to the disciples in the boat? Why do you think they were open to a stranger's advice from the shore?

248

3. What stands out to you in Jesus' exchange with Peter in verses 15–17? What does this say to you about God's response to you when you sin?

4. Why do you think Jesus asks Peter the question three times?

5. Why do you think Jesus confirms the call of Peter here, on the lakeshore, rather than in the Upper Room in Jerusalem, where the disciples had first seen him in his resurrected body?

6. *Reread verses 21–22.* In what area(s) of your life are you struggling with comparing what Jesus is doing with someone else's life to what he's doing in yours?

TAKE IT WITH YOU

1. What "big idea" will you take home from the Scripture today?

2. Take a few moments of silence so that each group member can meditate and pray, listening to Jesus. In what area of your life do you sense Jesus saying to you, "Follow me"?

3. How has this *Jesus Journey* study impacted you?

TALK TO GOD

Take some time to share personal prayer requests.

As you spend time in prayer together this week thank God for his love and forgiveness.

Pray that you will all follow Jesus no matter what is happening around you.

Thank God for the opportunity to learn about Jesus and grow closer to each other and him.

MAKE PLANS TO HAVE A CELEBRATION DINNER NEXT WEEK!

You could even celebrate with a first-century meal like Jesus might have eaten.

According to the experts who contributed to the "Ancient Israelite Cuisine" entry on Wikipedia, a typical Jewish meal of the day might have included lentil soup and flatbread (something like pita bread), fresh fruits in season (grapes, watermelon, cantaloupe, figs, apricots, pomegranates, and olives), or dried fruit (raisins, dates, apricots, figs) which ancient Jews really loved, and often took on journeys or while working. [56]

They also enjoyed goat cheese, and yogurt sweetened with honey. Almonds, walnuts, and pistachios were also very widespread, and are mentioned in the Bible.

Rice had been introduced a few hundred years before, and by the Roman period was a common food — and major export. Jews in the first century also ate a variety of legumes including garbanzos and peas, and enjoyed stew flavored with onion, garlic and leeks. Some recipes of the time also mention mushrooms.

Olive oil was used for cooking and for frying, and olive oil production was a major industry in biblical times. One ancient olive oil production site had over one hundred large presses in one location. Vinegar production was also widespread. Herbs and spices included capers, coriander, cumin, dill, hyssop, mint, mustard, saffron, thyme, salt, and various kinds of pepper.

For beverages, ancient Jews drank water, milk, freshly squeezed fruit juice, and wine.

The most common meat was probably fish, but people also ate goat, lamb, chicken, geese, duck, pigeon, and quail. Beef was known, but only eaten by the elite. And of course... *hummus*.

HUMMUS RECIPE

I crave it! You know you want it. Your small group will love it. But did *Jesus* eat hummus?

The most common accompaniment to hummus, pita bread, was invented by the Amorites about 2,400 years before Christ, and has been popular in the Middle East ever since. So I imagine there was some sort of spread for the bread — when you're eating pocket bread, you need something to put in the pocket!

Food historians suspect hummus has been serving that very purpose for thousands of years. Garbanzo beans, or chickpeas, were widely eaten in the time of Christ, and used in cooked food such as stews. So it's very possible people ate a cold mix of garbanzos with their pitas. But the earliest known *written* recipe for cold hummus only goes to back to the 1200s in Egypt.

Here's a modern variation:

INGREDIENTS

1 can of garbanzo beans
4 tablespoons lemon juice
2 tablespoons tahini (add more according to taste)
1 or 2 cloves chopped garlic (according to taste)
1/2 teaspoon salt
2 tablespoons olive oil
Little bit of parsley for garnish

DIRECTIONS

Combine ingredients in blender, saving a few beans for garnish. Blend for 3–5 minutes on low until creamy. Place in serving bowl, and create a well in the center of the hummus. Add a small amount (1–2 tablespoons) of olive oil in the well. Garnish with a few garbanzo beans left from the can, and parsley. Enjoy with fresh, warm or toasted pita bread, or cover and refrigerate.

JESUS JOURNEY

SMALL GROUP ROSTER

NAME	EMAIL	PHONE

JESUS JOURNEY

PRAYER REQUESTS

_____

_____

_____

_____

_____

_____

_____

_____

_____

_____

_____

_____

_____

_____

_____

_____

EXTRAS

JESUS JOURNEY

MUSIC PLAYLIST

These are songs I enjoy about Jesus! I hope you'll enjoy them too.

Hero ABANDON

Mighty to Save HILLSONG UNITED

You Are My King (Amazing Love) LOTS OF GOOD VERSIONS, TRY NEWSBOYS

The Power of Your Name LINCOLN BREWSTER

Forgiven and Loved JIMMY NEEDHAM

Follow You LEELAND WITH BRANDON HEATH

Give Me Your Eyes BRANDON HEATH

I Will Follow CHRIS TOMLIN

Rend GREAT SONG FROM JESUS' PERSPECTIVE / JIMMY NEEDHAM

Jesus Saves JEREMY CAMP

Lead Me to the Cross HILLSONG

Via Dolorosa LEELAND

Gethsemane STUART TOWNEND

Blessed Redeemer CASTING CROWNS

In Christ Alone LOTS OF GOOD VERSIONS; TRY THE ONE BY OWL CITY

Behold the Lamb STUART TOWNEND

Alive (Mary Magdalene) NATALIE GRANT

Overcome JEREMY CAMP

Christ Is Risen MATT MAHER

My Jesus LEELAND

Give Me Jesus FERNANDO ORTEGA

Jesus, I Come SHELLY MOORE BAND

Jesus Lover of My Soul HILLSONG

My Jesus, I Love Thee HYMN; TRY THE VERSION ON "THE HYMN PROJECT"

Untitled Hymn (Come To Jesus) CHRIS RICE

Your Great Name NATALIE GRANT

Friend in You; Jesus Loves Ya; Can't Live Without Jesus ALL OLD SCHOOL SOUL SONGS BY JON GIBSON

Jesus; Now Behold The Lamb BOTH BY KIRK FRANKLIN

And of course all those Christmas songs!

Here's a fun one: *Born is the King* HILLSONG

RECOMMENDED BOOKS

If you liked this look at Jesus that combines travelogue, history, and geography, you might also like these books. I enjoyed them as I prepared for our *Jesus Journey*.

Gary Burge, *Jesus, The Middle Eastern Storyteller* (Grand Rapids: Zondervan, 2009). (Burge has a whole series of these books — I got a lot out of them.)

Tim Keller, *King's Cross: The Story of the World in the Life of Jesus* (New York: Dutton, 2011).

Calvin Miller, *The Book of Jesus* (New York: Simon and Shuster, 1996). (A great digest of writings about Jesus throughout the ages)

R. Wayne Stacy, *Where Jesus Walked: A Spiritual Journey Through the Holy Land* (Judson Press, 2001).

Wayne Stiles, *Walking in the Footsteps of Jesus*, (Ventura: Gospel Light, 2008).

Ray Vander Laan's *Faith Lessons* DVD series (Grand Rapids: Zondervan).

Peter Walker, *In The Steps of Jesus* (Grand Rapids: Zondervan, 2006).

N. T. Wright, *How God Became King* (New York: HarperOne, 2011).

ENDNOTES

1 www.seetheholyland.net/herodium/ (accessed June 20, 2012).

2 Richard Crashaw, "Herod's Suspicions," in *The Book of Jesus*, ed. Calvin Miller (New York: Simon and Schuster, 1996), 127.

3 Material on Joseph informed by Scot McKnight, *The Jesus Creed: Loving God, Loving Others* (Brewster, Massachusetts: Paraclete Press, 2004) 77*ff* and by a great Christmas sermon by John Ortberg at Menlo Park Presbyterian Church.

4 Joachim Jeremias, *Jerusalem in the Time of Jesus* (SCM/Fortress Press, 1969), 304-305.

5 Ibid.

6 Ron Mehl, *Love Found A Way*, (Portland, OR: Waterbrook Press, 1999), 71.

7 Timothy Keller, *King's Cross*, (New York: Dutton, 2011), 39.

8 Ibid.

9 Brian Blondy, "Archeologists uncover house in Nazareth dating to time of Jesus," *Jerusalem Post*, December 22, 2009 (accessed June 6, 2012).

10 John Koessler, "Jesus Disappoints Everyone," *Christianity Today*, April 5, 2012.

11 Flavius Josephus, *Antiquities* 20.9.1 (This and all subsequent citations from Josephus can be found at http://perseus.uchicago.edu/greek.html).

12 C. S. Lewis, Walter Hooper, *Collected Letters: Narnia, Cambridge and Joy 1950–1963* (New York: Harper Collins), 75.

13 "Strata Answers," *Biblical Archaeology Review*, Vol. 38, No. 5, September/October 2012, p. 64.

14 Flavius Josephus, *War*, 3.10.

15 My information on this point comes from John Ortberg, "The World's Greatest Mission," a great sermon delivered on September 18, 2005, at Menlo Park Presbyterian Church, available at www.mppc.org.

16 Ibid.

17 N. T. Wright, "On Earth as in Heaven," sermon at York Minster, 20 May 2007, accessed at ntwrightpage.com/sermons/Earth_Heaven.htm.

18 Neil MacFarquhar, "Heavy Hand of the Secret Police Impeding Reform in Arab World," *New York Times*, November 14, 2005 (accessed June 18, 2012).

19 Gary M. Burge, *Jesus, The Middle Eastern Storyteller* (Grand Rapids: Zondervan, 2009), 58*ff*.

20 Ibid.

21 Ibid, 65.

22 Bill Hybels, from his introduction to the video curriculum, "Becoming a Contagious Christian" (Grand Rapids: Zondervan).

23 Teresa of Calcutta, "Daily Prayer," in *Eerdman's Book of Famous Prayers*, (Grand Rapids: Eerdmans, 1983), 99.

24 Adapted from Mark Driscoll, "Jesus and Religion" sermon, http://marshill.com/media/luke/jesus-and-religion#transcript (accessed on June 17, 2012).

25 Quoted in Timothy Keller, *The Prodigal God* (New York: Dutton, 2008), 46.

26 Keller, *King's Cross*, 75.

27 Ibid, 76.

28 F. F. Bruce, *Are The New Testament Documents Reliable?* (Intervarsity Press; Downers Grove, Ill, fifth revised edition 1992), 74.

29 Shelly Conhey, "The Second Temple at the Time of Jesus," www.jewishvirtuallibrary.com, (accessed June 6, 2012).

30 For a riveting account of the Aleppo Codex story, see Matti Friedman, *The Aleppo Codex* (Chapel Hill, North Carolina: Algonquin Books of Chapel Hill, 2012).

31 R. Wayne Stacy, *Where Jesus Walked* (Valley Forge: Judson Press, 2001), 158.

32 Corrie Ten Boom, *Each New Day* (New York: Revell, 2003) Devotion for May 26.

33 Miller, 273.

34 Josephus, *Antiquities*, 8.2.5.

35 *The Works of Flavius Josephus, Vol. 2*, translated by William Whitston (London: Chatto & Windus, 1897), 259.

36 Some commentators place the crowd very conservatively at 300,000–400,000 based on the assumption that Josephus may have been exaggerating, but either way it was a massive group. Imagine how much hummus they must have eaten.

37 D. A. Carson, *The Gospel According to John* (Grand Rapids: Eerdmans, 1991), 269.

38 Josephus, *Antiquities*. 14.109–13.

39 I've adapted these points from Mark Driscoll's sermon, "Jesus and the Temple," www.marshill.com (accessed June 11, 2012).

40 Josephus, *Jewish Wars* 5.1.5; 36.

41 C. S. Lewis, *The Weight of Glory and Other Essays* (New York: Simon and Shuster, 1980), 36–37.

42 Philo, *On the Embassy of Gaius*, 38.299-305.

43 Ibid.

44 Josephus, *Jewish Wars*, 5.207.

45 Eusebius, *The Life of Constantine*, 3.28.

46 www.pbs.org/empires/romans/empire/women.html (accessed June 18, 2012).

47 John Updike, "Seven Stanzas at Easter," in Miller, 471.

48 Anne Lamott, *Traveling Mercies: Some Thoughts on Faith* (New York: Anchor Books, 1999), 49–51.

49 C. S. Lewis, *Surprised By Joy* (Orlando: Houghton Mifflin Harcourt, 1955), 221.

50 Andrea Monda, "The Conversion Story of C. S. Lewis" http://www.ewtn.com/library/SPIRIT/cslewconv.HTM (accessed June 18, 2012).

51 Miller, 213.

[52] Transcript, "Bob Abernethy's Interview with Dr. Francis Collins," *PBS Religion and Ethics Newsweekly*, http://www.pbs.org/wnet/religionand ethics/transcripts/collins.html (accessed June 18, 2012).

[53] http://www.mtv.com/news/articles/1497529/brian-head-welch-talks-california-church.jhtml (accessed June 18, 2012).

[54] From Sheldon Vanauken, *A Severe Mercy*, Quoted in Francis Collins, *The Language of God* (New York: Simon and Shuster, 2006), 31.

[55] Vance Havner, *Hearts Afire: Light on Successful Soul Winning* (Westwood, NJ: Fleming H. Revell, 1952), 76.

[56] "Ancient Israelite Cuisine," Wikipedia. http://en.wikipedia.org/wiki/Ancient_Israelite_cuisine (accessed August 17, 2012).

ACKNOWLEDGEMENTS

It started with a wish. I mentioned my "bucket list" in a sermon — things I'd like to do before I kick the bucket. One of the first things on my list, I revealed, would be to take my wife and youngest son to Israel. Later, a man in our church, Lee Hanson, told me, "You know, René, that's not exactly the impossible dream!" He volunteered to set up a tour for me to lead. And the idea caught fire. Dave Hicks, one of our pastors, suggested I turn the trip into a book. And you hold in your hands the fruit of that journey. We ended up visiting both Israel and Jordan, and I'm so thankful to Lee, Dave, and Gina Weeks, who administered all the trip details.

Invaluable to our experience: Our charismatic, brilliant guide, Kenny Garon, from whom I learned so much. And obviously we could not have seen anything without Dov, our amazing bus driver. Kenny, a Jew, and Dov, a Christian, are a wonderful example of the kind of love and camaraderie we all pray to see one day everywhere in the Middle East.

Massive thanks to Kelly Welty, who produced all the small group videos and who, along with Philip Lima, beautifully photographed the trip.

Thanks to John Eric Paulson for his beautiful photograph on the cover, and to Priscilla Watson for her watercolor maps.

Major thanks also to Valerie Webb, who shepherded the whole project, wrote the daily questions, and, with Jim Josselyn, wrote the small group study questions.

Thanks also to José Santillán, who spent hundreds of hours translating this book into Spanish (*Los Viajes de Jesús*).

I'm indebted to layout artist extraordinaire Kevin Deutsch and the many, many others at Twin Lakes Church who contributed to the production of the book and editing of the manuscript, especially the talented writer Karen O'Connor, my wife Laurie, the aforementioned Dave and Kelly, Brian King, June Ettinger, Margie Bishop and my friend and co-pastor Mark Spurlock, who all read various drafts and made many valuable suggestions.

And I am grateful to every single person who joined us on our Holy Land trip. The ceaseless, genuine brotherly love we experienced gave me a glimpse of life in the Kingdom. I'm particularly happy that my wonderful wife Laurie and awesome son David could join me and make the trip a lasting family memory. Next time I hope my son, Jonathan, and daughter, Elisabeth, can join us as well!

Finally, all praise to Jesus, who joins us all on our journeys, making every land Holy Land.

Southern Steps, the main commoner's entrance to the Temple in Christ's day

1ˢᵗ-century steps to Jerusalem from priestly mansion ruins near Church of St. Peter in Gallicantu

Church of the Holy Sepulchre interior dome

Kidron Valley Tombs from the first century:
Absalom's Pillar (left) and Zechariah's Tomb (right)

The Bene Hazir family tomb from the time of Christ (Kidron Valley)

Main street of Beth Shean (Scythopolis), capital of the Decapolis

Tabgha as seen from the Sea of Galilee

First-century shaft tombs in Church of the Holy S

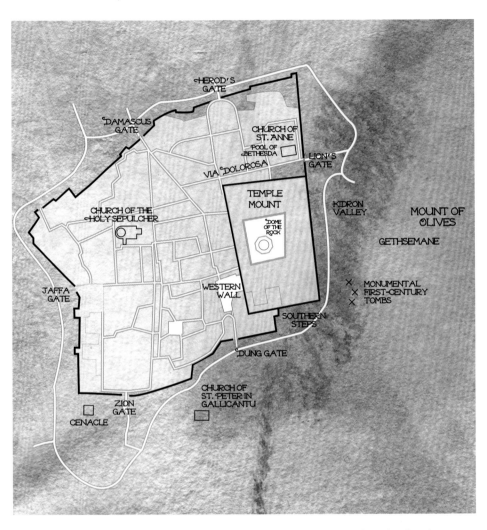

The city of Jerusalem, with points of interest mentioned in this book